FOG OF DEAD SOULS

FOG OF DEAD SOULS

A THRILLER

JILL KELLY

Skyhorse Publishing

Skyhorse Publishing books may be purchased in bulk at special discounts for sales promotion, corporate gifts, fund-raising, or educational purposes. Special editions can also be created to specifications. For details, contact the Special Sales Department, Skyhorse Publishing, 307 West 36th Street, 11th Floor, New York, NY 10018 or info@skyhorsepublishing.com.

Skyhorse® and Skyhorse Publishing® are registered trademarks of Skyhorse Publishing, Inc.®, a Delaware corporation.

www.skyhorsepublishing.com

10 9 8 7 6 5 4 3 2 1

Library of Congress Cataloging-in-Publication Data

Kelly, Jill, 1946-
Fog of dead souls : a thriller / Jill Kelly.
    pages cm
ISBN 978-1-62873-772-1 (hardback)
1. Older women--Fiction. 2. Life change events--Fiction. 3. Psychological fiction. I. Title.
[DNLM: 1. Romantic suspense fiction. gsafd]
PS3611.E44923F54 2014
813'.6--dc23
                                        2013038261

Printed in the United States of America

*For all the women who've found themselves
in the dark night of abuse, and for all the men
who've helped love them back to the light.*

1

Ellie McKay walked into the Maverick Bar about nine-thirty. The sun had set hours earlier, but the sky remained light to the west in the crisp September air. She'd been driving since mid-afternoon, and she was ready to get drunk.

She took a room at the Bide–a–While motel. The ambiance and the price had nothing to do with her choice. It was the convenient location of the Maverick, just down the street. She hadn't seen a grocery store or a liquor store on her way into Farmington, and she didn't want to drive anymore. Besides, she was tired of being alone.

Some nights she tried restaurants—the kind with a cocktail lounge that will bring a double rye on the rocks a couple of times without looking askance. But tonight it was too late to eat, too late to be hungry. She had promised herself that she wouldn't get drunk in the bar. The blackouts were unpredictable and she wanted to choose what happened. She wanted to face the end, if it was coming her way, with her eyes wide open. She just wanted a good buzz, some way to really slow down so that she could sleep and not dream of Joel and the hotel room. She wanted to drink to feel all right again and to feel loose enough to ask for a bottle that would carry her through the night with maybe a bit left over to start the next day.

When you've got one bag, it doesn't take long to unload the car, and by this time, she never unpacked—just showered off the road and put on clean underwear and walked on down to the tavern. There had been rain earlier in the day and the neon flashed in the puddles that remained: Coors Light, Coors Light, Coors Light. She noted with relief the half dozen pickups parked in front of the Maverick. Bars were easier if they weren't too crowded. Men got rowdy in crowds; they got mean.

She pushed the door open and walked right to the bar. It's always straight ahead in a country tavern, and she knew if she made a beeline for it, there'd be no need to make eye contact or suffer the reactions of the patrons to the newcomer. She felt more invisible that way.

The bartender, a young brawny redhead in overalls and a red denim shirt with pearl snaps, put a napkin down in front of her right away. "What'll it be, miss?"

She smiled. She liked kind bartenders who pretended she was still young. "Double Maker's Mark," she said. "Go easy on the ice."

"You got it," he said. The drink was before her in no time.

She let it sit a minute though the craving was strong. She'd thought in Santa Fe that she might stop again or at least slow down.

The bartender noticed her hesitation. "Something wrong, ma'am?"

She saw the worry that played at the corners of his eyes, so she pushed away her resolution. She needed him on her side. She laughed and said, "Just giving thanks to the bourbon makers of America. My way of saying grace."

The redhead chuckled and moved away.

She took a sip, then another. Alone, she'd have drunk it down, trying to get to that place of no fear. Instead she decided to pace herself, watched the digital clock next to the cash register. But after five minutes, the drink was gone, and the bartender—she decided his name was Billy—looked over at her from the beer tap. She nodded and he fixed the next one.

The Maverick had a big mirror behind the bar. She liked that because she could watch the action without being part of it. There were four booths over to one side of the front wall and three of them held couples. Two of those couples were kids. Boys barely old enough to shave, let alone drink. Cheerleader girlfriends. When did the world get so young? In the third booth, the couple seemed different, though they were necking and laughing, too. When they disentangled themselves, she saw they were both gray-haired and thick in the middle. Somehow that made her feel better.

The older woman, she decided to call her Maudie, got up and disappeared in the back, while her boyfriend, Roy—why not Roy?—went to the jukebox. There'd been two honky-tonk tunes in a row, but now George Strait's croon came on. "I still feel twenty-five, most of the time . . ." When Maudie came back, Roy whirled her around the floor a few times before they sat down and went back to nuzzling each other. Billy took them a fresh pitcher.

By now, her second bourbon was pretty well gone. Here came the hard part. Had she schmoozed enough with Billy Bartender to get him to sell her a bottle? She didn't like to drink more than two in the bar. She could get back to her room without a problem on two drinks. If she ordered a third, she'd be making a different kind of decision.

She glanced into the mirror. She still looked like herself. Dark straight hair, dark eyes and brows, skin surprisingly smooth for her age. The extra pounds—she'd lost count after thirty—were still there, but she didn't look half-bad, she thought. She'd never been a classic beauty—jaw too square, nose a bit too wide, a smile she'd never been fond of. But she was still shapely and she knew men still looked at her legs.

She stared a moment into her own eyes. She wanted another drink, a third or fourth, and if she drank them, she'd be able to yuck it up with Billy and maybe some guy and get that bottle and go home. Alone or not, she didn't care. And if it turned out to be him, whoever *he* was, then it did. And there'd be some relief in that. She was tired of running.

The woman in the mirror nodded at her, and Ellie nodded back. She looked down the bar. A couple of truckers sat to her left, wearing the road like a badge of honor. One winked in her direction. She smiled back. Then she turned and looked to the right. A cowboy with a gray beard was nursing a beer and a shot. He, too, smiled at her. But nothing sparked, and she decided to try her luck with Billy to get the bottle and go. The young man was busy unloading a tray of clean glasses, so she waited for him to get finished and look her way.

It was then that Al slid onto the stool next to her.

She saw him in the mirror first. He was tall, so tall that his head and shoulders showed well above the row of bottles that lined the shelf behind the bar. She was tall herself, but she had never been drawn to the tall ones, preferring men her own size. But this guy had a mane of thick silver hair that fell down over a weather-lined brow. Similar lines crinkled his eyes and creased the corners of his wide, handsome mouth.

The man grinned at her as he took off his black hat and laid it on the bar and, to her surprise, something in her went soft and felt safe for the first time in all these months.

"What'll it be, Al?" Billy asked, coming down the bar.

"Coffee," he said. "Big coffee." And he grinned at her again.

Billy filled a big glass beer mug with coffee from the hot plate next to the maraschino cherries and lime slices. She could smell that it was long past fresh. He set the mug down in front of Al along with a carton of half-and-half.

When Al had finished turning the black stuff white, he turned to her. "Where you from?"

"Not here," she said. She heard her words come out kind of snippy and she hadn't meant them to. She felt flustered all of a sudden, so she drained the ice melt from the glass. Billy tried to catch her eye to see if she wanted another, but she avoided him. Truth was she was waiting to see what Al would say next. But he said nothing. Just put his elbows on the bar and sipped at his coffee. *Maybe it's my turn*, she thought. She looked up at Billy and asked for a glass of water.

At that, Al looked over at her and at the empty glass on the bar. "My name's Al," he said. "I own a ranch about fifteen miles out of town. I do pretty well, considering that bush-whacking G. W. in the White House. I'm sixty-four, my hair and teeth are my own, haven't ever had a major illness and don't plan to have any."

She didn't know what to make of these revelations. She took a big drink of the water in front of her and thought about that third drink.

"Well," she said, finally, when she realized he was waiting for her to speak. "My name's Ellie. I'm sixty, and I've been a teacher most of my life. I, too, have my own hair and teeth. I have also had two major illnesses that are none of your business."

Billy had his back turned to them and was wiping between the bottles, but Ellie could see his shoulders shaking with laughter.

Al didn't say anything in response, just nodded solemnly. Then he signaled Billy for a refill and the smell of overcooked Folgers wafted towards her again.

He took his time with the coffee, pouring dollops of cream into it and stirring them in. All Ellie could imagine was that there was an exact shade of brown he was looking for. Then he asked her if she wanted another drink. She thought about it for a moment, then lied and said no. Al nodded to Billy, who brought her a cup of the coffee. She poured in a little cream, but she knew it would make her sick, so she left it sitting there on the bar, moving the cup around a little to be polite. She held on to the whiskey glass as if it were a life preserver.

"It's nice, isn't it," he said after a while, "just sitting here together like this."

Again that feeling of being safe and soft came over her, and Ellie felt her shoulders relax—really relax—as she looked at the aging cowboy sitting next to her. "Yes, yes it is," she said and smiled at him.

They were quiet another few minutes. Then Al drank down the last bit of his coffee and he turned to her. He put his hand ever so gently on her forearm, which lay on the edge of the bar. "Ellie, have you ever wanted to be a rancher's wife?" His eyes were serious, dead serious.

She managed a smile. "I've never thought about it." She paused. "Say, does Jesus enter into this somehow?"

He frowned. "What do you mean?"

"I mean I need to tell you that I am not religious. No way, no how. I'm not cut out for Sunday School and prayer meetings and being the good little woman at home. I'm more the hell and damnation type, if you know what I mean."

He leaned toward her and she caught a whiff of Old Spice. "Do you have to do it alone?" he said.

"Do what?"

"Raise hell. Can someone else come along? Be there to pick up the pieces? Bring you back home to yourself?" Then he smiled at her with that wide, handsome mouth and she couldn't help herself, she went weak in the knees.

"Sure, I guess," she said to Al. "Why not?" And Ellie pushed the coffee away, held up the whiskey glass, and nodded at Billy, who brought over the bottle.

2

It took Al the usual twelve minutes to leave the lights of Farmington behind, to have the land open up and the stars start to wink in the black velvet above. He loved that thirteenth moment, loved the night closing in around him and the truck, the soft electronic lights of the dashboard the only reminder of the century he lived in.

The pavement ahead was dry. Alert by second nature to the wild eyes along the roadside that might suddenly dart out, he let his mind go blank, a trick he had learned in the long, difficult months after he had buried Annie. He tuned into his breathing, into the ache in his chest and the fullness in his throat. He didn't want to think about the impetuous encounter he had just had. Although people knew him as decisive, he wasn't much of a risk-taker, and now somehow he had jumped in with both feet before his mind could say otherwise.

He had liked Ellie right away. There was something endearing about her bravado, her certainty that was most likely a mask which made him want to stand between her and the world. Funny how you could see that hidden place behind the eyes in some people—and in some animals. It took no time at all to see it.

He looked over at Beemus, who was stretched out on the seat beside him, his graying muzzle resting lightly on Al's thigh. Annie had thought it stupid to have a house dog on a ranch, but Al had wanted a companion dog, not just a working dog, and Beemus was a true companion. He gave the cocker a rub behind the ear and the old dog thumped his tail softly against the seat.

Al had gone to the Maverick that night in the hopes of running into Gracie. She and a couple of girlfriends usually showed up on Tuesday nights for the buffalo tacos, and he'd taken to coming later, when they were through eating and had had a few pitchers. He would wait patiently at the bar drinking his coffee until she was ready and then Gracie would let him go home with her. Sometime after the first few months, they'd stopped talking about Annie and they'd started sleeping together. Rumors of revenge had circulated in the small town, but Al knew it wasn't that. It was just something to hold him and Gracie against the loneliness of the night. Now it was a routine, and though neither of them felt anything more than affection, they had stayed with that routine—or they had until tonight.

He thought about Ellie, how she'd teased him about bad bar coffee, wondered why he hadn't gone to Starbucks. He'd started to defend himself but didn't want to explain about Gracie. And they'd teased each other and then he'd asked those questions that somehow just fell out of his mouth. And she'd agreed. He felt the weight of Ellie in his arms at the motel door, the soft taste of her lips, the way she had leaned into him. His whole body stirred at the possibility.

"I'll be here at eight," he'd said to her at the door of her room. He remembered the silly grin that had come unbidden to his lips and she had grinned back and said, "Make it ten." Then they'd looked at each other a long moment and she'd gone inside.

Up ahead on the right, the old gas station came into view, its rusted canopy and pumps a relic of the road's history before the Interstate. He shook himself from the reverie and signaled a right, though his was the only car for miles in any direction.

3

Ellie waited twenty minutes after Al had left and then headed back to the bar. She hoped he'd gone home but just in case she'd concocted a story about dropping her car keys. But he wasn't there and she had no trouble buying the bottle from Billy, who winked at her and wished her a good evening.

She poured herself a stiff drink when she came back to the room, but she'd had enough to drink at the bar that she no longer needed to hurry. She wasn't drunk though. Over the last several months, she'd built up a tolerance again, and besides, she was wired from what had just happened with Al. She felt giddy and nervous and somehow guilty.

She thought about Sandy. But it was ten-thirty and that meant close to midnight at home. And what could she say? It was still safer that Sandy didn't know where she was, safer for both of them.

She thought about checking out, moving on. She could drive to the next town, wherever it was, and find a motel there. She hadn't planned to stay in Farmington, and maybe Al's proposal had just been a bar joke. In any case, how disappointed could he be if a total stranger stood him up for breakfast?

She glanced around the lonely room with its chipped veneered furniture and its old blue carpet with the threads showing through near the door and the bedside. She thought bitterly that it was an apt metaphor for her life. Then she took another big swallow of bourbon to loosen the grip of the self-pity. As she set the glass down, her glance fell on a glossy stand-up triangle on the coffee table that announced free wi-fi, and she thought of how plugged into the electronic world she had been before Gettysburg. The old lure of news and connection sang out to her, so she got her keys and went out to the trunk for her laptop.

There were nearly a thousand messages in her college email account and she deleted most of them quickly: committee meeting minutes, textbook advertisements, potluck solicitations for a faculty evening, a nasty note from the registrar about her overdue incomplete grade for a senior.

She lived her old life for an hour, reading the messages one by one and deleting them. She kept only the ones from Sandy, although after the first couple, she couldn't read them—the worry in them so stark, so pleading. *Maybe I should send a reply*, she thought. Then she came back to her senses and deleted those, too.

Stiff from sitting, she turned the computer off and stowed it away. In the front compartment, where she stored the remote mouse, her hand touched paper. She pulled it out and there were Sandy and Arlen grinning at the camera on that October Saturday and there was Joel, frowning off to the side. She glanced at it for only a second, then tore the photo into tiny pieces and flushed it down the toilet.

4
—

"Find something else, will you?" Joel's voice was just this side of belligerent. He didn't usually care what they listened to on long car trips as long as it kept him awake, but tonight he was the kind of angry he got when he was wrong and, clearly, the angst-ridden hits of Steve Perry and Journey weren't working.

Ellie opened the glove compartment to get some light and looked through the CD carrier. "Van Morrison?"

Joel shook his head.

"James Taylor? The Eagles?"

Joel gave one of his famous you-just-don't-get-me sighs and then shrugged in agreement.

Quickly the music churned up the silence and Ellie could turn away, back toward the night rolling past.

They'd left Greensburg late, well after six, even though they'd agreed to meet up with Sandy and Arlen in Gettysburg for dinner. Ellie had left campus at three so she could shower before they left. She'd packed her bags that morning, and getting the cats situated had taken only a few minutes. By four, she was ready. By quarter after four, she was calling the hospital.

"He's in surgery," Nadine said. "Gunshot wounds. Went in at three, probably be a couple of hours."

"He told me he was off at noon." She tried to hide her frustration. It wasn't Nadine's fault.

"Well, you know how he loves to ride to the rescue."

"All too well." She and Joel's assistant had had this conversation before. "Will you see him later?"

"I doubt it. I'll be leaving at five; it's Friday. But I can leave a message."

"It won't make any difference. Thanks anyway."

Ellie closed the phone and made some chamomile tea. She felt calmer, okay with waiting, so she took the novel she was reading out of her suitcase and went up to her bedroom and lay down. The early October dark was creeping in the windows when she heard his key in the door.

"Ellie, are you ready?" he called. She could just see him standing in the doorway in the long leather coat he always wore, looking for all the world like a cowboy gangster from the 1880s.

"I'll be right down," she called, though she felt leaden from the sleep and more inclined to suggest they leave in the morning. But she knew Joel would be hyped up from the surgery, so she washed her face and hands, hurrying in the threat of his impatience.

Now they'd driven nearly three hours, mostly in silence. When she'd asked about the surgery, he'd scowled and said nothing, a code she'd learned to recognize that told her the patient had died. She softened her heart and body then, put her hand on his knee, and leaned into him in support. But he didn't soften back. After a few minutes, she pulled away and went back to watching the road, watching her thoughts.

Mutual acquaintances had fixed them up at New Year's. She'd been eager to meet someone new, and he'd been looking for a date for the hospital fundraiser. Joel was attractive and stylish. What's more, he was the right age and the right amount of single. His work as an ER surgeon was a bonus. It gave him an edge of drama and sophistication that the other men in her world, academics and administrators, could only talk about.

Ellie was a bit surprised when Joel pursued her. There were flowers and candlelit dinners and sweet notes in the mail. For all of his cynicism and sophistication, she thought she saw through to the ardent heart of the young man he had once been, and she fell in love with that. And there was something else about him, a streak of renegade that she admired. Always too much the good girl, she hoped Joel could teach her how to kindle that streak in herself.

The honeymoon, as she saw it now, had lasted two months. Then they had settled into a pattern of dinners out and sex and a little conversation—a pattern, he said, that matched his chaotic work life. She thought briefly of asking for more, but her own career was busy enough with committees and publishing, and she let the moment pass. Now she felt hungry for an intimacy that seemed out of reach.

Outside of Bedford, they moved off the freeway and into the countryside. Ellie turned off the climate controls and rolled down her window. The warm humid night rushed in. Crickets singing, moths flying into the windshield, the occasional white rails of a thoroughbred farm whizzing by . . . The little town of McConnellsburg slept on as they drove through it and the clear, starlit night. Then five miles from Gettysburg, the first few tendrils of fog appeared in the headlights.

5

—

S he heard it as distant thunder, a faint rumbling noise, and half
awake, she wondered if a storm was brewing. The rumbling
drew nearer and louder and then moved away, and she opened
her eyes to the hotel room and realized that a housekeeping cart was
passing down the hall.

Straight over her was the ceiling of nubby plaster. She found it
oddly fascinating in the dawn's early light and smiled at the stupidity
of her fascination. She felt groggy and languid in an old familiar way,
and she realized she was stoned. She smiled at the absurdity of that
too—it was years since she'd touched a drink or a joint—and she
closed her eyes and assumed she was dreaming.

She slept again, and when she opened her eyes, the light
through the sheer inner curtains had changed, fuller now as though
the morning were well into itself. The grogginess was gone, but it
had been replaced by a headache and a queasiness that also was
familiar. A wave of distress and disbelief washed over her. *I couldn't
have had anything to drink*, she thought. *I just couldn't have*. Maybe
she had the flu.

She groaned and moved to roll over on her side, but she couldn't.
Wide awake in an instant, she felt rather than saw that her wrists
were tied to the bed posts. Fighting the panic, she willed herself to
calm down. She closed her eyes, took several deep breaths, felt her

heartbeat slow a little. She could feel the sheets against her bare skin and that her feet were free. Somehow that helped calm her, too. She began a mental scan of her body. Her arms and legs were stiff and ached. So did her lower back. She pulled her knees up to relieve her back and a pain in her genitals shot through her. They were sticky and sore. The nausea and panic rose up again and she started to cry. For what seemed a long time, she let the fear and self-pity take her. Then self-preservation kicked in.

The room felt empty. The bathroom door stood ajar, but only the faint glow of the night light on the hair dryer shone out. Most of the bedroom also lay in deep shadow from the heavy curtains, just a stripe of muted white coming onto the bed through the inner sheers.

She pulled and struggled for a moment against the bonds that held her. There was some play in them and she hoped they would come loose. The gold braided cords that held her looked familiar, and she realized they'd been swagging the curtains the night before. She remembered thinking how elegant they were, like the down comforter and the fruit basket. Joel liked to go first class and she'd been happy to go along if he wanted to pay for it. *Joel,* she thought. *Where was Joel? Was he hurt too?*

She pulled her knees up farther and inched upward in the bed. She tried to reach the cords with her mouth, thinking that she might be able to undo them with her teeth. The one on the left was too tight and too far, and after a minute she gave up and tried the other. It was a little closer and a little looser and she worked and worked it, desperate to get free and desperate to pee. Finally her bladder could hold no longer and she wet the bed. She didn't care. That seemed the least of her problems.

She kept working on the cord and finally she worked it free. Sobbing with relief, she moved away from the wet sheets and towards the other bedpost to free her left hand.

She pulled herself up and sat on the edge of the bed. Strangely, the panic subsided with the freedom and an odd sense of calm washed over her. The room was warm—she was sweating from her efforts, but she didn't want to be naked even with herself, so she pulled the comforter around her and then turned on the lamp.

Joel sat in the armchair in the far corner of the room. His head was leaning against the wingback and his thinning dark hair looked as though he had just run his fingers through it. His skin was pale and smooth—he looked very young. His open-eyed gaze was turned toward her, like he'd been watching her sleep. She didn't cry out, she didn't speak his name. Where he had gone, he couldn't hear her, and she knew it.

6

The police weren't long in coming. Ellie called the front desk and asked the clerk to call 911. She stared at Joel for a long moment after she put the phone down, then went into the bathroom, peed again, and brushed her teeth. She'd watched enough police procedurals on TV to know she shouldn't shower, though she ached to do so. But she hoped that brushing her teeth wasn't a violation of some statute.

Then she wandered around the room, dragging the comforter with her. There was no sign of struggle, no furniture overturned, no clothes strewn about. None of this made any sense to her, but the order in the room somehow made her feel calmer, safe even.

She opened the curtains to let the daylight in and saw that the sky was blue overhead, the fog of the day before gone. On the small table next to the armchair were two bottles and a glass. Without looking at Joel, she reached for the glass. It was half-empty and smelled of scotch. There was a second glass on the nightstand. She went over to it and picked it up. Her lip gloss was on the rim. She sniffed it, then tasted it. The neutral nothingness of club soda. Relief flooded her. She went to her suitcase, found clean underwear and slacks and a sweater, and took them into the bathroom and closed the door. When she saw the marks on her body, her hands trembled so hard she couldn't put the clothes on.

The knock on the door was loud and it startled her even though she was expecting it. When she opened the door, a man her own age stood there, a photo ID in his upraised palm. His suit was as tired-looking as he was. She said nothing, just tightened the comforter around her, and moved back into the room. There were two other men, both much younger, both in suits as well.

The tired policeman wanted her to sit on the bed but she refused, so the hotel manager, the youngest of the three, brought in a straight chair and placed it in the middle of the room. The second policeman ushered him out, and then Ellie sat in the chair and answered the first man's questions. She was aware that the room stank of urine and sweat and her fear, but the tired detective didn't seem to notice. He just went on asking questions in a soft, kind voice.

She told them of waking up in the bed. She showed them the cords, the marks on her wrists. Her hands shook, her voice shook. She told them she thought she'd been raped.

There was another knock on the door. The second policeman opened the door and a young man brought in a tray with a coffee pot and several cups. The young man looked at Ellie with frank curiosity, then left. The older detective offered her a cup and though she didn't like coffee, she didn't want to offend him, so she took it. It was warm in her hands and it helped her stop shaking so much.

She told them how she found Joel once she had freed herself. No, she knew nothing of the needle in his arm. No, she hadn't touched the body, even to see if he was dead—she could see he was dead. No, no one else had come back to the hotel with them after dinner, not Arlen or Sandy. No one.

The truth was she didn't remember. She didn't remember anything between dinner and waking up that morning. No, she hadn't been drinking. She was four years sober. Ask Arlen. Ask Sandy. She couldn't tell if the men believed her or not. She began to cry from fatigue and frustration.

A woman officer had arrived by then, and the men asked Ellie to get dressed. The tired detective asked the female officer to help her, asked Ellie if she needed immediate medical attention, but Ellie shook her head and the two women went into the bathroom. When Ellie dropped the comforter, she heard the woman suck in her breath.

She glanced over at the officer, and the woman turned away. Ellie took a deep breath and put on her clothes. The burns and strap marks and bruises made her wince with pain and the bra was impossible, but she managed to put on a pair of soft cotton slacks and two layers of knit shirts.

When she came back into the room, more people were there, taking photos, examining Joel's body. She couldn't manage to get the socks on so the woman officer helped her with them and with her trainers. All the while, she avoided looking at Joel. She felt desperate to get out of the room, to get some fresh air. She said as much to the female officer, then sat back on the chair and closed her eyes, hoping it would all go away.

7

The *beep-beep-beep* of a garbage truck pulled Ellie from the dream. A dream of hallways and empty rooms, of fleeing and pursuing, she wasn't sure which. The only memory that had lasted was of a whiteboard in a classroom, the words on the board erased by an invisible hand faster than she could write them.

The lamp beside her was on, for she couldn't sleep in the dark now if she was alone. The truck beeped one more threesome. Then the driver shifted gears and it rumbled off out of the parking lot, the sound growing faint as it moved onto the street.

The clock on the nightstand glowed 3:47. The room was as silent as the street outside. Ellie ventured a foot toward the other side of the bed, but the sheets were cold. She was alone and awake in the night, and relief alternated with fear.

She got up, used the bathroom, and opened the curtains a bit so she could find the bottle. There were a few shards of ice floating in the plastic bucket. She fished them out and into the glass that stood next to the bottle, then drank down the cold water straight from the bucket. She was surprised to see that the bottle was mostly full and she relaxed as she poured some into the glass. Then she pulled on her nightshirt against the cool of the room and sat down in the faux-leather chair by the little table that held her salvation and tried to remember the night. She remembered the long day of driving, the Maverick Bar. Her stomach rumbled and she realized she hadn't eaten since lunch the day before. And then Al's handsome face came back to her. She felt a wave of something, desire maybe, the first she'd felt in all those months, and then a twinge of hope. Could she hide here? Had she run far enough? Could Al protect her?

She sat for a long time in the half-stupor that drink-induced sleep created for her—that friendly relaxed place where she didn't have to worry. She let her mind go blank and she left the bourbon untouched. When she came back to awareness, the clock now showed 4:38. So she drained the glass and got back in bed, willing herself to go back to sleep. The days were already long enough, empty enough, she thought, without adding on a couple of hours in the dark.

She slept soundly for nearly two hours, turned off the alarm before it went off at seven, then slept again until after eight. She ignored the huge mirror and unflattering light in the bathroom. Since Gettysburg, she'd given up looking at herself in the morning—assessing the deepening marks of hangover and fatigue had not been a great way to start the day. She made coffee in the little coffeemaker and took a shower, running the water cold at the end to jolt herself into the day.

Once dressed, she was unsure again. It was only nine, plenty of time to leave. So why didn't she?

The truth was, she was too tired to go. Too tired to run anymore. And the fact that Al had wanted breakfast instead of sex made everything different. That little spark of hope flared up once more and she saw that she had put on the rumpled black knit slacks and t-shirt that she traveled in and went to change into something more, well . . . she wasn't sure what exactly, but just more.

8

Ellie went to Gettysburg Hospital in a squad car, accompanied by the woman officer, whose name badge read HARTWELL. Ellie asked after the detectives—she'd assumed they would come with her, protect her. But Hartwell said no; they had work to do at the crime scene. Ellie nodded, though she didn't really understand. She felt a bit sick and her head ached, but Hartwell let her roll the window down and the fresh air made her feel better and a little more normal.

There was no long wait at the hospital, only an intake form and copying of her insurance card from the college. It was early Sunday afternoon, and the emergency room was quiet. Ellie relaxed a little. The cold and trembling had eased up, and the staff was kind as they took her information and her vital signs.

A young woman doctor came to the ER cubicle right away. She asked Ellie if she could stand so that photographs could be taken of the bruises and burns and strap marks on her back and her buttocks and her thighs. Then her fingernails were cleaned onto special sticks, and every orifice swabbed and inspected. Ellie tensed at each new intrusion, but the doctor was kind and gentle and respectful. She asked Ellie what she remembered and Ellie felt apologetic that she couldn't help much.

"It doesn't matter," the doctor said. "Your body will tell us a lot of what we need to know."

"Do you know what drugs he . . ." She couldn't say it. "What drugs I was on?"

The doctor hesitated, then sighed. "I can guess. A sedative of some sort, a benzodiazepine, and most likely rohypnol. Do you know what that is?"

Ellie nodded. "The date rape drug. It's happened on our campus to a couple of girls."

The doctor nodded in return. "I'm sorry," she said. "It would explain why you can't remember. And why you're not more upset. The sedative is still in your system. I'll give you a prescription for more when you leave."

"I can't take them," said Ellie. "I'm in recovery."

The doctor paused. "I understand that, but you're going to need some help when the drugs wear off. You've been through a lot."

Ellie didn't say anything. She didn't have to fill the prescription.

"We're also going to admit you overnight, just to keep an eye on things."

Ellie nodded. "I want a shower."

"Of course. As soon as we can transfer you to a room. And then I want you to take something and sleep."

Ellie protested. She didn't want to be sedated anymore, but the doctor convinced her that a few hours of sleep would help her heal.

Within the hour, she had been taken upstairs, given a clean gown and a clean bed, and something to eat. All the while Hartwell waited silently in the room. Ellie found that comforting and she took the pill offered to her and slept.

𝕩

When she woke up, the night had come, and the two detectives from the hotel stood by her bed.

"How are you feeling, Ms. McKay?"

Ellie let the tired detective's face come into focus. Soft hair, more gray than blond. Brown eyes. A nice jaw, soft now with age. "Okay, I guess," she said and struggled to sit up. The detective reached over for the remote and raised the head of the bed.

"I'm Detective Hansen," he said as he stepped back. "We met at the hotel."

Ellie nodded.

"And this is Detective Skopowlski. And you know Officer Hartwell."

Ellie nodded again.

"We need to ask you a few more questions. Are you up to it?"

After years of TV cop shows, Ellie half expected to be bullied or badgered or even disbelieved, but that didn't happen. The detectives had verified who they were: a college professor, a respected surgeon. They were kind, the questions simple and logical. What kind of mood had Joel been in on Friday? On Saturday? Saturday night? Had he ever tied her up or hurt her before or had there been sex games of any kind? Had he ever talked about doing violence to himself or others? Had he talked about suicide? Did he have a history of mental illness? Did he do drugs?

She answered the questions the best she could. Joel had been quiet—maybe even moody—on Saturday, but he was often quiet when surgery hadn't gone well. Besides, she said, Arlen talked enough for everybody. "Have you met Arlen yet?"

"Yes," said Hansen, "he and his wife are outside. They're waiting to see you."

Ellie felt a huge wave of relief. She wasn't alone in this.

"Did you argue over the weekend?"

"Joel and I? No. We never argued." She told them how she'd seen his temper once or twice but always aimed at inanimate objects, like the TV remote. He'd never directed it at her. And Joel had never suggested any kind of rough sex to her, no handcuffs, no silk scarves, nothing.

"I'm not naïve," Ellie said finally, "but Joel wasn't very inventive in the bedroom. Pretty much straight intercourse."

A look passed between the two men that she couldn't interpret, but she suddenly felt foolish.

"How would you describe your relationship with the deceased, Ms. McKay?" Skopowlski spoke this time.

Ellie took an instant disliking to the man. "Dr. McKay," she said. She seldom pulled the PhD card, but Skopowlski's tone had changed.

The gentleness seemed to have disappeared with the look between the two men, and even though his voice wasn't sinister or demanding, there was a sharp edge to it that had not been there before.

"Dr. McKay," he said. "How would you describe the relationship?"

"He was my boyfriend." Ellie didn't want to sound seventeen. "My lover."

"Were you serious about each other?"

"We hadn't talked about marriage if that's what you mean. We didn't live together. We didn't mix our finances."

Hansen nodded and spoke then. "What we're trying to get at, ma'am, is how well you knew Joel Richardson."

Ellie thought for a moment, took a deep breath. "I knew what he told me. I had no reason to think that what he said about himself wasn't true. Isn't that really what we all have to go on?"

Hansen nodded but Skopowlski shifted his feet impatiently, stepping back and then stepping closer to the bed. "What do you know of his past?"

"Not all that much, I guess. He was in Vietnam. He was a surgeon there and served two tours. He married a Vietnamese girl to get her out of there, but they'd divorced a long time ago. No kids. He came to Pittsburgh a few years ago to take the job at the hospital from some place in Florida. Or so he told me." She looked at Skopowlski and then at Hansen. "Is that not true?"

There was a moment of silence and another look passed between the two men. "It seems to be," Hansen said at last.

Skopowlski spoke up. "We're just trying to figure out what happened. What happened to you, what happened to him."

It was Ellie's turn to pause. Then she said, "Like I told you at the hotel, I don't know what happened to me—or to him. I don't remember anything of what happened last night. I got into the car—Joel's car—at the restaurant. I was laughing about something Arlen had said. That's the last thing I remember—laughing and getting into the car. Until I woke up this morning in . . . in the hotel."

Detective Hansen nodded. "Okay. That's enough for now. We'll wait until the lab reports come in. We need you to stay in Gettysburg until then. Can you manage that?"

For the first time that day, Ellie thought about her real life—her classes the next day, letting the dean know where she was, what had happened, all the inconvenience. She felt a surge of annoyance, but then she was relieved. At least she was feeling something. "I guess so. I'll have to sort some things out."

"Perhaps your friends can help with that. Do you feel up to seeing them now?" Hansen asked, touching her arm.

When she nodded, the three of them left and Arlen and Sandy came in. Her friends looked worried—worried and weary. Sandy gave her a tentative hug, and Ellie suddenly felt fragile and damaged, something that hadn't occurred to her before then. Arlen took her hand and patted it. There was an awkward silence.

Ellie broke the silence. "How did you know to come back?"

"That detective, Hansen, called my cell. He'd gotten the number from your phone. And we just turned around and drove back."

"So you know about Joel."

"Yes," said Sandy quickly, "but we can't believe it. I mean, we just had dinner with you guys last night and we all had such a good time. How could this happen? How could he do that to you?" Then Sandy looked at Arlen and said, "We always thought there was something . . ."

"Don't say it," said Ellie. "Don't say anything about him. We don't know what happened yet. I'm okay. I'm okay."

"But you've been tortured." The look of horror and fear on Sandy's face as she said this struck some deep part of Ellie and a sense of loss washed over her. But she said nothing.

Arlen stepped in then. "What can we do for you, honey?"

In that moment, Ellie felt so glad to have him for a friend. "I need Sandy to call the dean," she said. "I have to stay here in Gettysburg for a few days. I suspect I'll miss a week of work."

"Honey, you'll need more time than—"

She raised her hand to silence Sandy. "One day at a time, okay?" Sandy nodded.

"You two should go home," Ellie said. "There's no reason your lives should be disrupted because of this."

Sandy shook her head. "Don't be crazy. We're not leaving you to face this alone, so shut up already. We'll sort this out together. Arlen and I will be here for you."

And Ellie was glad to let them.

9

Like always, Al was up before the sunrise. Since Annie had been gone, he'd trained himself to get up when he first woke. The nightmares, the dreams of anger and humiliation, came in that second round of sleep, and he avoided them that way.

It didn't hurt the ranch any for him to be up before dawn, having time to think before the crew arrived. And now that most of the crew was Mexican, he'd learned to siesta with them after lunch, mastering what Gracie told him was a "power nap."

He fed Beemus, made coffee and toast for himself, pulled on a jacket against the chill, and then they went out to the old rocker that had belonged to Annie's grandmother. Most mornings he and the dog sat there on the big porch for a half hour or so until the light came on behind the hills in the distance. He liked this quiet time. He had a wide view of the property, a view he'd grown up with. It was his world. The land belonged to him and he belonged to the land.

These days, he sat and rocked, went over the day's work, and made peace with his God. Today, when his plans and prayers were through, he went on over to the barn to meet with the foreman. He was nervous about meeting Ellie later and work seemed a good distracter. At nine, he showered, shaved, and, nervous as a schoolboy, got dressed and drove into town.

He wasn't at all sure he would find her at the motel, but when he knocked on the door at ten, she was there, smiling shyly, more dressed up than the night before in slim gray slacks and a long, black sweater. Behind her, he saw that the covers on the bed had been straightened, the room tidied. Her neatness pleased him.

Her greeting did, too. After the shy smile, she looked him in the eye and then stood on tiptoe and kissed his cheek softly, the way he had kissed hers the night before. Then she picked up a black leather satchel and pulled the door closed behind her.

"Where to, cowboy?" She smiled at him and a much younger, more open woman appeared in her eyes. "I've always wanted to say that."

He couldn't help but laugh. "Breakfast!" he said and opened the passenger door of the SUV. He'd parked next to an aging red Honda Civic with Pennsylvania plates.

He drove them to the other side of town, a few blocks into the barrio. There was a diner there he liked where he wouldn't run into the usual folks in his life. There'd be talk among them soon enough.

Ellie sat as far from him as she could in the cab, up against the door, but she turned to face him, to watch him, and so it wasn't fear or hostility that put the distance between them. When he looked over at her, she would smile but the laughing girl in her eyes was gone, replaced by a wary creature, a fox perhaps or a deer. He wondered if she had always held both in her.

"I'm not much for talking first thing," she said after they'd ordered, so he held off until the huevos rancheros had come and gone, until the coffee mugs were full once more, and the bill sat waiting on its little plastic plate.

They'd taken a booth near the window and she sat angled so she could look out at the street. Finally she took a sip of the fresh coffee, put down the cup, and smiled, the wary smile. "What you said last night . . ."

"I meant it." He realized he must sound abrupt, crazy even.

She nodded, then looked out at the street again, seeming to find the passing of an old rusted truck of supreme interest. Then she turned again. "I don't do complicated. I don't do drama. I've had enough of that for several lifetimes. I don't do secrets. You can ask me anything and I will tell you the truth. But my past is just that. Over and done. Nothing to do with you or what might be with you. And I won't talk about it."

She took another sip of coffee and toyed with her earring. It was gold and shaped like a cat. "Do you have a past? Old complications and dramas?" She leaned into the table and looked at him intently.

"I do."

"Can't imagine otherwise for a handsome man who's lived sixty-four years." She smiled her open smile.

He felt his body relax a little.

"Does that past need to have anything to do with me?" Her voice had deepened somehow, taken on a smoky quality that wasn't sexual exactly but definitely came out of her body.

"No," he said right away, and then "No" again, more forcefully this time.

"I need a fresh start. I need a clean slate, a chance to start again. Isn't that what the West is all about?"

He nodded.

She was silent then for a long moment. "How about we each get to ask three questions? My answers will be the truth and I'm counting on yours to be the truth as well. And then we'll talk about now and tomorrow and the days after that. Is it a deal?" She reached over and touched his hand and the open-hearted girl smiled at him.

Her touch was soft and gentle and he wanted to lie down with her and hold her. He felt charmed by her earnestness and her straightforward way of speaking and yet he felt confused by all she was saying. But he didn't want any of it to end so he nodded his agreement.

"You first," she said. "What would you like to ask?"

He was suddenly afraid of what she might tell him, but he gathered up his courage. "Are you in trouble with the law?"

She smiled and shook her head. "No," she said. "And no creditors on my tail either."

"Your turn," he said, hoping he wasn't showing too much of the relief he felt.

"Have you ever hit a woman or a child or beaten an animal?"

The question took him by surprise, and he looked at her as closely as he dared. "No, no, never. I don't believe in that. I . . . I just don't . . ."

"I believe you," she said quickly, and she touched his hand again. When he remained silent, she said gently, "Your turn."

He thought a moment, then said, "Are you married?"

"No," she said right away. "I've never been married."

He sat back then, satisfied.

After a moment, she said, "And you, Al, are you well and truly free to be with me?"

That was an easy one. "Yes," he said without hesitation, although a thought for Gracie fluttered by. But Gracie knew, as he knew, that no claims had been staked.

They were both silent then for a few moments. The waitress came by. She filled Al's cup without asking and then hesitated. Ellie smiled up at her but placed her palm over the cup and the waitress walked away.

"One more each," said Ellie.

Al felt at a loss. He had dozens of questions to ask but they seemed impertinent. What side of the bed did she sleep on? Did she like to have her neck kissed? Did she like dogs? What did she do all day when she wasn't traveling? Did she have to watch TV in the morning? How did she feel about horses? Could she ride? Yet he knew these were all things he could find out without asking. And they were small things. This was the time to ask the big questions.

"Ask me yours," he said.

"Okay." She took a deep breath. "I want to stop drinking. Will you support me in that, no matter what it takes?"

Again, the question surprised him. It was such a personal thing to ask for. Why did she think she could trust him with this part of herself? He wanted to ask questions in turn, but that wasn't how they were playing this. He could feel her waiting for the answer. "Yes, I'll support you in whatever you need."

She sat back then from the table and a look he couldn't decipher crossed her face, but she nodded and her eyes were lighter around the edges. She clasped her hands on the table, a gesture of patient waiting that was oddly reminiscent of his grandmother, a thin strong woman named Violet. And he remembered he had one question left—and he knew what he needed to ask.

10

Ellie had rightly predicted a week in Gettysburg. After one night in the hospital, she was released to the care of Arlen and Sandy, who took her to the B&B they'd been staying in, one not far from the battlefield but away from town and the hotels and the police station. Arlen wrangled a discounted rate for two rooms with adjoining bath for the week and convinced the owners to cook for them as well. Ellie was sure he'd told the elderly couple her story, as they treated her like royalty, but it was quiet and comfortable and she was glad not to be in a hotel.

Sandy found a naturopath for her. The kindly young man, fresh out of school in Seattle, gave her several herbal concoctions, including drops for her wounded spirit and an arnica salve for the bruises, which Sandy helped her apply. Sandy had burst into tears when she saw Ellie's body: the line of burns along her inner thighs, the criss-cross of belt welts on her back, the finger marks on her ankles and upper arms where she'd been gripped by whatever maniac had done this. Ellie submitted docilely to the treatments, covered herself with a flannel nightgown Sandy had bought for her, and kept to her bed. Her body began to heal.

On Monday, she called her AA sponsor. She thought she would surely break down in the telling but she managed to get through it, Sunday's confusion now replaced by a strange calm and the relief of survival. Octavia urged her to take the tranquilizers the ER doctor had prescribed. It would not damage her sobriety to take prescription medication as directed. To be extra safe, she could give them to Sandy or Arlen for dispensing. So Monday night and Tuesday during the day, Ellie slept the restless sleep of the drugged.

Then, in the deep of Tuesday night, Ellie woke in a sweat. She had been teaching a class in the dream. She recognized Sarah Jane Lewis in the front row. Sarah Jane was a poor student who should not have been majoring in French, but Ellie admired her persistence and her efforts. Sarah Jane was reading from the last page of Albert Camus's *The Stranger* when Joel appeared at the door of the classroom. He held a large barbecue fork in his hand and pointed it at Ellie. "Come with me," he said, his voice surprisingly soft and pleading. Ellie looked at the clock above the blackboard. Quarter to three. Class didn't end for five more minutes. She looked at the students but now there was only Sarah Jane there before her. "Come with me," Joel said again, this time his voice deep and familiar. She turned to the desk, reached into her bag, and withdrew a string of condoms in plastic wrapping, then headed to the door. Once over the threshold, Joel pulled her by the hand along a corridor with big frosty windows. In the rooms, Ellie could see sides of beef, pigs, lambs—all skinned, all frozen. She was surprised to feel little beyond curiosity. Then Joel stopped abruptly, pulling her up beside him. He motioned to her to tie his hands behind his back with a gold cord. Then the corridor disappeared and they were in a barn—a shaft of sunlight streaked down from a wide crack in the wall. Joel stood before her on a high stool, another gold cord around his neck. "Kick it," he said, looking deep in her eyes. "Kick it."

It took a moment for Ellie's heart to stop racing, for her to recognize the bedroom in the B&B, to smell the cloying Victorian potpourri that clung to the bedding. It took another moment to remember the hotel room, the bedposts, Joel watching her with his dead eyes. Her chest filled with anguish and her throat ached but the tears wouldn't come.

She pulled herself to sitting, then got out of bed. She put on the new robe over the soft flannel gown Sandy had bought for her and slipped on socks against the autumn chill that had settled into the quiet house. She padded silently down the carpeted stairs and wandered around until she found the kitchen. There was grapefruit juice in the fridge and she drank three glasses before her thirst was quenched. Then she sat down at the small table in the bay window and looked out at the night.

Fog blanketed the garden, wisps and tendrils of white streaming across the lawn, skirting the old oak, which was ringed with benches.

For the first time in years, she thought of Danny, long gone from her life, his love of sitting in silence in the night, the firefly glow of his cigarette, the clink of ice in his glass. He liked to watch her sleep. Claimed it calmed him to know that one of them could do it.

She felt clearer in her mind. The afternoon before, she'd put the Valium away. She was afraid to get hooked, and she knew she couldn't put off the thinking forever. She inhaled deeply, then opened her mind to the questions she had been keeping at bay. In the space of another two breaths, the breakfast nook was crowded with them.

11

Wednesday morning Detective Hansen showed up at the B&B with Ellie's purse and her suitcase, which the police had hung on to. Sandy answered the door, then went upstairs to get her friend. A few minutes later, the two women emerged. Ellie had put on a pair of black knit slacks and a gray turtleneck, which had been in the suitcase. As she came down the wide staircase, Hansen suddenly felt as if he were in a movie, watching the love interest make her big entrance. He had an inexplicable urge to take her in his arms and embrace her.

Instead, he nodded at her solemnly, then asked Sandy where they could talk in private. Sandy showed them into the dining room, almost as if she were the maid, and then closed the pocket doors behind her as she left.

Hansen held out a chair for Ellie, then sat down across the table, his chair pulled out so that there was more distance between them. He didn't want her to feel pressured by his presence.

He asked how she was, then said, "Tell me everything you remember about Saturday. Anything and everything, details and all."

"Okay," she said. "I woke up about at seven-thirty. I could hear the shower running. Then I went back to sleep for a while. When I woke up again, Joel was dressed and sitting across the room—in that same chair." She paused. "He was reading the paper and drinking coffee."

"Paper cup?"

She looked at him and shook her head. "His travel mug."

"He'd been out?" Hansen said.

"No, I don't think so. He asked if I wanted some. I said no, not yet, but there was coffee in the hotel's coffeemaker when I went into the bathroom."

"What time was that?"

Ellie frowned. "Eight-thirty, maybe. I took a shower, dried my hair. When I came out, he was still reading the paper."

"Could he have left while you were in the shower?"

"I suppose so. I was in the bathroom about fifteen minutes. But it didn't look like he'd been out."

"Okay, then what?" Hansen made a note in a little notebook.

"We met Sandy and Arlen downstairs for breakfast. Do you want to know what I ate? I had two eggs over easy, hash browns, sausage. Do you want to know what Joel had?"

Hansen smiled in spite of himself. "Sure, why not?"

"He had oatmeal with butter and white sugar and skim milk. He always eats oatmeal."

"Who picked up the check?"

"Joel. Joel always picks up the check. It's a thing with him."

Hansen made another note and then looked up at Ellie.

She sighed. "Then we went to the battlefield. Arlen had . . ."

Hansen held up his hand. "Did either of you come back to the room before that?"

"Sandy and I did. I used the bathroom. She did too. I got a warmer jacket because it was damp and foggy out. That took maybe ten minutes."

"And Arlen and Joel?"

"I don't know what they did." Ellie frowned. "I assume they waited downstairs. They were in the lobby gift shop when we came down. Arlen was buying gum. Juicy Fruit. I hate the way that smells."

"Go on," said Hansen.

"We drove—we took Arlen's car—to the battlefield. He had a fancy guidebook of the different sites and battles—skirmishes, he called them—over those three days of fighting, and we drove and got out and looked around and he'd read a bunch of stuff, some of it pretty interesting actually, and then we'd pile back in the car and drive some more. I would have preferred to just walk—I like to walk—but Sandy has a bad hip so we got in and out of the car. It became pretty tedious, especially because the fog never lifted. It was cold and damp and unpleasant."

"Anything else you remember?"

Ellie shook her head. "Arlen took a lot of pictures. He has a scrapbook of battle sites. Frankly, the patches of grass and woods all look a lot alike to me—I guess if I was a botanist, I could tell the difference between the trees and grass in the various places, but I can't."

"Did Richardson ever leave the group? Did he get a phone call or step away to make a call?"

Ellie shook her head again. "No, but Sandy and I did stay in the car at one of the stops. Arlen wanted to walk up a fairly steep hill and Sandy didn't want to, so we just stayed in the car and talked about how hungry we were and how we'd had enough."

"How long were they gone?"

"Twenty, thirty minutes maybe. I don't know."

Hansen wrote in his notebook and studied Ellie a moment. He could tell she was growing weary, but whether of talking or remembering he couldn't tell. "Just a few more questions. What happened after that?"

"We went to a deli and had lunch."

"Anybody drink?"

"Joel and Arlen each had a beer." She paused. "Arlen had two."

"Joel didn't have a second?"

"No, he doesn't . . . didn't drink much. I couldn't have been with him if he did."

Hansen looked her in the eye for a moment, briefly wondering what her whole story was, and then he looked down at the notebook.

"Okay, tell me about the rest of the day."

"After lunch, Arlen and Sandy dropped us at the hotel. That would have been about three, I guess. I was really chilled and I took a hot bath and soaked a long time. Joel watched a football game on TV until I was through. We read and napped a little although I didn't really sleep. I don't think Joel did either. We watched CNN for a while, got dressed, went to dinner about seven."

"Anything unusual happen at dinner?"

"No. Arlen drank a little too much maybe. He and Joel split a bottle of wine and Arlen seemed to drink most of it. Arlen and Joel got into a discussion about the Civil War. Joel was defending the South and the right to secede. Arlen got pretty heated but nothing came of it. Arlen had been showing off with all his Civil War facts and I suspect that made Joel feel, well, I don't know. Joel didn't like to be wrong."

Hansen closed the notebook. Even though they'd been talking less than a half hour, he knew it had probably felt like an eternity for her. While he'd learned a few things that might prove helpful, she wasn't a good witness because of the drugs she'd been given that night—and the ones she was probably still taking. And that meant they'd probably have to do this all again.

"I haven't been much help, have I?" Her face was full of worry.

"Yes and no," he said after a moment. "Everything helps us see the whole picture, so all these details are important. It's just hard to know exactly which ones hold the key." He waited another moment. "You sound pretty clear about Saturday."

"Yeah, I guess I do. I remember it, up until we left the restaurant." She looked out the French doors onto the back garden. "I remember it, but I don't understand it."

She turned to look at Hansen and he saw the terrible darkness in her eyes that he'd come to recognize in the victims of sex crimes. "I tell my students that there are almost never answers to 'why' questions, that we can only ever really know 'how' something happens. And I do want to know how this happened, but that's not good enough. I want to know why and who. Who did this to us? And why would he?"

Hansen's eyes never left Ellie's face as she said all this, though he kept his own look neutral. But inside, his heart and lungs felt squeezed by her pain and what she didn't understand, and he felt both ashamed and angry, dirty somehow, and outraged.

"Yes," said Sandy, "about nine-thirty."

Hansen nodded. "Time is a factor." He turned back to Ellie. "Your bruises and burns were at least twelve hours old when the doctor examined you at the hospital, meaning the abuse occurred sometime not long after midnight, but Richardson died between six and eight in the morning—a number of hours later. His involvement explains the gap."

"Explains it how?" said Arlen. He sounded indignant. "Couldn't he have gone out, Joel, I mean, and then come back and found Ellie, and killed himself from shock?"

"Instead of calling the police, you mean? Instead of calling an ambulance? Do you know something we don't, Mr. Gerstead?" Skopowlski had turned from the window and Ellie saw the interest in his eyes.

"No, no, I'm just guessing." Arlen seemed to shrink away. "I . . . I just can't imagine he would sit there and watch while someone tortured her. That's unbelievable." He wiped the tears from his face. Sandy took his arm and steered him over to the other end of the table where she helped him into a chair and then sat beside him with her hand on his arm.

Hansen shifted his body so he was facing Arlen. "You're a drug salesman, isn't that right, Mr. Gerstead?"

"Yes," said Arlen. "But what does that have to do with anything?"

"Do you have access to syringes? Do you carry samples of pentobarbital?"

"No, I don't." Arlen's voice sounded defensive, vehement, even to Ellie, and she wondered why he felt that way. "Barbiturates are a whole different class of drug than what I deal with. I deal in asthma drugs and anxiety medications, things like that. Pills and capsules. I don't have samples of anything that would be injected."

"Okay," said Hansen. "Thanks for clearing that up."

Ellie suddenly felt she counted for little or nothing in this conversation. She reached across the table and touched Hansen's sleeve. "Tell me everything you're thinking. I want to know."

"It isn't nice."

"None of this is nice," Ellie said. She wondered at her own detachment.

Hansen gave one of his tired smiles. "Okay," he said. "We don't think this was a spur-of-the-moment thing." He let that sink in.

"That's why he didn't want you two to stay here at the B&B with us," Sandy said, looking at Ellie.

"Makes sense," Hansen said. "We think he either knew someone here in town or the guy followed you from Pittsburgh. At first we thought Richardson might have passed him a key at the restaurant so that he was in your room when you returned or Richardson could have let him in once you got back to the hotel. But that doesn't match the security camera tapes. No one was seen entering or leaving your room other than you two, and the other activity in the hallway was into and out of rooms quite a ways from yours. There were two waiters on room service duty, but they didn't service any rooms on your floor."

"Then how did he get in or out?" Sandy asked.

"We don't know. We suspect he went out of the window to a floor below. There was a big party going on in a couple of suites on the second floor with a lot of coming and going of people not registered at the hotel. He could easily have slipped in among them." Hansen shrugged and shook his head.

"We've also been checking his calls. Richardson only made calls from his cell to his answering service Saturday morning and Saturday afternoon. Though there were two calls made from the room phone—one to the Three Coins and one to this B&B."

"Joel called the restaurant to check on the dinner reservations," Ellie said. "And he called the B&B to tell Sandy and Arlen what time to meet us."

Arlen spoke up. "I talked to him briefly. We agreed to meet at seven-thirty."

Sandy nodded in agreement.

"Dr. McKay, did you hear his call to the restaurant?" Skopowlski moved closer to the table and stood a bit behind Hansen.

"No, but I was running a bath part of that time," Ellie said. "He just told me he'd done it."

"Do you think the other man was at the restaurant, that he worked there?" Sandy was pale, Ellie thought, and she bit her lip in that familiar way as she spoke.

"We don't know—that seems a long shot," said Hansen, looking down the table. "The reservation girl at the Three Coins couldn't confirm that it was Richardson who called although the name was checked off, but they were busy in the late afternoon and the phone rang a lot. Several calls came in for the chef, one of the waiters had a sick kid—everything checked out."

"Will you find this man?" Ellie's voice was small and tentative as if all the fear was now taking hold.

Hansen sighed and looked her in the eye. "I don't know. We will certainly try. But I don't know. However, we don't believe you are in any real danger now. We actually don't think this was about you, not you personally. We think it was sexually motivated, that Richardson was a voyeur and that he had planned to kill himself once this was done. We don't think the other man will have any interest in you now that Richardson is dead."

"But are you sure?" said Sandy.

"No," said Skopowlski, "but we think Richardson paid him—he withdrew a lot of cash on Friday afternoon, which we didn't find in his things. So if the man was paid for his work, he won't be working for Richardson again."

Hansen looked over at Ellie. Her eyes had turned empty, lost. He touched her hand. "Dr. McKay? Ellie, are you okay?"

She blinked and looked at him. "No," she said, "but that's my problem now, not yours."

14

In the fall, the dining room at the Grand Canyon lodge closed down at eight. After the cake, Ellie and Al soon found themselves alone in the big room. The waitress encouraged them to take their coffee into the great hall and sit by the fire. She'd come for the cups later. But they left the table empty-handed and headed back toward the guest rooms.

As they approached her door, Al put his arm around her shoulders. She stiffened and he loosened his grip but didn't let go. With his other hand, he pulled the key out of his pocket and opened the door.

"May I stay with you?" he asked. His voice was gentle and he looked into her eyes, but then looked away, hoping that would give her more space.

Ellie took a deep breath. "No," she said and then let the breath go. "But I'll come to you. I'll come to you a little later."

Al nodded. "414," he said. "Back toward the main lobby, take a left and then follow the signs. And take your time. We're in no hurry." He smiled at her and saw that she seemed a little calmer, a little more sure. He handed her a key to his room.

She went in and closed the door. He waited a moment to see if she would change her mind, but he heard nothing, so he turned and went to his room. He hung up his jacket, took off his boots, then stood there a bit perplexed. He wasn't a pajama kind of guy. He'd slept in the all-together for most of his life, married and single. But he couldn't answer the door naked or get into bed before she came. What if she just needed to talk for a while? He wished they'd already been through this part so they could be easy together.

In the end, he stripped his fancy clothes off and hung them up and put on an old, soft pair of jeans. Then he flossed and brushed his teeth and used mouthwash a couple of times. He didn't know what else to do with himself. He felt fifteen again—and not the good part of fifteen.

He turned down the bed, propped up the pillows, and lay against them. The digital clock read 8:30. For the first time in years, he thought about June Marie. She'd been the daughter of his mother's closest friend and she came to stay summers with them to get out of the noise and dirt of Chicago. Those summers had been happy ones. He taught her to ride and rope as he learned for himself to be a cowboy. In high school, they'd written to each other every week or two, long-distance sweethearts—soul mates, she'd called it. He pined for her when he went away to college, told her he'd marry her when he was through. She'd never said yes, but he assumed it was understood. Then his senior year, there was a long silence between them, and his mother wrote that she had married a Jewish boy from her neighborhood and they'd joined the Peace Corps and gone to the Philippines. That summer he'd come to the Canyon to work in the park and Nature had worked her magic, helping him to heal his heart. Three years later, he'd met Annie and married her and they'd had thirty-five years on the ranch together before she was gone.

He hadn't thought he would marry again. And certainly not a stranger, a stranger with troubles he couldn't even fathom. His friends would think he'd lost his mind. And maybe he had. But he was tired of worrying about his own life problems, tired of using Gracie as a false kind of comfort, tired of being alone in his life. He believed that people needed each other, like that corny Barbara Streisand song, and in an instant in the Maverick Bar, he'd decided to need Ellie.

He woke to find her sitting on the bed next to him. She wore a long, soft black coat with a hood that made her look like a priestess from the King Arthur book he'd read when he was eleven. He reached up and touched her face and a wave of sadness came over him for this wounded creature who'd come into his care. But he wasn't at all sure that he was magician enough.

"I was tempted not to wake you," Ellie said.

"I'm glad you did." He stroked her cheek and she leaned into his hand and then lay down beside him, tucking the coat around her. They lay like that for a few minutes until he moved his head and looked at her and saw that she was watching him. He kissed her then and felt her kiss him back, a deep kiss, and he was glad.

After a few minutes, she sat up and undid the one button of her coat and he saw that she wore a white cotton gown underneath. The sleeves were loose wings of sheer fabric and lace and went almost to her wrists. The lacey neckline left her throat bare and accentuated the fullness of her breasts and the near roundness of her shoulders. It was simple and elegant, modest and provocative. Desire surged through him and he put his hand on her waist and pulled her down to him. She lay for a moment with her head on his shoulder and her hand moving on his chest as if to take his measure. Then she turned her face up and they kissed for a long time.

But when he moved his knee up between her legs and pressed against her, she flinched and pulled back, her breathing suddenly sharp and ragged. He slowed his pace then, stroked her flank through the gown and held her close until she quieted again.

"Ellie, it's okay," he whispered. "I won't hurt you and I won't let anyone else hurt you."

She pulled back to look into his eyes. She searched them for a long time and then pressed her mouth to his. He unbuttoned the gown, pushed it aside, and saw the marks. He stifled a gasp and then gingerly moved away from her. She lay still, barely breathing, her eyes shut tight. Only the few tears sliding down onto the pillow betrayed her.

He kissed her eyes and said in a low, gentle voice. "Ellie, look at me."

After a moment, she opened her eyes and met his. "It doesn't matter to me," he said. "The past is the past. Our lives are from now on."

The skittish animal in her looked out at him. He was unsure how to treat her, whether to acknowledge the marks or ignore them.

Her impassive face gave him no clue. Finally, he propped himself up on the pillows and pulled her to him. He waited a moment to find the right words. "For better or worse, Ellie. That's how it works with me. I've married all of you. You've married all of me. I come to you battered, scarred, old. I don't care. You come to me battered, scarred, old. I don't care about that either. We don't know each other but we will. We have the rest of our lives to sort that out. Or at least I hope so. And I want you, naked or not. When you're ready."

She said nothing, but her breathing grew even and slow after a while, and her limbs slowly relaxed. He reached down, pulled the comforter over them and turned out the light. When he awoke hours later, he was alone.

15

After her conversation with the detectives, Ellie went up to lie down in her room at the B&B. She felt exhausted and wired at the same time. She felt as if she'd been assaulted again, and yet she could fathom little of what she'd heard.

All that week, she'd clung to the idea that she and Joel were both victims, even though some part of her knew that wasn't logical. She needed to believe that he had been murdered and that she had been hurt by someone else. She'd told herself a story about the killer being interrupted before he could kill her too. All that week she'd refused to talk about what had happened. She didn't want Arlen's or Sandy's speculations. She didn't read the paper or watch TV. She spent the time instead mourning Joel and his untimely death and feeling the absence of a man she'd come to care for. Now that illusion was shattered, yet she didn't know what to do with all that she had found out. She felt a pressing need for it not to be so.

She knew she should call her sponsor. That's what the program said to do. But how to talk about all this? Her sponsor wasn't a therapist, wasn't a professional who could help her make sense of what Joel had done. She knew she should go to a meeting, but she didn't have the energy to find one, let alone sit through the readings and sharing with people who had no idea what she'd been through. She hoped Sandy would come in and talk to her but she didn't.

Sandy was in shock, too, probably. And what could she say anyway? That she'd never really liked Joel? How would that help anything now?

She paced the room, restless, anxious, a taut-wire tension ratcheting up in her body. On a pass by the window, she saw Hansen and Skopowlski talking on the sidewalk. She hurried down.

Hansen wasn't surprised to see Ellie come out the front door. After decades of this work, he was no longer surprised by anything that a victim or perpetrator did. He sent Skopowlski off with the car and followed her into the dining room. He closed the pocket doors on both ends, nodding to Sandy and Arlen, who stood talking in the kitchen.

Ellie had taken up a post at the French doors so he sat himself at the end of the dining table, a good distance from her. He relaxed his shoulders and jaw, a technique he'd learned in a stress-reduction course. He found that it helped him and it helped people talk to him more easily. Then he waited.

"The Joel I knew wouldn't have done this to me," she said, shaking her head. "He was a gentleman, you know, the old-fashioned kind who opened car doors and held out a chair and stood up when I came into the room. I didn't care about any of that but he insisted. He was polite. He was respectful. There was a—I don't know—a kind of elegance about it, about him."

She looked over at Hansen, who was watching her face. He nodded so she would go on.

"I didn't think Joel liked sex much. We saw each other for five or six weeks before we slept together. He wasn't eager or pushy about getting me in bed and that was fine with me. He was my first sober relationship." She looked at him to see if he understood.

"Tell me about that," he said. He watched her whole body shift as she went into teacher mode.

"I started drinking pretty young, in college. And I drank for many years. So sex and drinking, well, they went together, you know. Sex is easier somehow when you're drunk or stoned. At least it was for me. When I got sober two years ago, I didn't really know how to be with somebody. In the first year, they tell you to stay out of a relationship because the drama can get you drunk again. But after two years, I was ready to try and Joel, well, he made it easy. He was not very affectionate but he made few demands, let me take it at my own pace. It all seemed perfect."

"Did you ever see a mean streak or anything that told you there was another side to him?" Hansen kept his voice low, neutral, just talking.

Ellie shook her head. "No, I don't think so. He was very intense when it came to his work. And he was often moody if he lost a patient, like he had that Friday."

Hansen felt a spark of something. "Tell me about that."

"I don't know the details. It was a young man with gunshot wounds. He must have died, Joel was irritable on the trip to Gettysburg. I learned that when he got moody, he hadn't been able to save the patient. I do know that what he liked was the challenge of the surgeries. Once he'd saved a woman who'd been thrown through a windshield. She was badly hurt, like liver and spleen and intestines all mangled, and he was able to patch her up. And there was a Latino kid who was bleeding to death from knife wounds all over his body and he saved him too. He seemed very proud of those things, and I was proud of him for doing it. That's not work I could do."

Hansen wondered if she could hear the eulogy in her voice—and the denial. "Did he care about these patients?"

She looked at him and a curious expression crossed her eyes. She pushed off from the wall and came over and sat down next to him. "I teach literature, you may know that."

Hansen nodded.

"Literature is about stories, the stories of people and relationships. The first couple of times Joel told me about his cases, I asked questions about their stories. How had they ended up in the ER? But he didn't know. He was only interested in their bodies, their wounds. He wasn't interested in their lives or their . . . their selves, their spirits. Don't get me wrong, he wasn't cold about it. He just seemed to care about getting the job done. I figured he'd seen so much carnage and violence that he'd had to tune it out and focus on his technique."

She reached out her hand and touched the edge of his sleeve, as she had done earlier that morning. He could feel the warmth of her hand through his jacket and shirt. "There was something wrong with Joel, wasn't there?"

"Yes, I believe there was." He paused.

"I feel so foolish," she said, "so stupid. All these things I've told you add up to something, don't they? Something I couldn't see."

"This is not your fault." He could feel himself overstepping his role as detective, but he couldn't stop. "You had no reason to look for it." He saw her go pale then and he knew they were done.

"I'll go find your friend. You should rest now," he said and he got up and left the room.

Sandy helped her upstairs, insisted she take off her clothes and get back into bed.

"You've had a terrible shock, honey. Sleep a while. It will help."

Ellie felt worn out, wrung out, but a little clearer for having talked to Hansen. She rolled over on her side, curling up as tightly as she could. Then she closed her eyes and saw Joel's face, and suddenly she felt like she was choking. She got up from the bed and went to the closet. She found the valium stuffed deep into the pocket under her dirty clothes and she took two. In less than ten minutes, they had worked their magic.

⚘

Ellie woke with a start. She had dreamed again of Joel. He was sitting on one bed in a cheap motel room and she sat on the other. He was handing her bottles of whiskey and she would drain each one and then lay it carefully down as if it were a sleeping baby. His look was clear, charming even, and she felt a deep surge of desire for him. Then there was a knock on the door and she went to answer it. When she turned back, Joel was gone but the bed was littered with bottles.

She heard the knock again and found herself in her room at the B&B. The door opened quietly and Sandy stuck her head in. "Are you awake?"

"Yes," Ellie lied. "Come in."

Sandy sat on the edge of the bed. She patted Ellie's shoulder where it lay under the comforter. "Arlen needs to go home. He can't take any more time away. And I need to get back too. Are you feeling up to going home? Detective Hansen says they don't need us to stay any longer." She smiled sadly at her friend. "Maybe you can start to put this behind you."

Ellie was tempted to laugh, but she knew it would come out bitter. She couldn't imagine putting this anywhere. But she took a deep breath and said yes, she could pack up and go. The sooner, the better.

Within an hour, they were in the car. Their drive retraced the route from the Friday night before. Ellie stared out the window at the countryside. It had been the longest week of her life.

16

"Good morning." Al found Ellie in the dining room at the same table they'd shared the night before. Her head was bent in concentration over a notebook. He watched her for a moment before going up to the table, then waited until she looked up before sitting down across from her. She smiled back at him and closed the notebook.

"Hi," he said. "Have you been up long?"

"About an hour," said Ellie. "I like to write first thing each day. You?"

"I got up before dawn. Went for a hike. Felt good to be on the trails."

"Did you miss Beemus?"

He chuckled. "Yes, although it's been a while since that dog's been trail-worthy. He's pretty old."

"I have a couple of old cats," she said. "I know what that's like. Hard to see our loved ones fail."

Al liked the way her face lit up when she talked about her animals. This was the first time she'd mentioned them and he wanted to ask more. Hell, he wanted to ask all kinds of things of this woman he'd married. And he didn't know what was okay and what wasn't. He decided to say so. "About last night . . ."

Her whole body stiffened and a frank look of fear crossed her face. That wasn't at all what he'd wanted. The young waiter came by and poured him coffee. "Later," he said, when the boy tried to hand him a menu. The boy skulked away.

He tried again. "Please, Ellie, just listen. I meant what I said last night, that's all. I accept whoever you are, and whatever has happened to you. Clearly, you've been through a lot and I respect that. And if you ever want to tell me about it, I want to know. And if you don't, that's okay. But I can't pretend you didn't have a life before now and I want to know about who you are and what you like and what you don't like and I want to be able to tell you those things about myself, too. I want us to be able to say what we need from each other."

The whole time he was saying this, she was looking out the window at the far side of the Canyon. Huge clouds scudded across the late fall sky, and there were shadows playing along the layers of rock. She kept silent a long time and he felt discouraged. *I'm not cut out for this horse-whisperer role*, he thought, *not with a woman with scars like those.*

Ellie turned back to him and her eyes were surprisingly calm. She gave a little wry smile and took a deep breath. "I'm not who you thought I was at the bar that night, am I?"

He realized this was a rhetorical question and he kept his mouth shut.

"I'm different when I drink. I know that. Maybe it wasn't fair of me to say yes to you if I wasn't going to keep on drinking. Maybe it was the drinking woman you wanted. She's a lot more fun. She's not scared of much at all." She looked him in the eye, but he didn't know if she wanted a response or just wanted to see if he was paying attention. "The sober me, well, that's a different story."

"It didn't have anything to do with your drinking." He paused. "No, that's not strictly true." He ran his hand through his hair. "I don't know. I'm not very good at talking about these things."

"Why did you ask me, Al?" She was looking straight at him.

"Why did you say yes?"

She shook her head as if at his foolishness.

Al decided just to plunge in. "I was married for a lot of years, more than thirty. Her name was Annie and we were in love for a long time. It was a good life. My dad passed the ranch on to me. Annie and I had a son. We had some good years when there was money and we had a few when there wasn't much." He looked out at the Canyon.

"When our boy was eleven, he died." He could feel his breath shuddering in his chest, even after all these years. He breathed steadily and slowly for a few seconds to right himself. "Some couples don't make it past that," he said, "but we did. We worked at it. It was hard but we did it. I think Stevie must have found a way to hold us together."

Stevie came and stood beside him then. He could smell the sun on his boy's skin, and for just a moment, he felt the weight of his boy in his arms, first wriggling with life, then leaden with drowning. Something sharp and jagged closed his throat and it was a moment before he could speak again. This time he leaned into the table, resting his forearms on the checkered cloth.

"Three years ago, I lost Annie too. Three years is a long time. Three years I've been alone at the ranch. No wife, no son, just Beemus and a few hired hands. It's not enough. It's not good to be lonely like that. I'm a man who needs a woman." He looked at Ellie and saw that she was watching him, really watching. He saw her nod. "And something in the Maverick told me I needed you. I don't know how else to explain it." He saw now that there were tears in her eyes.

"Tell me about the boy," she said. "If you want to."

And he did. He told her the stories that he had told himself in the middle of the night. Of a little patch of garden where Stevie killed a snake with a miniature hoe. Of a bicycle without a paved road to ride it on. Of a 4-H calf that won no prizes at all and Stevie's broken heart when it went to slaughter. Of reading together, *Gulliver's Travels* and *Huck Finn* and Sandburg's *Lincoln*. Of watching the clock each afternoon and being at the end of the long drive every day to bring his son home from school.

Somehow in this telling, breakfast came and was eaten. The check came and she put cash next to it. Coffee, and more coffee, was in his cup. And he kept on talking, filling the well of his memory with a flood of stories. And when he was done and sat back, he could see in her eyes that there was more between them now than a marriage license.

♎

Ellie and Al spent two more nights at the Grand Canyon. Al realized the days would be better spent in courtship than honeymoon, and he let Ellie set the pace for what they did and what they talked about. He hiked alone early each morning even though the deep frost made the predawn hours bitterly cold. But it gave him time to think and the movement to work off his restlessness and curiosity.

He'd join her each morning in the dining room where she sat writing. They'd taken to telling stories of their childhoods, their school years, safe ground for them both. They both had been shy children, happiest alone—he outside with his dog, she inside with her books. But their early lives had been very different. She'd grown up in a suburb, he on the ranch. Her exposure to wild spaces was a Campfire Girl camp she attended each summer for a week. His exposure to a library hadn't happened until he went to college. He began to worry that she wouldn't be happy as a rancher's wife.

The first night repeated itself twice more. She would come to him late in the evening and he would hold her and soothe her until they both slept. At some point, she would go back to her room. Although they kissed and touched each other, he did not try to make love to her again.

It was snowing the day they left, tiny flakes that spun and whirled in the breeze. It delighted her and he caught a glimpse of the girl she'd been and his feelings deepened.

They were crossing the border into New Mexico when he finally brought up the future. "Are you okay with a motel for a while? We could get you a suite at the Residence Inn? I want to do some work at the ranch before you come out there—maybe a week or three."

She looked over at him and he saw gratitude and relief in her face.

"Good," he said. "That's settled then."

17

At seven in the morning on the Monday they all returned to Greensburg, Sandy Gerstead was in the kitchen making coffee when the doorbell rang. Puzzled, she ran her fingers through her hair, tightened the sash on her robe and opened the door to two men in suits.

"Good morning, ma'am. Is your husband at home?" The two men smiled, fake friendly smiles, the both of them, and showed her their badges.

"Yes," she said, "he's in the shower."

There was a moment of awkward silence and Sandy realized the men were waiting to be invited in. Not knowing what else to do, she opened the door wider and the two men came into the foyer and stood there patiently. Sandy went up the stairs.

Arlen was shaving, a towel around his waist, the bathroom door ajar and leaking steam. He frowned when he saw her face. "What's up?"

"There are two policemen downstairs wanting to talk to you."

"Don't look so worried, Sandy. I'm sure they just want to get my opinion on what happened to Ellie. We're key witnesses, you know. They're bound to want to hear what we have to say."

Sandy didn't feel reassured. "Should I offer them coffee?"

"Of course." Arlen went on shaving. "Tell them I'll be down in ten minutes."

Arlen was true to his word. In exactly ten minutes, he came whistling down the stairs. The two men, both in their forties, stood in his living room, one holding a mug of steaming coffee. The smaller and stouter of the two men held out his hand. "Mr. Gerstead? I'm Detective Capriano. This is Detective Jackson. We need you to come downtown with us."

Arlen shook his head and smiled. "Happy to tell you what I know about the case, gentlemen, but I've got a client meeting at eight-thirty."

"I'm afraid that will have to wait. We promise not to take too much of your time, but we need to do this now. I'm sure you understand," Capriano said.

Sandy noticed that although he wasn't a handsome man, he had astonishing eyelashes on beautiful dark eyes.

"Why can't we talk here?" Arlen's struggle to maintain his good humor flashed across his face. Sandy, who stood at the edge of the room, was suddenly afraid.

"We need a DNA sample, sir. We are trying to eliminate as many potential suspects as possible so we can find out who did this to your friends."

"You mean I'm a suspect?" Arlen's face had gone pale.

"No, sir, but we do have to look at anyone who might have been involved. Do you object to giving us the sample? We can get a warrant."

"No, no, I don't object. That's not what I meant. I just can't believe you would think that I could hurt Ellie or Joel."

"We don't think that. This is just procedure. It helps us narrow the scope of the investigation."

Jackson spoke for the first time, his deep bass rumbling in the quiet room. "Do you need a coat, Mr. Gerstead? It's chilly this morning."

Arlen nodded and Sandy went to get it.

After the three men had left, Sandy stood for a long moment in the foyer. How had they gotten on this runaway train? She wanted to call Ellie, tell her what had just happened, what she was afraid of, but she knew she couldn't.

⚘

It was a long drive into Pittsburgh, out onto the Interstate and then into town. They entered police headquarters through a parking lot and a basement door. Somehow Arlen had expected to enter through the front door amid cameras and reporters. He felt disappointed. They parked him in a small windowless room on the fifth floor, and he watched the clock for thirty minutes, growing more and more impatient as time passed. At one point, an acne-scarred kid with gangly arms and huge wrists took a mouth swab, filled out a lengthy form, and had Arlen sign it. When he left, Arlen wondered if he should have read the form first. He waited nearly another hour, more and more incensed at the treatment he was receiving.

Just before ten, Capriano came in alone. He had a manila folder with him, which he placed on the table between them so Arlen could see that it bore his name.

"What's that?" he said. "I don't have a record."

Capriano smiled. "You don't have a criminal record, Mr. Gerstead, but you do have a record. Tell me about Melanie Trumbo."

Arlen gave a small humph of exasperation. "I'm never going to live that down, am I? I made a stupid joke. It was off-color, I get that. I didn't think about it at the time. I didn't mean anything by it. I wasn't trying to come on to her or hassle her. I was just telling a joke to a bunch of guys. She overheard us, thought it was about her, and reported me. It wasn't a big deal."

"You don't think sexual harassment of a co-worker is a big deal?"

"I didn't say that. I didn't harass her. I didn't touch her or try to come on to her."

Capriano waited.

Arlen rushed on. "I'm a happily married man. I wouldn't risk my marriage for someone like her."

"What happened after her complaint?"

"There was a kind of hearing. In the end, I got reassigned to a different territory."

"Why did you stalk her afterward?"

Arlen looked up, surprise and something else in his eyes. "Do I need a lawyer?"

Capriano shrugged. "I don't know. I'm not accusing you of anything. We're just having a conversation here."

"Okay, okay, I went by her house a couple of times. I just wanted to let her know that I was, I don't know, I was angry. That new territory wasn't nearly as profitable as my old one—the hospitals were much smaller—and I'd lost all the hard work I'd put in making contacts, all because of a reaction to a stupid joke."

Capriano kept silent a bit, but Arlen didn't speak again, so he did. "Tell me what's in your juvenile record."

Again Arlen looked surprised. Then he shook his head. "That's sealed."

"I know," Capriano said. "But you are certainly free to tell me what happened. Like I said, we're just having a conversation here."

Arlen seemed to weigh his options. "I was in love with a girl and I used to follow her home. I hoped she'd notice me."

"Sounds pretty innocent," Capriano said. "I've followed a girl home a couple of times in my time."

"Yeah, see, it was no big deal."

"But somebody pressed charges."

"Yeah, her old man. He didn't think I was good enough for her."

"Well, men do want to protect their daughters. Do you have a daughter, Arlen?"

Arlen shook his head. "I have boys, two boys, but they live with their mother."

Capriano nodded in sympathy. "It's tough not to see your kids." He waited for a response but when none came, he went on. "So that was it. You followed her home. The old man didn't like it. He called the police. That's the whole story. There wasn't any more to it?" He looked at Arlen.

Arlen nodded but he bit his lip and tipped his chair back from the table.

"You know," said Capriano. "I was telling the truth this morning. We don't think you had anything to do with the death of Dr. Richardson or the assault on Dr. McKay. You weren't in that hotel room at all that weekend, were you?"

Arlen looked relieved. "No," he said. "My wife was. She went up to use the bathroom. I'll bet you found her prints there."

Capriano smiled at him in encouragement although he gave no sign of agreement. "How well did you know Dr. Richardson?"

"I met him through Ellie. They came to dinner at our house and Ellie had us over a few times. We went to a movie once or twice with them. Joel and I went to a basketball game at Pitt one Saturday. I had a great time but he wasn't much into sports so I didn't ask him again."

"Did he talk about his past?"

"No. I knew he'd been in 'Nam. One time when we went by for a drink at his place, he showed me a collection of some sort of daggers that he'd brought back. I guess as a surgeon he'd be interested in that kind of thing."

"Did you ever see him use these daggers?"

"No, I don't think I ever saw them again."

"And that was it? A few dinner dates, a ball game. Your wife and Dr. McKay are good friends, aren't they?"

Arlen nodded.

"So, wouldn't it be logical for you to become good friends with Richardson?"

"I guess, but he wasn't the good-buddy kind of guy, if you know what I mean." He looked at Capriano for agreement, and the detective nodded and waited. "He was, I don't know, kind of weird. He had secrets."

"Did he ever tell you any of those secrets?"

"No, why would he?"

"What was the name of the girl you followed home?"

"Karen, Karen Schuster. Why?"

"Just curious. Why did her father have you arrested?"

"I told you. I followed her home."

Capriano waited. A minute ticked by.

"Okay, okay," said Arlen, "I had a gun. I wanted to show it to her. I wanted her to think I was somebody."

"And then what happened?"

"She freaked out, and her father came to the door and he started yelling and I pointed it at him."

Capriano waited.

"That's it. Her father took the gun from me and the police came and I went to jail for about an hour and my folks came and got me and that was that."

Capriano smiled and nodded, then stood up. "Someone will drive you home now, Mr. Gerstead. Thank you so much for cooperating with us. It helps a lot." He watched the relief flood Arlen's face and he knew there was more, perhaps much more, to all this, but he decided to bide his time. Arlen wasn't going anywhere.

18

When he suggested she stay in town a while longer, Al hadn't been thinking of just Ellie. He really did want to do some work on the place—have Consuelo and her crew come out and clean it top to bottom, maybe repaint the bedroom—but he also knew he had to talk with Gracie and tell her what he had done before he moved Ellie to the ranch. It seemed only right. So after he dropped Ellie at the motel, he drove by Gracie's to see if she might be home. Her 4x4 was in the driveway. He parked behind it, went in through the open garage, and knocked on the kitchen door.

"Come on in," he heard her say. She was wrapped in a Navajo-plaid fleece robe and big wool socks, her red hair tousled as if she'd just gotten up. She was sitting in the recliner, watching *Oprah*. She grinned when she saw who it was and muted the TV. "Hey, where you been?"

"Traveling," he said.

She raised her eyebrows and gave him a quizzical look. Then she shrugged and smiled again. He moved toward her and she put up a hand. "Don't come too close, honey. I've got one hell of a cold and you sure as hell don't want it." It was then he noticed the box of tissues and the lineup of cough syrup and medicines on the table next to her.

"Thanks for the warning." Al went over and moved the newspaper aside and sat down on the couch.

"Sorry about the mess," she said. "I've just felt like crap the last couple of days." She blew her nose loudly in a tissue and pitched it into the wastebasket that sat a little ways from the recliner.

"That's okay, Gracie. I know you weren't expecting me."

"Well, I did think you might come around, especially when I wasn't at the Maverick on Tuesday."

"I was out of town." He paused, hoping the right words would come. He could see her waiting for information. "Look, Gracie, there's no easy way to say what I've got to say."

A flash of pain crossed her face, then resignation. "I've heard this one, before, Al. You've met somebody else."

"Yes, and the thing is, I've married her."

"You what? I don't get it. Is this a joke?"

"No, Gracie, it's no joke. We went to Flagstaff and got married last Sunday."

"We who?"

"You don't know her. She's not from around here."

"Where is she from?"

"I don't know." Al realized how stupid that sounded and that it hadn't occurred to him until this moment that he didn't know where Ellie had come from.

Gracie looked at him for a long moment. "How long have you known her?"

"A week or so. I met her at the Maverick last Tuesday."

"Our night. Let me get this straight. You met another woman on our night at the Maverick and you married her. And you don't know where she's from."

"Yup," he nodded, "that about sums it up."

"What's her name, this woman who's bewitched you?" He could hear the jealousy choking her voice and it surprised him.

"Ellie."

"And I suppose she's twenty and got legs up to her ass and long blonde hair and she thinks you're a big, strong cowboy sugar daddy who's going to take care of her."

"You watch too many TV movies, Gracie. Ellie's my age and she looks it. I need a companion, Gracie. I need to share my life again."

"And it was never going to be me, was it?" There was a bitter set to her mouth that reminded him of Annie. He hated to have put it there.

"No," he said finally and paused, wondering how much he should say. "Annie was always going to be . . ."

"Fuck you, Al," she said. "No wonder Annie left you. Now get out of my house." And she turned up the TV so loud it hurt his ears. He could hear Oprah's voice all the way to his truck.

19

Ellie planned to go back to work the first Monday after Gettysburg but Sandy talked her out of it. "You need more time, honey. You need to rest. You've been through a terrible ordeal. No one will fault for you taking another week or two. Maybe you should even consider taking a leave this semester."

And so she'd agreed to stay home and rest. Not that home was all that restful. The first Saturday morning, she woke to find the morass of the media at her door, microphones and cameras and reporters. They rang the bell incessantly until her landlord, Duncan, a home-town boy who lived downstairs, called his uncle, who called the chief of police. Warned about trespassing on private property, the reporters retreated to the street. Duncan called again and they were all cited for holding a parade without a permit. Soon, only the diehards were left, sequestered in their cars.

Things quieted down then. She didn't go out. She stopped answering the phone, stayed off email. Some of her faculty friends called to see how she was doing, but Ellie didn't know what to tell them. She didn't want to describe anything. She didn't want to talk about it. It was easier to just see Sandy, who brought her groceries and Thai take-out. It was Sandy who called Ellie's doctor, made her an appointment for early in the week, got the name of a rape counselor. It was Sandy who fended off reporters with ease, protecting her friend.

Saturday was hard. Ellie didn't want to be alone with her feelings, so she and Sandy played Quiddler and Canasta, watched old movies, exercised to an old Jane Fonda tape—anything to not think and not talk. Sandy stayed while she napped, ran her a hot bath in the late afternoon. At seven, she took two more Valium and sent Sandy home and went to bed.

Sunday morning, she found she didn't have the energy to get up. She fed the cats and went back to bed. The cats were happy to follow her into the bedroom. She dozed and dreamed and slept some more. She woke thirsty from the drugs but with little appetite. When Sandy showed up, she was asleep on the couch. Sandy made tomato soup but Ellie let the bowl grow cold on the coffee table.

She slept through the next five days. She slept through her doctor's appointment but got the woman to agree to refill the Valium. Sandy, who worked at the college library, came by on her way home to fix supper. But most of the nights, Ellie lied and said she'd had a late lunch and not to bother fixing anything.

Late Friday afternoon, her cell phone rang. Only a few people had that number: Joel, Sandy, her sister, her best friend in Virginia. But it was none of those. It was Detective Hansen.

"Did I wake you?" His voice was already familiar and somehow comforting, and she found it odd that she felt that way.

"No, yes. I've done nothing but sleep all week. I think I must be depressed." She heard a low chuckle from the other end.

"I would think you have a right to be," he said. "How are you doing, other than sleeping?"

"I don't know. I just get through the days. I'm looking forward to going back to work next week."

"Isn't that a little soon?" She heard the concern in his voice and it made her feel somehow safer though she knew that was silly. He was two hundred miles away.

"You sound like Sandy," she said. "I need to work. I need to get back into my life. I can't watch any more game shows or soap operas. I'm not cut out to be idle."

"Well, don't rush it. You've been through a lot."

He paused and she waited.

"I don't have a lot to report," he said. "We've eliminated all the possible suspects that we came across. We're pretty well convinced that it wasn't someone you knew."

"Like who?"

"Some of Dr. Richardson's colleagues, men he knew socially."

"Arlen." She didn't know why that occurred to her.

"Yes, we looked at Mr. Gerstead, but his DNA was not a match."

"You tested his DNA?"

"Ellie, Dr. McKay, we're very thorough at what we do."

"Arlen? You suspected Arlen? He's my friend. He's married to my best friend. He's . . ."

"Not that kind of guy?"

"Touché," she said. "What do I know about men and what they're capable of?" She could hear the bitterness in her own voice.

"Whoa," he said. "We looked at every man we could think of. We have nothing that puts Mr. Gerstead in that room with you and Joel, nothing at all. We have no evidence that you should feel uncomfortable with him."

"Would you tell me if you did?"

"We don't suspect him." Hansen's voice sounded weary and patient. She remembered his tired smile. He went on. "We're looking in other directions."

She felt a deep sinking in her gut. "You're not going to find him, are you? The man who did this. He's going to be out there in my world."

"I'm not going to stop looking, Ellie. That's all I can say."

"Yeah, I got it. Okay, I'm going to hang up now. Thank you for calling." The coldness in her voice spread through her body. She went upstairs and got into bed and turned the heating pad on as high as it would go.

20

After Hansen hung up, he sat in his car outside Ellie's apartment for a while. He wanted to go up and knock on her door, convince her he was doing all he could. But it wasn't really true. Once the coroner ruled that Joel Richardson had taken his own life, the case faded quickly from priority in the Gettysburg Borough Police Department workload, there were plenty of other cases to handle. And Ellie McKay wasn't a resident or a local taxpayer. She was a tourist who'd brought her own bad fortune to town with her. After the initial gossip and titillation, the locals, including the police chief, saw it as a Pittsburgh matter. Hansen argued that the second man could have been a local, and the chief gave them permission to spend a bit more time looking into it, but he clearly didn't see it as critical.

He had heard twice that week from Arlen Gerstead, who said he was calling for Ellie, wanting to know if there was any news. The first time, his DNA results had just come back and Hansen wondered if Arlen were gloating, rubbing Hansen's nose in it that he wasn't a suspect any longer. Capriano had pegged Gerstead as a *prima donna* witness: someone enamored of crime and delighted to be involved. But something deeper nagged at Hansen about Arlen, something for which there was no evidence whatsoever. Maybe he just didn't like the man, didn't like someone who'd want to be friends with Joel Richardson.

To both phone calls, Hansen had said no, no news. That was half true. They still had no clue as to the identity of the second man, but over the two weeks, they had learned a lot about Joel Richardson.

The Vietnam story was true. He had served two tours of duty, first as a medic, then as a surgeon. He'd been twice decorated although a doctor in DC named Kirchner, who had worked with Richardson in a field hospital, said he wasn't convinced that he'd deserved the medals. "But then, I didn't like him much," Kirchner had told Hansen over the phone. "He often worked drunk or hungover, and he had a temper and took it out on the nurses. But he was a wizard with the knife, I'll say that for him. He saved a lot of lives—and limbs—and didn't lose too many. In the off-time, he liked to cruise the bars and the prostitutes. He even married one, I heard. That wasn't my scene. I had a wife and kids here in the States and all I wanted to do was survive and come home." He paused and then gave a deep sigh. "He's dead, you say? Was it a suicide?"

"At this point, we don't know."

"Hmmm. That war did strange things to a lot of us. Were you old enough to serve back then?"

"I volunteered when I turned eighteen," said Hansen, "but the war ended while I was in basic."

"Just as well," Kirchner said. "Just as well."

Richardson's Pittsburgh General colleagues said much the same thing when Hansen showed up there toward the end of the second week. Excellent skills, undaunted by the most impossible cases, a great track record but tough to work with. The nurses weren't interested in being on shift with him, as he made things difficult for them.

"How so?" Hansen had asked one ER nurse practitioner.

She ran her fingers through her short gray hair. "Nothing specific, really. Just an attitude of impatience and intolerance. He wanted everything at warp speed—instruments, test results, answers. On a busy night, and there aren't many that aren't busy in the ER, it's chaotic enough here without a doctor cursing the technicians."

"Anything odd about his personal life?" said Hansen. "I know sometimes doctors and nurses . . ."

She laughed. "Around here we called him Flash. All style, no substance. He looked good but there was nothing really there."

"Anyone who tried him out?"

"You might ask Janey Colson. She dated him a bit when he first came to the hospital."

But Janey had little to say when Hansen tracked her down. "We went out a few times. He was good-looking, a sharp dresser. Took me to a few nice restaurants. But I was looking for a husband and there was something missing."

"Missing between you?"

"Yes, but more missing in him. To be honest, the sex wasn't all that great. He had, well, technique, he knew everything to do, but he wasn't really there with me. I wanted a man who was present, not off in his head carving up a spleen."

"Did he ever suggest anything kinky?"

"No," she said. Then she frowned and looked at him.

"What?" said Hansen. "Anything will help."

"Well, one time I saw some books in his bedroom. *The Story of O* and a collection by the Marquis de Sade. I knew what they were about—I've been around a little. But he never suggested we do anything out of the ordinary and I'd forgotten about them."

"He ever suggest a threesome?"

"No," she said, then she paused. "Well, there was this one time. A friend of his met us for breakfast after work. The guy seemed kind of nervous but decent enough. After we ate, Joel invited us both back to his apartment. We played music and drank until dawn and the men smoked a joint and talked about motorcycles and accidents they'd had. It wasn't all that fascinating to me, and I kept waiting for Jerry to go home so Joel and I could go to bed."

"That was his name? Jerry?"

"Yeah. I remember wondering if he was a J Jerry or a G Gerry. Funny what the mind gets up to when you're bored."

"Then what happened?"

"Nothing really. There was an odd kind of tension in the room as the morning came on, and I suddenly didn't feel too comfortable. So I went to the bathroom, got my coat, and went in to say goodbye. Joel didn't seem to care much one way or the other, gave me a peck on the lips and didn't even walk me to the door, but Jerry looked disappointed, like he was expecting something to happen. Later, after

I broke it off with Joel, I saw Jerry a couple of times at the hospital waiting for Joel and we chatted. I thought he might ask me out, but he didn't and I met my husband and that was that."

Hansen spent a couple more hours talking to Richardson's neighbors, other ER doctors, guys at his gym. Nothing turned up. He checked in with Capriano, who shared what he had.

Capriano had handled Richardson's electronic and financial records. The dead man had no landline and his cell phone and rarely used pager records led them nowhere. There were calls to the answering service and the hospital, quite a few to Ellie and three or four to the Gersteads over the months Ellie and Joel had seen each other. There were calls to a lot of take-out restaurants in Joel's Pittsburgh neighborhood. He saw a dentist and a chiropractor. The detectives got excited when they found the number of a Monroeville massage therapist, but it turned out that Joel had twice bought Ellie a massage gift certificate. He had never been in the place himself. And none of the numbers he called belonged to a Jerry or a Gerry or a Jerome or a Gerald.

Richardson had money. He made a great deal, had paid for his condo and his Lexus outright, owned expensive art. He had an American Express card, which he seemed to use only for travel and the occasional phone or email purchase. He withdrew $1,000 nearly every Friday—weekend cash spending, they assumed, but on what?

Capriano traced his clothes to several clothing importers online, one in Italy, one in Hong Kong, and other labels revealed a tailor in Squirrel Hill, who was most distressed to hear that such a good customer was no more. But there was nothing suspicious, or rather nothing that led anywhere.

That was the problem: Nothing led anywhere. There was no trace of the second man. Capriano and Hansen both knew that there's always a trace, that something *would* turn up but it was impossible to predict when. The Pittsburgh police put it in pending and Hansen headed home.

Hansen was more than reluctant to let the case go. What had happened to Ellie in that hotel room filled him with shame and anger. First, he was a career cop and a true believer. Protect and serve was what he lived by. While he wasn't always so sure about

misdemeanor drug busts, he didn't like to see any creep
with a heinous crime. And this was a heinous crime. They a
that Richardson had been in on it, probably arranged it,
paid for it. If he had abused her himself and then killed hims
the shame of his sickness, well, that would have been terrib
would have satisfied the right order of things in Hansen's wo
Richardson hadn't done it. He'd let it happen, had it done,
it done. And he'd most likely watched. In his jacket pock
forensics team had found two matching linen handkerchief
full of semen. They couldn't pinpoint the time of ejaculatic
could tell that the emissions had happened several hours
Hansen prided himself on knowing a fair amount about hu
nature, but this was one sick guy.

Hansen was angry on another level, a deeply personal one.
always found rape despicable. That and child abuse were the w
forms of bullying and power play a man could indulge in. So w
his younger daughter was raped in their backyard by a neighborh
kid who'd repaired her bike, Hansen had struggled to stay wit
the law, to just catch the kid and put him away. When the boy w
convicted, knowing the kid would experience rape himself behi
bars seemed only a small consolation. Just like knowing Richards
was dead was small consolation.

The night had descended and it was hours back to Gettysbur
Hansen thought one more time of knocking on Ellie's door, but h
knew his motives weren't entirely professional. He started the moto
and with one more look up at her windows, he drove away.

21

Ellie wasn't sure how she was going to make herself a life in Farmington, not in town or eventually on the ranch. She had never seen herself as living for her work but teaching had been fun, at least at first, and it had always given her life structure. So she met with the dean at San Juan College and although the man was clearly impressed with her credentials, there were no openings. There was, he said, a community education program if she wanted to offer French conversation for no credit. Ellie told him she'd think about it. As she drove away from the treeless campus, so different from the full-leafed splendor of gothic Greensburg, she realized that Joel was still calling the shots, pushing her into a retirement she did not want.

She wasn't drinking. After breakfast with Al that first morning, she'd poured out the bourbon. She'd had several hard days of craving but that had eased with sleep and good food and long, long walks. She went to a couple of AA meetings but it didn't seem to help much to be with strangers. She could hear her sponsor's voice urging her to return but she didn't go back.

She also didn't know what to do with Al. She and Joel had seen each other once or twice a week, sometimes once or twice a month. That had been plenty. But being a wife was going to mean something quite different. For one thing, Al expected her to make decisions

about redoing the house, expected her to want a say in wall colors and rug patterns and crockery. And he wanted to see her every day.

"I want to get to know you, Ellie. I want you to get to know me, to get to know this life we'll make together here. There's plenty of room here for you to have an office or a studio or whatever you want to do. It doesn't matter to me what it is. I just want you around," he told her one afternoon when she'd gone out to the ranch to have lunch with him. They had returned from the Grand Canyon a week earlier.

She'd taken to going out at noon most days. He'd show her the progress on the house. He'd talk about his day, ask about hers. She wanted to look forward to seeing him, she wanted that to be the highlight of her day, the structure she craved. But it didn't work. She felt a genuine fondness from him that both warmed her and made her feel guilty, for she did not return it. She found Al attractive, endearing even, but she did not love him. She thought about drinking again. When she drank, it was easier to be with men. The chemistry of attraction seemed heightened by a little bourbon and she was easier in her body. She could tell Al she'd changed her mind about wanting to stop. They could drink some wine together, get to know each other in that easier space. She liked him, she really did. But so much lay between them, so much that he didn't know and that she didn't know how to say.

The truth was that none of it seemed real. Not the wedding in Flagstaff, not the erstwhile honeymoon at the Grand Canyon, not their return to Farmington. She had thought that when she sobered up again, things would take on the awesome clarity of her first sobriety, when every leaf on every tree seemed vibrant and special, when she was so aware of her good health and her good fortune. She had believed that if she stopped drinking again now with Al, somehow the whole experience with Joel could be sorted out, put to rest. She saw now how naïve she had been. Joel's death, the rape, the second man—they weren't gone. She had not drunk them away, she had just drunk them into hiding. Now that she was not using alcohol to keep them at bay, these other men loomed in her dreams, in her unguarded moments.

And she found that she could not relax at the ranch. In many ways, it was a lovely home, airy and spacious with views of the mountains and the desert light pouring in. The stone work was local and handsomely done, the furniture massive and masculine but comfortable. The new paint gave everything a clean, fresh feel. Al had given her free rein to get what she wanted. She'd never had that before. But after the thrill of choosing and getting, it all felt empty to her. *She* felt empty.

"We should be ready for you to move in by next weekend." The touch of Al's hand on hers was warm and gentle, although she could feel the calluses that ridged his palm.

Anxiety swept over her. She didn't see how she could do that. She wasn't ready.

He must have seen something in her face, for he put his arms around her very loosely and said into her hair. "No hurry. Just wanting you around, that's all." He pulled back a little and looked into her eyes. "You know you can tell me anything, don't you?"

She smiled and nodded, knowing full well that she meant nothing by either one of the gestures.

22

The day after she talked to Detective Hansen on the phone, Ellie got dressed and left the house. She was relieved to see the reporters were gone. The long drive up the hill through the one-hundred-year-old elms was reassuringly familiar, as were the turreted brick buildings at the top. Campus was mostly deserted on a Saturday morning, and she had no trouble finding a faculty parking spot. She went in through the back of the building to the post office. Her mailbox was crammed full: student papers, committee meeting minutes, announcements of conferences and calls for presentations. She scooped it all into a canvas shopping bag and headed up the maze of hallways to her office. She passed no one save an elderly demented nun who regularly wandered the halls of the main building on the weekends. They nodded at each other and Ellie went on her way.

Taped to the heavy wooden door were cards and good wishes from some of her students. Her heart eased a little. She unlocked the door, stepped over the cards and papers on the polished wood floor, and put her satchel on the desk. The next three hours afforded her a sort of freedom: She sorted the mail and left phone messages in the empty offices of colleagues. She talked to the two colleagues who had taken her classes the week before. They were surprised to hear from her, surprised to learn she was back at school. She was relieved that they didn't press her for details.

Shortly after two, she went downstairs to the student lounge and got a couple of candy bars and a soda. She wasn't hungry, but she knew she needed a break. She took the long route back through the chapel. More elderly sisters sat reciting the rosary or praying. One snored as she passed by. She sat a moment amid the incense and watched the pale sunlight come through the stained glass rendering of the Stations of the Cross. She felt that God, if He or She existed, was very far away.

When she came back to her office, she found a note on her desk. The dean wanted to see her right away. Ellie retraced her steps through the chapel, then down the stairs and into the administrative wing.

Sister Joseph Marie stood looking out the window, but she moved to her desk when Ellie came in. She motioned for Ellie to sit across from her. The dour biologist and Ellie had a history, and it was not a good one.

"How are you?" the nun said.

Ellie opened her mouth to tell the truth, then remembered the power the woman had. "Better each day," she said finally. "How are you?"

"Concerned about you. We all are. Frankly, I'm surprised to find you here. I just happened to be going by and saw that your office was open."

"I wanted to come in and get some work done—get caught up before Monday."

"And escape the reporters."

"That too."

"Ellie, I'm sure you know this has been all over the news."

"Yes, I assume so. I haven't seen any of it though."

"Well, the school has gotten a lot of publicity, not very good publicity." Sister Joseph Marie leaned forward and folded her hands on the desk.

Ellie frowned. "I don't understand. What happened to me doesn't have anything to do with the school."

"Well, you work here, and the questions and rumors that are circulating are not very good for us."

Ellie frowned. "I don't know what you're talking about."

"There's talk that you and this doctor were part of a sex group, couples who shared partners, and did . . . I'm not sure how to put this . . . unnatural things with each other."

"None of that is true. Joel and I had a normal relationship—a very normal relationship." Ellie took a deep breath. "Sister, you seem to forget that I was raped and beaten. Are you suggesting that I consented to that, that I chose to have it happen?"

The nun grimaced. "No, no, you've misunderstood me. It's the college I'm concerned about it. Gossip of this kind does not serve us."

"I can't control what people say, what they want to make up," Ellie said. She could feel the tears coming and she willed them away.

"I am aware of that. That's why President Finney and I agree that you should take a medical leave for the rest of the year and let things die down. Come summer, no one will care about this."

"And if I refuse?"

"We're confident you won't refuse. You will receive your salary and we hope you will see this as a sabbatical for research, perhaps even a trip somewhere. Your classes are already being covered. I suggest you take anything you need from your office and head on home." The dean looked at her for a long moment and then took a folder from her inbox and opened it. Her dismissal couldn't have been clearer.

23

Hansen got busy with other cases—a missing child most likely kidnapped by the divorced father and a series of garage fires in an upscale neighborhood. He gave the cases his attention. He was too good a cop not to. But he did not forget about Joel Richardson or the second man. And he did not forget about Ellie.

One Friday, he took off at noon and drove to Pittsburgh, showing up at Detective Capriano's desk just before five. The detective sat squinting at his computer screen, and he smiled when he saw Hansen.

"Hey, Doug! What's up? In town on business or pleasure?"

"Oh, a little of both. Thought I'd take you out and buy you a beer."

Capriano nodded. "Okay, just let me call the wife."

They went to a little bar two blocks south of the station. Capriano swore they had the best burgers in town and a local microbrew on tap. They got there just ahead of the after-work crowd so Hansen held down the booth while Capriano put in their order. They talked police politics, small-town versus big-city, until the beers and the food came. After they ate, Hansen ordered another pitcher and spoke what was on his mind. "Anything new on the Richardson case?"

Capriano tilted his head. "Not really. We went over his apartment again but we found nothing. I mean, nothing. A few clothes, a few toiletries. No papers, no documents. The place felt like a motel.

Even more interesting is that there was no home computer or laptop. That struck me as odd. Yeah, I know not every sixty-year-old is computer-savvy, but this is a guy living in a high-tech world. He didn't have friends he emailed, information he looked up on the Web? So I checked with his accountant and Richardson had bought a new Asus six months before he died. So where did it go? It wasn't at the hotel, it wasn't in his car, it wasn't in his work locker."

Hansen had been watching the bartender, a blonde girl about twenty-five who reminded him of his daughter. He turned back to Capriano. "Somebody took it."

Capriano nodded. "But why? What's on there that's problematic?" He sighed. "And there's something else: there were surprisingly few prints in Richardson's apartment. Not just very few prints besides his, but very few of his."

"But the house hadn't been cleaned recently."

"You got it. Not by his regular service anyway."

"Whose prints did you find?" Hansen topped off the other man's beer.

"The professor's. Her friend Gerstead's as well. And here's something interesting—Gerstead's prints were in the master bedroom."

"Hmm. Maybe he used the bathroom?"

"Maybe, but no prints in there."

"Didn't Gerstead tell you that Richardson showed him a collection of Oriental knives—maybe he showed him in the bedroom."

"Maybe." Capriano finished his beer and looked at Hansen. "I'd love to get my hands on that laptop."

"What are the chances it's still around?"

"Depends on who took it."

Hansen was silent for a long moment. "I can't shake the feeling that Gerstead is in this somehow. I've got no proof, but I've got that feeling. What do you think?"

Capriano shrugged. "Are you thinking there were three men in the room that night? Gerstead and Richardson both watching?"

"No, I think Gerstead was genuinely upset that Ellie—that the professor had been abused. I don't think he knew about that. But something just seems off with him." Hansen finished his beer.

"You got a place to stay tonight?" Capriano asked as they left the bar. "We've got one of those futon things in my son's room. You'd be welcome to it."

"Thanks but I've got some place to go."

Capriano raised an eyebrow and grinned. "You sly old dog."

Hansen didn't bother to tell him it wasn't what he was thinking.

§

Hansen found a cheap motel just off the turnpike in Monroeville. He watched the sports channels for a while, then slept restlessly. When he woke the next morning, he knew he'd dreamed of Ellie and the hotel room where he had first seen her. A shadow of a figure had passed by the doorway, but the light shone bright in his eyes and he could not see who it was.

He showered and shaved, put on the clean shirt and jeans he had brought with him, and then drove to Ellie's apartment. She lived in a handsome neighborhood that had been elegant and expensive several decades earlier. The houses were still probably expensive. They had two and three stories, were fronted by old elms, and sat on oversized lots, but many of them needed new roofs and the brick re-pointed. It was just after nine in the morning when he climbed the outside stairs to the second floor and knocked.

There was no response and he was about to knock again when the door opened a cat's width and a long-haired orange cat darted out. The chain was on, and Ellie looked out at him over it. He could hear her exhale in relief.

"I didn't mean to frighten you," he said.

"I know," she said, "but everything does."

She unlatched the chain and opened the door wider so he could come in. He found himself in a small alcove with a landing and then followed her up four carpeted steps into a big, light kitchen that looked out over a small backyard and the cobblestone alley. She'd clearly been sitting at the kitchen table. Her journal was open, a green pen lay in the trough of the spine, and something steamed from a red mug. A black velour hoodie was draped over the chair.

She clicked on the electric kettle. "I have black and green tea, and some herbals, and maybe some decaf coffee." She looked over at him, where he stood by the window.

"Any kind of tea is fine. I don't want to be any trouble." He smiled at her but she didn't smile back. She had aged some since he'd seen her last, put on weight.

A glossy black-and-white cat meandered in and came over to sniff Hansen's leg. He stooped down and petted it, who purred loudly. "This is one friendly cat," he said.

At that, Ellie finally smiled. "She is. Her name is Nellie. She's my favorite."

Hansen remained near the floor petting the cat, which made no effort to move away. The kettle clicked off and Ellie poured water in another red mug and set it on the table across from her own.

"I haven't given up on the case," Hansen said after he sat down.

Ellie looked at him but said nothing.

"It's important to me that you know that," he said and held her gaze for a few seconds.

She nodded, looked out the window, then sighed deeply. "The college has asked me to take an extended leave."

Hansen felt a surge of surprise, almost confusion. "How come? Are you ill?"

"No," she said. "Sick at heart, maybe. Suffering from terminal foolishness for trusting Joel, perhaps. No, they—the administrators—don't want the publicity. I'm somehow tainted now by Joel's sickness."

"They can't possibly fire you over this." Hansen was appalled.

"No, but they can push me into an extended paid leave. Replace me for now. I'm welcome to come back next August and start the new school year. They hope it will all have blown over by then—or maybe they hope I'll go away." She turned towards him and he saw that she was frightened.

"I was counting on school," she said, "on the routines, on the effort it takes to teach and do my life. I was counting on that to keep me, I don't know, sane."

Hansen nodded. He couldn't imagine not having his job to go to. He wasn't one of those eager to finish his years on the force and take the pension. His job and its twenty-four-hour nature shaped his life.

"I'm sorry," he said, and he touched the back of her hand. She didn't seem to notice. "What are you going to do instead?"

Ellie got up from the table and poured out the tea from her cup. Then she sat back down and looked at him. "I don't know. Six months ago if you'd offered me a year of salary and my freedom, I'd have been ecstatic. Do some art courses somewhere. Travel for a few months. Read to my heart's content. Now all I want is my job back."

"Are you seeing someone? A therapist, a rape counselor?"

"Yes, three times a week, but I don't know how much help it is. I just can't get over the fact that I trusted a sick man with my life and he paid someone to brutalize me."

"Are you going to AA meetings?" Hansen wasn't sure it was okay to ask that, and he could tell she was surprised he had.

She shook her head. "I'm not drinking, if that's what you're asking, although I'd sure like to. But I can't sit still long enough to go to a meeting." She got up again and left the room this time.

Hansen couldn't tell if he'd been dismissed. He heard a door close and then water running. He looked around. Even in depression, Ellie was tidy. The counters were wiped, the floor clean, the dishes stacked neatly in the drainer. He went over to the fridge. There were deli salad containers and packages of cold cuts and cheeses, a roasted chicken, and a pan of lasagna. Someone was taking care of her . . . Sandy Gerstead, probably.

At the entrance to the kitchen, he noticed a cork board. The large rectangle was covered with photos, greeting cards, postcards from Greece, Costa Rica, Goa, and several from France. Photos of a dark-haired woman who looked like Ellie, her sister maybe. School photos of two boys, one blond, one African American, and one of the two boys and the sister. There were several quotes typed out, and then from behind a recipe for almond cake, he saw Arlen Gerstead looking out at him. He moved the recipe and took down the photo. It was a recent picture of Ellie and Sandy and Arlen. They were dressed for summer in shirtsleeves and Ellie was laughing. They were facing into the sun. All three were squinting and the photographer cast a dark shadow over them. *Joel Richardson*, Hansen couldn't help thinking. He slipped the photo into his pocket and moved the recipe back into position.

When Ellie came back into the kitchen, Hansen was pouring himself a fresh cup of tea. She smiled at him but he couldn't read it. Glad he was still there? Just being polite? She'd brushed her hair and a minty smell of toothpaste reached him. "I can put this in my travel mug if you want to be rid of me," he said.

She shook her head. "No, I . . . It's okay. I can use a little company, especially if I don't have to explain anything."

He gave a little laugh. "I won't interrogate you."

She shook her head again. "That's not what I meant. You already know what happened. I don't have to pretend it didn't or pretend that I'm okay."

He sat back down with the tea and she joined him.

"Are you married, Detective?"

"Doug."

"You're married to Doug?"

"No," he laughed. "My name is Doug. Please call me Doug."

"Doug." She waited but he said nothing. "Are you married, Doug?"

"Yes, but . . ." he paused. "It's complicated."

She nodded and gave a little smile, but her eyes remained wary and dark. "A 'yes, but' is always complicated," she said.

"My wife lives in Montreal. She's Canadian and moved home to take care of her mother and an aunt who are both in poor health. Is this too much information?"

"No," said Ellie. "Someone else's complications are a relief."

"I haven't seen Claire since she left. We . . . we've had our share of problems and it seemed better to go our own ways."

"I'm sorry," said Ellie. "That's hard."

"It was harder when she was still in Gettysburg."

"How long has she been gone?"

"Four years."

"Oh," Ellie said, and Hansen saw a small look of surprise come into her eyes.

"Oh," he repeated.

They sat in silence for a moment. Then Hansen spoke again. "I have two daughters, Marie-Hélène and Jeanne. One in Philadelphia—she's a teacher. One in Montreal—she works with computers. You don't have kids?"

Ellie shook her head. "Only students."

"Probably plenty," Hansen said.

"It is."

Hansen drank down his tea, which had grown cool in the cup. "Okay if I use your bathroom?"

"Of course. It's just to the left on the landing."

When he came back, she was washing the cups. He stood and watched her from the doorway. Her movements were neat and efficient, her long, slender fingers easy at their work.

After she wiped her hands on a towel, she moved toward him to show him out. "Doug," she said, and as though he was a teenager again, he felt thrilled at hearing her say his name. "Is it okay if I leave town? Okay to travel?"

His heart sank but he smiled and said, "Sure, there's no reason not to. Will you email me with a way to reach you in case I have news?" He handed her a business card.

She smiled but the look in her eyes was bitter. "I have several of these already."

"Of course you do. Sorry. Force of habit."

"If I settle somewhere, I'll let you know." She moved down the four stairs to the door. "And I'll make sure the college knows how to reach me."

He knew that would have to do even though it wasn't enough. He, too, moved to the front door. Then he turned and said, "I forgot to ask you something. Your friend Arlen. Does he ever go by Jerry?"

Ellie shook her head. "No, I've never heard him called that. Sandy calls him Arlie sometimes and I've heard him introduce himself as Al once or twice, but never Jerry. Why?"

He saw a flash of hope in her eyes that he'd seen in other victims, a thin thread that might lead to understanding or forgetting. He shrugged. "Just a vague lead. Nothing substantial. Just trying to check out as many things as we can."

"No . . . yes . . . no. In part, I've come to ask your blessing on us."

"Ah . . . are you asking about a church wedding?"

Al considered this for a moment. Then he said, "No, I don't think that is what . . ."

Broadacre waited and, when Al said nothing more, he spoke again. "Are you having second thoughts?"

"No." The response was immediate, firm. "I've wanted a wife again for too long and nobody here . . . Let's just say that nobody here seemed right."

"Not even Gracie? I thought you two were serious."

"No, at least I wasn't. I see that now."

"And this woman does seem right."

"Yes."

"And you'd like to understand your attraction to this woman?"

Al frowned. "No, I know all about that. Ellie's intelligent and educated. She's kind and thoughtful."

Broadacre smiled when he saw Al blush. "Sounds like she'll make an excellent partner for you."

Al nodded. He said nothing more, but he made no move to leave.

Broadacre waited and then said quietly, "What is it, Al?"

Al looked out the window at the church parking lot.

"What is it, Al?" Broadacre repeated. "Is it that she doesn't share your Christian faith? Is it that you got married in some chapel in Arizona?"

Al looked over at him. "No, not at all. We just wanted to do it and do it quickly. It was really fun. I felt like a kid again."

"Is this woman asking you to give up your faith?"

"No, nothing like that. In fact, we haven't talked about it at all, not since the three questions."

"Questions?"

"When we were getting to know each other, we each asked each other three questions, things that were important to us. That was her idea—the three questions. In one of my questions, I asked her if she believed in God."

"And she said no."

"No, she said she believed in the Great Mystery. That she wasn't sure what that was or how it was, but she knew something connected us all and worked in our lives."

"That sounds just like God," Broadacre said, relieved. "Does she believe in Jesus?"

"Only as a wonderful human being, a great teacher. Not as the Son of God."

"I'm not sure this is anything to worry about, Al. I suspect she'll come to a different understanding after she's come to services with you for a while. And, of course, I'd be happy to talk with her."

"That's not going to happen, Jim. She's made it clear she's not interested in church. She doesn't believe in organized religion, only in personal beliefs."

Broadacre sighed. "It's too bad you didn't have this conversation before you married her."

Al looked back at the minister. "We did, Jim. I knew this when I married her."

Broadacre frowned. "Excuse me, Al, but I'm not sure what you're looking for here. You seem disturbed by your new wife's beliefs but you say you aren't having second thoughts."

"I'm not disturbed by this, Jim. I'm satisfied that my wife has values and beliefs that are compatible with mine. You're the one making it a problem." He waited a moment and then stood up. He leaned over and threw his cup and napkin into the trash. "I shouldn't have come," he said. "I thank you for your time."

"No, Al, wait. I've misunderstood something here. Let's talk some more."

But Al was already out the door.

25

Hansen put the photo of Ellie and the Gersteads on the refrigerator in his kitchen, using a kanji magnet that Jeanne had given him when she came back from her year in Japan. He didn't care that he'd stolen the photo. He didn't fool himself into thinking that he'd wanted a photo of Gerstead. He could have access at any time to the mug shot the Pittsburgh PD had taken when they tested Arlen's DNA. All he had to do was ask Capriano. No, he wanted a little bit of Ellie in his house.

Hansen lived in a townhouse condo a few blocks from the center of town. He and his wife had had a lovely old farmhouse with a couple of acres out toward the highway, but after she left, he couldn't bear to go on living there alone. And he wanted Claire to know it was over, so he sold the place before the economy tanked and he made good money for them both. He sent her half in a check that was accompanied by a terse note. "Proceeds from our life together."

He realized later that might have seemed like a bitter gesture, but he wasn't sure how to undo it. He wasn't bitter, but he didn't love her anymore. He hadn't loved her for years, maybe not all that much even to begin with. She was a beautiful woman and her Montreal accent was exotic and sexy. It had been a matter of pride for him that such a beautiful woman would marry him. He had been the envy of his buddies on the force who had married hometown girls. And it was true, Claire had style and a kind of grace that pulled people—men—toward her.

Hansen didn't regret the marriage. Their partnership had worked for quite a few years, and he loved his daughters more than anything. But once the girls were grown, he realized that none of these women needed him. With Jeanne and Marie-Hélène, that was as it should be. They needed to move on, make independent lives, find their own husbands to rely on. But with Claire . . . well, he wanted a woman who needed him around, who asked his advice, who was happy to see him. And that wasn't Claire, not even from the beginning. It was probably time to file the papers he'd had in his drawer for months.

He sighed and pulled out the Richardson file he'd made for himself and read through everything again. He made notes on his discussion with Capriano. He was convinced Richardson had had a double life and that somewhere there was evidence of it. But how to find it?

Two hours and three beers later, he called Capriano.

"Don't you know this is my day off, Hansen?"

"Detectives don't get days off." Hansen could hear a game in the background.

"Don't tell that to my wife." Capriano paused briefly. "Okay, what's up?"

"Do you guys have access to a profiler?" He heard Capriano inhale and then let out a long sigh.

"Yeah. There isn't one on staff that I can just go to, but there is somebody the department uses. You want to try to profile the second guy?"

"Well, that would be a help, but I'm actually thinking of a profile on Joel Richardson." Capriano said nothing, so after a minute, Hansen went on. "As far as we can tell, Richardson is guilty of a sex crime. Clearly, we can't prosecute a dead man. But maybe a profile would help us crack his double life, and that might lead us to the second man."

Again Capriano said nothing, but this time Hansen stayed quiet. He knew the value of space and quiet for thinking.

"Yeah, okay," Capriano said finally. "I could run this by my lieutenant. We're stalled in the case and it's the kind of open file that he hates. Maybe he'll kick loose a few bucks for the profiler."

"That would be great. Maybe we can find something that way. Thanks."

"You got it. Anything else?"

"Yeah, just one thing. Would you send me a copy of Gerstead's mug shot? I'm still convinced he's in on this although I don't know how. Something's not right about that guy."

"Sure, I'll email you the photo on Monday morning. That soon enough?"

"Yeah, okay. Thanks a lot."

26

Four weeks after Gettysburg, Ellie was paralyzed by inactivity and indecision. A week after her conversation with the dean, a revised contract had come in the mail, offering her 80 percent of her salary through September plus several thousand dollars in travel funds from the Dean's Special Account. The contract was accompanied by a stamped return envelope "for her convenience" and a handwritten note from the president, offering her sympathy and her encouragement to go to France or to Africa for the remainder of the school year. "We'll look forward to seeing you next August," she wrote.

Sandy had at first been appalled by the school's stance. She shared Ellie's anger and disgust at what she called "saving their own asses first." But after the contract arrived, Sandy's stance shifted and she urged Ellie to take the money and run.

"It's been four years since you were in France. You're always talking about the need to go, to refresh your slang, your knowledge of the culture. You always have a good time there. Now, money isn't an object, so go."

"But I'll be running away."

"So what? You've got nothing to prove to any of these people."

"How can you say that? The school thinks I colluded with Joel, that I participated in his . . . his games, that I brought this . . . experience on myself."

"Your friends don't think that. I don't think that. We know you. And we want you to be safe and heal from this. I don't think you can do that with the media buzzing around."

Ellie couldn't argue this last point. The media had been relentless. That morning a woman reporter had thrust a small tape recorder in her face as she was pumping gas into her car. The woman's voice was shrill, impatient. "Tell us what it was like, Ellie, waking up in that hotel room." The woman had followed her into the convenience store, barking questions. "Do you still have bruises? Did you kill your lover?" The other customers stared. Ellie had pushed to the head of the line, thrown $40 down on the counter, and hurried out. The harassment was also keeping her from going to AA meetings. Her sponsor had advised her to stay away from meetings as it would interfere with the anonymity of others. Ellie felt relieved. She didn't want to disrupt the meetings and she couldn't sit still anyway. She wasn't worried about her sobriety. She had no interest in drinking and she was taking the Valium as prescribed.

"So, will you make plans and go?" Sandy's voice was still there on the phone. "I really think it would be best. It would give you some space to be yourself. I can't imagine anyone in France will care about this."

"You seem awfully insistent about this, Sandy. Is the dean pressuring you to pressure me?"

"No, honey. No one at school is pressuring me to do anything. They're just concerned about you, the way I am, the way Arlen is. We want you to be okay and we aren't sure that being here right now is the best thing for you."

"All right," Ellie heard herself saying. "All right, I'll look into it. I'll make some calls."

"Good," said Sandy. "Shall I come by tonight? Need anything from the store?"

"No, thanks. I've still got lots of food from Sunday." She didn't tell Sandy that all she was really interested in was ice cream, that she didn't have much appetite for anything else. Ice cream made her feel safe somehow, more relaxed, and she made sure she had a freezer full. She knew she was gaining weight—so much ice cream, so much sleeping, so little exercise. But she didn't care. Being thin and healthy and attractive hadn't saved her from Joel's cruelty. He had used her with no more thought than those people who trained dogs to fight and kill using small dogs or cats as bait.

She had no way to think about Joel and what had happened. Her therapist had tried to convince her that what Joel had done wasn't personal, wasn't about her as Ellie, just about her as a generic woman, but Ellie couldn't buy it. She had spent a lot of time with Joel, laughing, talking, kissing, touching each other in the most private of places. Had he faked all that? Had she misread his ways with her?

Sometimes there are no signs, the trauma counselor had said. Many psychopaths are highly intelligent, know how to charm and adapt. They aren't ordinary people with a mental illness. They are extraordinary people with an extraordinary illness. She urged Ellie to stop blaming herself, to blame Joel and the second man. She urged her to grieve for herself, to cry, to shout and be angry, but Ellie found it difficult to do those things. She felt like she was faking it, trying to please the counselor, not healing herself. And on some level, she realized that staying numb from all the feelings around Gettysburg meant she didn't have to feel the fear that was underneath it all.

Maybe going away would help, she decided. Maybe getting away from places where she'd been with Joel would make a difference. It was worth a try.

27

Ellie didn't go back out to the ranch while the last of the painting was being done. She talked to Al on the phone each day the rest of the week and he talked of coming into town to spend the night with her, but then one of the horses took sick, so he stayed at the ranch and her move got postponed. Ellie was relieved—being on her own gave her more space to breathe, more space to figure out what she was going to do.

She still didn't feel ready to move to the ranch. Moving there meant telling Al everything. She couldn't be his wife, his everyday partner, and keep this big secret. She felt guilty having married him. She'd wanted the safety of someone to be with, to hold her in the night. She'd wanted a way to stop running. Al had held out his hand and she had taken it. She needed to find the courage to be honest if they were going to have a life together.

Even more worrisome were the dreams. Few nights went by that Joel didn't appear. Some were nightmares and in them she'd wrestle with the gold cords and the hotel sheets and Joel's staring eyes or she'd feel the weight on her body of a man she didn't know, his breath hot and sour on her face. Other dreams were more benign: sitting in a restaurant across from Joel, him pushing a glass of sparkling water her way or standing in the cold fog on a hillock overlooking the battlefield, Arlen and Joel pushing and shoving each other.

She even dreamed of Hansen, his eyes smiling at her, but fatigue and worry etched on his face. She knew that Joel could not hurt her, but the second man . . . the second man could be anybody. He could be the barista at the Starbucks, the man behind the counter at the dry cleaners, the guy who took her money at the gas station. She saw him everywhere though she had no way to know his face. She couldn't live like this much longer, and she couldn't start a life with Al with this between them.

She knew she needed to talk to somebody, but she didn't know how to find someone. She didn't see how she could ask Al to recommend a therapist without telling him everything . And she couldn't do that, not yet. Finally she resorted to the Internet. There were mostly family therapists in town, many specializing in marriage counseling, none of them specializing in trauma that she could see. However, there was a woman with the unlikely name of Desdemona Feldstein-Two Horses who not only had degrees, but who also advertised alternative therapies.

♏

Mona was about forty, pretty and dark, a slight East Coast overlay on her speech. Her office on the third floor of an old bank building was warm and welcoming with Navajo rugs and watercolors of the high desert and a ceramic mug for tea. She surprised Ellie by not asking questions, by just waiting until Ellie was ready to start. Ellie wondered if she would have waited the whole hour.

In the end, it took Ellie ten minutes to start telling the story, and thirty minutes to tell it, from Joel to Al—thirty minutes during which she surprised herself by not crying, not choking on the words. *Maybe this was progress*, she thought. She looked out the window or down at her hands while she talked. She didn't want to see the reaction on Mona's face. After she finished, Ellie took a deep drink of the tea, which tasted of mint and lemon and something cool and green, tarragon maybe. Then she sat back and realized that she'd been stiff and tense the whole time. She willed herself to relax.

Finally she looked up. Mona sat quietly across from her, her pen and paper still, her face serious and concerned. "What an ordeal you've been through," she said at last.

Ellie nodded.

"Do you feel safe here in Farmington?" Her voice was low and cool.

Ellie looked her in the eye. "Yes," she said, "and no. Yes, because I'm far away from Pittsburgh and no one except you knows who I am or what happened to me. But that man is out there, that other man, the one whom Joel paid, and I worry that he will find me, and that he will do something terrible to me again."

"That seems a very reasonable fear."

Ellie looked at her in surprise. The twenty-something rape counselor in Pittsburgh had tried to convince her how unlikely it was that this paid thug would come after her since he knew she wouldn't remember him and Joel wouldn't be paying him again. Now, she was relieved to feel understood.

"Have you spent time in therapy around this already?" The concern stayed on Mona's face.

"Yes, I saw a rape counselor the police recommended right after the event. Then I saw a trauma counselor for a few weeks. It helped some but I couldn't figure out what either of them wanted from me. The trauma counselor wanted to hypnotize me but I didn't want to know what had happened and I don't want to know. I don't need the details. I just want to stop having the dreams. I want some peace from this."

Mona nodded and wrote something on her steno pad. "I can offer you a chance to talk about it, Ellie. The nightmares, the fear, your body's and spirit's ways of dealing with this. And I'm glad to do that, but it will just be talk. Are you open to something else . . . to other kinds of healing?"

When Ellie nodded, Mona got up and went around to her desk and retrieved a card from a small box. She handed it to Ellie.

BROWN BEAR WOMAN

SHAMANIC JOURNEYS, VISION QUESTS, TRADITIONAL HEALINGS

Ellie looked up at Mona, who smiled. "Sofia has been known to work magic on soul sickness. You'd have to go to Chama to see her and you might have to wait a few days once you get there. She takes her time, figures out what all is needed for your healing. Do you have time that you can take to do this?"

"Yes, I can figure that out. I have some, well, I guess you'd say, things to sort out, but I could go, I could go right away."

Mona nodded. "Ellie, I know you don't know me. We haven't built up a relationship of trust and maybe you want to explore some other options or come back and see me again before deciding to do this. I just don't honestly think that more talk is what you need. I think some spiritual healing is called for, and Sofia is gifted at this kind of post-traumatic work. She works with a lot of the vets coming back from Afghanistan—and she works with rape victims."

It struck Ellie as odd that she might have something in common with war veterans. Then she realized that of course she did. She, too, was a victim of power and violence.

"Actually, not talking about it anymore is appealing to me," she said finally. "I want my power back and I can't talk it into happening. Maybe this Brown Bear Woman can help."

"Shall I call her now?"

Ellie felt the familiar fear of the possibility of knowing what really happened, of going crazy from the pain. Mona must have noticed, she said, "Sofia won't let anything bad happen to you. She will protect you from evil, and you'll be safe with her."

Ellie took a deep breath. "Okay, please call her. I can go any time."

Richardson got off seeing not McKay with a man, but his lover with McKay."

Hansen exhaled in disgust. "Yeah, but it was about violence, not sex."

"For Richardson—and for the second man—they're the same."

"I know," said Hansen, "but I don't get it."

"Yeah, well . . ." Capriano slid out of the booth and moved toward the back, to the restrooms.

Hansen paid the bill while he was gone, then sat reading the report. The idea that the second man was Richardson's lover made sense, but it didn't bring them any closer to finding him. And nothing in the report could help him figure out the nagging mystery of Arlen Gerstead's part in any of this.

He brought up Gerstead when Capriano came back.

"I agree there's something off with that guy," said Capriano. "He's a suck-up. I know there's a fancier, psychological word for that."

"Sycophant."

Capriano shrugged. "That's it. But there's no evidence that he's the second guy. And he's not smart enough or cool enough to lie that well. Not after how quickly he told me stuff in the interview. He's not good at keeping secrets, and Richardson would have needed someone as secretive and devious as himself."

"I know. That makes sense. But there's something Gerstead isn't telling us."

"Do you think he knows who the second man is?"

Hansen frowned. "Probably not as such. Like you said, he doesn't keep secrets well. But if he hung out with Richardson more than he's telling us, he may have met Richardson's lover."

"Let's interview him again then."

"Yeah, let's."

♄

The Gersteads' phone went straight to voicemail and a call to his wife at the college told them that Arlen was in Akron but headed back that afternoon. She gave them his cell number. Again Capriano got voicemail, but he asked Arlen to stop by police headquarters on his

105

way home. He was sure that Gerstead would be too curious to pass up a chance to find out what they knew.

Hansen took off then and spent a part of the afternoon checking out garage and tool shed arson cases in the small towns around Pittsburgh, looking for connections. At four-thirty, he found himself in Greensburg, across the street from Ellie's apartment. Her red Honda was parked half-way down the block and he started to get out, but then he noticed the silver Mazda in the driveway with the trunk up. He suddenly felt unsure, so he sat back into his car.

About ten minutes later, Ellie's door opened and a young man came down the stairs and went over to the Mazda. It was a kid, Hansen saw, in his mid-twenties maybe. He had trouble telling the ages of the young anymore. Despite the cool weather, the guy was dressed only in a blue t-shirt and jeans, some kind of fancy trainers on his feet. His dark hair was longer than fashionable and pulled back into a ponytail. Diamond studs glinted from both ears.

The kid stacked two cartons together and then grabbed a full black trash bag and took them up the stairs. Hansen could feel his envy for the younger man's light step and his ease with the weight of his packages. The boy made two more trips to the car. The second trip involved a suitcase and another carton. The third time he carried two paper grocery bags up the stairs. On the last trip, the long-haired orange cat slipped out. The kid came back out and tried coaxing the cat in but the cat was having none of it. The cat padded down the stairs, leapt off the last step, and headed around to the back of the house.

Hansen got out of the car then and headed to the stairs. He knew he had no business there. He should just call Ellie and check in with her. But he was curious and somehow uneasy, whether for her or for himself, he couldn't tell.

Hansen had to knock twice to get an answer. Finally he heard a muffled voice saying "Coming. I'm coming." And the young man opened the door.

Hansen had his badge ready, but the young man barely glanced at it. "Hi," he said with a friendly smile. "Can I help you?"

"Is Dr. McKay here?"

The kid smiled again. "No, she left for France this morning. She's going to be away several months."

"France, huh?"

"Well, yeah. She teaches French."

"That's right." Hansen put out his hand. "Detective Hansen with the Gettysburg Police."

The kid's hand was warm, his grip firm. "Roger Gerstead," he said. "I think you know my dad, Arlen Gerstead."

"I do," said Hansen. "I do. So you're house-sitting for Dr. McKay."

"That's right. She needed somebody to take care of the cats and watch her place and I needed a place for a while, so it works out well." Sadness came over his face. "My wife and I just split."

"That's tough." Hansen paused.

"Hey, where are my manners? Do you want to come in?"

Hansen followed the boy inside but remained on the landing. "Did Dr. McKay leave an address?"

The younger Gerstead shook his head. "Her mail is going to school and my stepmom—do you know Sandy?"

Hansen nodded.

"She's paying the bills and stuff."

"That's fine," Hansen said, turning to leave. "I have her email. I didn't know she would leave so soon."

The kid shrugged. "I'm just glad to have a place."

"Hey, where are those beers?" The voice was male and came from the stairs and to the left.

"Hold your horses," the kid said. "The detective is just leaving."

"Just be sure he doesn't arrest you, bro," said the voice with a laugh.

"Such a kidder." Roger Gerstead looked embarrassed and held the door for Hansen.

As Hansen pulled away from the curb, Capriano called. Arlen was at the downtown station and they would wait until he arrived for the interview.

29

Gerstead and Capriano were laughing and sharing mugs of coffee when Hansen walked into the interview room. Gerstead had obviously told the joke and Hansen was glad to see he was relaxed. They'd get more out of him.

"Coffee, Doug?" said Capriano.

Hansen smiled and shook his head. "Too late in the day for me." He pulled up a chair and sat off a little to the side. This was Capriano's show.

"Arlen was telling me more about his job. He's a pharmaceutical rep, remember? What's your territory again?"

"Eastern Ohio, southwestern Pennsylvania, northern West Virginia." Gerstead looked pleased and relaxed.

"What does a drug rep do exactly?" said Hansen.

"I visit doctors' offices, try to interest them in prescribing our products. We give them literature on the research, benefits, side effects, that sort of thing. The big Merck Manual can't keep up with all the new products so we educate doctors about what's out there."

"And you give out samples," said Capriano.

"Yeah, but probably not the way you think. It's all pretty regulated. We have to account for all our samples, checking them out, signing for the amounts, and getting signatures from the doctors who accept them. We have to show what we took and where it went and what's left over. These are controlled substances after all."

"Sounds like a lot of paper work," said Capriano.

Gerstead looked annoyed. "Tell me about it. Twenty years ago, it was a lot easier. They trusted us. We took what we needed, gave the stuff away. The company was just mostly interested in upping the numbers of prescriptions and the doctors who wrote them. And we had a system of perqs that really enhanced our sales. Then the FDA tightened up. Now it's all business. And everything has to be signed for and counted. It's really hurt sales."

"What do you mean?" Capriano said. "Aren't there more and more drugs out there?"

"Well, in the old days, we used to do a lot of wining and dining in some pretty nice places. I had doctors who were really good friends of mine. Now we aren't supposed to socialize."

"Like with Joel Richardson." Capriano's face showed nothing.

"Well, Joel wasn't my customer. I met him through another surgeon I'd been repping to for years, a guy Joel had worked with years before, after Vietnam."

Hansen spoke up, his voice casual, calm. "I thought you said you met Joel through Dr. McKay." He sensed the increased interest in the tension of Capriano's body although the other man kept his demeanor cool, too.

"Did I? I don't think I said that. Actually Ellie met Joel through me. Well, it was Sandy's idea. Sandy's my wife."

"I remember," said Hansen.

"How long did you know Joel before you introduced him to Dr. McKay?" Capriano was back in the conversation.

"Oh, a good while, most of a year probably. Joel seemed lonely. He liked to eat well, good wine and good food. He was looking for a buddy and I was happy to do that."

"He ever come on to you?" Capriano tossed out the question as if he was talking about the weather.

"Joel? Hell, no. Joel was as straight as they come. He wasn't looking for that kind of buddy."

"You sure?"

"Am I sure? Yes, I'm sure. Look, we went clubbing together. Joel was a good-looking guy and good-looking women were interested in him. He had no trouble getting the women."

"What kind of clubs?"

Gerstead shrugged but Hansen could see that he was uneasy.

"Oh you know," he said finally, "the kind that men go to. Clubs with girls . . . women who dance mostly naked, and let you buy them drinks and where you can . . . you know."

"Sex clubs?" Capriano said. Again Hansen was impressed by how cool Capriano stayed—he made it sound like no big deal.

"Yeah, I guess."

"Aren't they expensive? To be honest, I can't imagine you make that kind of money."

"Well, I, I don't. I . . . I paid for drinks a few times but Joel paid for the rest."

Hansen leaned in and spoke. "Joel paid for the sex." It wasn't a question.

"Well, uh, yeah, I guess you could say so."

"Tell us about it." Capriano moved his chair to the right so he and Hansen were more clearly aligned against Gerstead. Hansen wondered if this was a conscious thing on Capriano's part.

Gerstead looked stricken and guilty, like a small boy caught playing doctor. "Come on, guys. I don't usually talk about this stuff."

"Look, Arlen, we're not interested in the details of your performance. We just want to know about the clubs and what went on there and if anything unusual happened. I don't need to remind you that your good friend Ellie was the victim of a violent sex crime that we're trying to solve and you owe it to her to give us any information that can help us," said Hansen.

"Well, of course I want to help."

"We know you do," Capriano said more softly. "Just tell us about it."

Over the next hour, Gerstead described half a dozen visits he and Richardson had made to three sex clubs in the city. Capriano was familiar with two of them but he let Gerstead describe them.

One was a strip joint in what had been the lobby/restaurant of an old hotel. There were two levels of cover charge: One included drinks and lap dances, and the other included a room upstairs above the club. Richardson had paid the higher cover charge for both of them, and Gerstead had spent a couple of hours in a room upstairs— "a really nice room, like the best hotels"—with a redhead named Tiffany, though he didn't think that was her real name.

Had Richardson gone upstairs, too? Hansen wanted to know.

Gerstead thought so. "We were sitting with a whole group of people. Two guys in their thirties maybe. They said they were law students. And there were four dancers. When I came back down, Joel was there with two of the dancers. I assumed he'd gone upstairs with the girl he had been paying the most attention to. She was Asian and Joel told me she reminded him of his ex-wife."

They'd gone back to that club twice more. Once the law students were there again. Several weeks later, Richardson had taken Gerstead to a private club somewhere on the edge of town. They'd driven there late at night. "We'd been drinking and I didn't know that part of town. Pretty poor from what I remember of the streets. Like a ghetto. The club was in a big old house, a boarding house type like from a movie. It was clean, but boy, it needed a lot of work."

The girls there were mostly black, though again there was an Asian girl, but not the same one. "Joel wanted me to go with the Asian girl, but I figured he was just being polite, that he really wanted her for himself. So I chose another girl. She was pretty in that way that black girls are who are mostly white."

"Anything unusual happen there?" Capriano had brought them all fresh coffee and he took a sip from his mug.

"Not much happened at all, as I remember. I was too drunk and I couldn't, well, you know. Funny thing is, Joel knew I couldn't do it. He found that pretty funny. Said he'd been watching us and it was pretty comical."

"How did that make you feel? His watching you," said Capriano.

"Oh, he wasn't watching. He was just kidding. I think he just guessed by how drunk I was and how sheepish I must have looked staggering out of the girl's room. I don't even remember getting home."

"Were the law students there?"

Gerstead shook his head, then suddenly looked up. "Whoa, do you think one of them was the guy in the hotel in Gettysburg?"

Capriano shrugged. "We don't have a clue as to who that guy is, so yeah maybe. Did you catch any names? Was one of them Jerry?"

Gerstead thought for a moment. "No, nothing I remember."

"And the third club?" asked Hansen, who was tired and ready to be done.

"Now that was something special." Richardson had insisted that Arlen wear a tuxedo. "Hell, I don't own a tuxedo. Why would I?" So Richardson rented him one for a month.

"We got dressed to the nines and drove to this house, well, really a mansion, in Squirrel Hill. A big iron fence and gate, a guy at the gate to check our invitation. Man, I felt like I was in a movie."

Hansen sat back, squelching his impatience. He didn't like this guy and couldn't understand how Gerstead and Ellie could be friends.

There were two dozen people in the house. Men in tuxedos, women in evening gowns. Everyone drinking champagne. At first, Gerstead thought it was just a party for rich people. But Richardson encouraged him to select a woman who interested him. Just as in the other clubs.

"And he encouraged me to ask for whatever I wanted. That the woman would do anything, anything I could imagine."

"And did you?" asked Capriano.

"Did I what?"

"Ask for what you wanted?"

Gerstead blushed and nodded. "This is going to sound so dumb but I'd always wanted to make it with a nurse. I wanted to be the patient and have the nurse come and have sex with me. And that's what happened. There was a room upstairs that was just like a hospital room and she put on a white uniform and everything. It was so cool."

"Did Joel pay for this?" Hansen spoke from the corner.

"You know, I never saw any money change hands. Like I said, it was like going to a party. And Joel had the invitation."

"Did Richardson tell you what he did that night?"

Gerstead shook his head. "No, I just figured he asked for what he wanted too."

"Any idea what that was?" Capriano asked.

"No, Joel was a pretty private guy."

"Did you go there again?" Hansen asked.

"Once more, about a month later. Joel seemed disappointed when I wanted to have the nurse again. He said I had no imagination. That seemed really unkind. I've got plenty of imagination. But I did get the nurse again."

"Anything else you can tell us?" Capriano said. "We appreciate your being willing to spend so much time with us this afternoon." He looked at his watch. "This evening."

"No problem. Anything I can do to help."

"So, anything else you can tell us? Anything out of the ordinary that might help explain what happened to Ellie?" It was Hansen asking now.

Again Gerstead looked guilty, found out. "A couple of weeks after the second time at the mansion, Joel sent me a DVD in the mail. It was me and the nurse. Both times. At first I felt kind of creeped out, but then I figured it was a service that the party people provided and Joel had forgotten to tell me about it. Gotta tell you, fellas, I've gotten a lot of mileage out of that DVD."

After Gerstead had left the station, Capriano and Hansen talked for a few more minutes. Hansen wanted to pursue the sex clubs the next day, but Capriano told him that he didn't work weekends when he didn't have to and that it would keep until Monday. "Go home, get laid, watch a ballgame. I'll pursue the clubs and let you know what happens."

So Hansen found himself on the turnpike headed east. He was halfway home before he realized he hadn't told Capriano about meeting the Gerstead boy at Ellie's apartment or that Ellie was gone.

30

At first Ellie found herself indecisive about going to see the shaman Mona suggested. She was open to such ideas but she didn't place much faith in what might happen. She couldn't see how there was any kind of a cure for her fear, her nightmares, her mistrust. Then she began to feel even more paranoid. She couldn't get over the feeling that someone was watching her. But when she looked around, there was no one, or only someone benign. An old woman, a banker type, a homeless guy.

Then she began to think that someone was going through her things when she left her motel room. Hand lotion that had been on the nightstand was in the bathroom. Her pajamas were on the bed, not on the hook on the bathroom door where she left them after she had showered. There was maid service and it was possible that the friendly young woman was moving things around, but it seemed so unlikely. One morning when she came back from breakfast, her computer was on and she knew she hadn't touched it since the day before.

To ease her mind, she decided to go to the Rio Chama Valley. The drive took her about three hours, out of the desert and ranch country into a much greener landscape of winter snow melt. The air was still dry and clear—it was still New Mexico—but the valley had a lushness that she missed from the East. She had taken a route that drove her through Taos—but she didn't stop. She'd do that on the way back, for Al thought she had gone to do some shopping for art for the house. She thought about the few days she had spent there before Farmington. That now seemed a lifetime ago, not just a few weeks.

She had reserved a cabin at the Elkhorn Lodge. Mona told her that in the off-season she could get a cabin for little money—especially if she paid cash—and have the kind of privacy that she might need before and after her sessions with the shaman.

"Houston, wow! You've come a long way. I see you're staying with us all week." Tom Willis, the owner of the Elkhorn, was a thin, wiry cowboy with a waxed handlebar mustache that dwarfed his already small mouth. "Business or pleasure?"

Ellie pulled out her politeness. "I've been traveling quite a bit and need a good rest."

"You couldn't have picked a better place or time for some R&R. This is what Shirleen and I call the 'off-off-season.' Mostly just us here so nobody will bother you. Café's open, of course, for the traveling trade, but you're also welcome to cook in your room."

Willis was friendly in that country way that still surprised her. Years of living in Eastern cities had made her wary and closed, and her experiences of the last year had sealed off any natural friendliness. Ellie nodded and filled out the card with her new name and the New Mexico license plate, which still looked odd on the Honda. "Is there a phone in the room?"

"Yup, though you'll need a prepaid card to call long distance. We sell them right here. Get good cell service on the property, too."

She looked at him and shook her head. "No cell phone."

"Don't blame you. I don't much think we need all that technology they keep trying to sell us. You expecting calls?"

"No. Just want to be able to call my kids. You know how it is."

"Sure do. Got pictures?"

"I beg your pardon?"

"Of your kids. Those are mine up there on the wall." Willis pointed to a Sears portrait of himself: a tiny blonde woman with her hair in a French twist and two boys who looked unfortunately like their dad.

"No," said Ellie, wishing she'd never started this lie. "Mine are grown."

Willis nodded but looked disappointed somehow. He passed the key over the desk, the old-fashioned kind on a plastic handle with the room number. "I've given you Cabin 3. It's the coziest and you'll be able to hear the river."

She thanked him and went back out and drove her car to the cabin with the 3 emblazoned on the door. She got her bags out and the groceries she'd brought with her and put everything away. She fixed herself a sandwich and took it and her tea mug down to the river where she sat for a long time, thinking about as little as possible.

About two-thirty, she roused herself and went back to the cabin. She had a four o'clock meeting with Brown Bear Woman and she'd have to find the house. She went into the lodge office and pushed the bell on the desk. The woman from the Sears portrait came out from a room in the back. She beamed at Ellie. "Hi, you must be Ellie Robison. Hope you're settling in okay."

"I am. Thanks, the river is lovely."

The woman beamed again. "Do you need something?"

"I have an appointment and I need to find this address." She handed her the paper that Mona had given her.

The woman read the paper and the beaming smile dissolved. "This isn't a good idea," she said.

"I beg your pardon?"

"This woman Sofia is crazy, she's an old Indian witch. You look like a God-fearing woman, Mrs. Robison. You don't want to have anything to do with her."

Ellie took a deep breath, then said as patiently as she could, "I just need to know how to get there."

The woman harrumphed, then pulled out a tourist map, the kind with sketches of local attractions in little circles around the edge. She took a big marker and put an X on the Elkhorn and then traced a route out of town heading north. "Turn right on El Norte Road about a half mile past the high school. I don't know if she has a sign or the address on the mailbox. I've never been there."

Ellie thanked her and hurried to her car. She was glad to be away from the fear wafting off the woman.

Ellie followed the map the woman at the Elkhorn had given her. She had no trouble finding the high school or finding El Norte Road, but she missed the second driveway somehow, going on a long way with nothing to the right or the left. Finally she came to a row of mailboxes and a gravel road. That didn't seem right, so she retraced her steps to the highway and found the second driveway and its mailbox just past the first one. It was a few minutes after four.

The trailer was not what she expected. It was a manufactured home of some kind, but it sat neatly painted and tidy on the lot surrounded by a wide deck lined with pots of flowers in a riot of pinks and reds and oranges. The porch was guarded by two well-fed dogs, a black Lab and a bigger, white dog that looked part wolf. They got up and stretched and ambled over as she got out of her car.

The door opened and a small woman came out. From a distance, she seemed glittery somehow, and then Ellie saw that she was dressed in black and gold batik harem pants and a long golden tunic. Her straight black hair was streaked with silver and hung down her back, and she had a dozen shiny bracelets on one arm. When she made eye contact with Ellie, her face opened into a warm smile and Ellie felt a tiny bit of her anxiety dissolve.

After the sunshine of the driveway, the room she entered was dark. Candles lit two corners of the room. Sofia showed her to an overstuffed sofa in a pink and gray pattern that had been ubiquitous a decade before. As her eyes adjusted, Ellie saw the walls held handsomely framed wildlife photos: a timber wolf, a black bear, an eagle perched on a snag. When Sofia came back with two cups of tea, Ellie asked about the photos.

"My husband takes them," she said. "He spends a lot of time in the wild."

She took a seat on the sofa right next to Ellie. The proximity felt disconcerting. Ellie was even more uncomfortable when the woman took her hand and said, "Let us just be together for a few moments."

So they sat. After a few minutes, the silence seemed endless. Ellie glanced at the woman next to her. Her eyes were closed and there was an expression of utter peace on her face. Ellie closed her eyes and tried to feel the same, to match the woman's slow, deep breathing. But panic crept in anyway. It wasn't the unknown, what the healing might involve or what the woman might do to her. The opposite was true. Ellie's fear was that the woman couldn't help her, wouldn't know how to help her

117

find a way to live in her body again—that she was a charlatan who would just take her money, give her a harmless potion, and send her on her way.

"Breathe," Sofia said, the pressure of her hand on Ellie's firm and warm.

Another few minutes went by. Sofia hummed softly to herself. Then she released Ellie's hand, stood up, and moved across the coffee table to a small straight-back chair.

She smiled at Ellie, the same warm smile, and shook her head. "The guides say that the time is not right to journey on your behalf."

Ellie felt something drop in the middle of her body. "Why not? What does this mean? Can't you help me?"

"Yes, I can help you. But not now. What you want now I cannot seek for you."

"I don't understand." Ellie felt close to tears.

Sofia smiled again. "I can't really explain it to you. The timing is just not right. Perhaps you need more clarity about what you are seeking to learn, what part of yourself you wish to reconnect with. Sometimes we wish to reconnect with an old self that is not useful anymore." She paused. "I sense you are in a new life."

Ellie nodded.

"Something in your old life is incomplete, something deeply restricting."

"Yes, of course it is. That's why I came to you." Ellie could hear the impatience in her own voice. She took a deep breath. "I was . . . I was badly hurt and I want to start over and forget all about that."

Sofia nodded and Ellie saw a great look of kindness come over the woman's face. She took another deep breath and willed herself to relax.

"That is not what is standing in your way," Sofia said quietly. "You do not know what you want. You know only what you don't want."

The truth of the words stung, and Ellie couldn't deny that that was true.

"To move forward in life," said Sofia after a moment, "we have to want life. We have to want to live." She stood up. "When you know what you want, when you are ready to choose, come back and we will see if we can put the past to rest."

For a moment Ellie stayed where she was. Then she, too, stood and went toward the door. The sunlight was blinding. She turned back to Sofia and said, "How do I do that? I don't know anymore how to do that."

The same kind smile reappeared and Sofia touched her arm. "Set yourself apart from the others in some way. Be receptive. Wait patiently. The answers will come." She took a card from her pocket and handed it to Ellie. "Call me when you know."

31

Ellie slept all the way to Paris. Between the Valium from her doctor and the sleeping pill samples Arlen had given her, the seven hours passed quickly. She was met at the airport by Michelle, a French major from the college who was now working as an au pair. Ellie offered to get them a cab, but Michelle insisted they use the bus system. Ellie realized the girl wanted to show off her knowledge of the city. She felt slow and hungover from the drugs and the jet lag, but she tried to seem interested in Michelle's chatter about her new life, which was vastly different from small-town western Pennsylvania. Before Gettysburg, she would have enjoyed Michelle's company, as the girl was clever and gregarious. Now all she wanted was to get to the studio apartment in the 5th arrondissement on the Rue des Ciseaux near Saint-Germain-des-Prés and go back to sleep.

Michelle insisted on bumping Ellie's big roller bag up the narrow, twisting stone stairs to the third floor. Apartment #4 opened into a small kitchen with gas stove top, toaster oven, and refrigerator plus a small sink and counter space just long enough for a dish drainer and cutting board. In French style, the dishes and cutlery were on open wire shelves. A few steps further on was a living room crowded with a chocolate brown velour sofa, a coffee table, a miniscule TV, and against the wall a wooden table and two dining chairs. To the right,

the glass of scotch, its fumes filling her senses, on the table as he pulled her down into his lap. A wave of desire surged through her and then she heard the shout from the street and awoke on the Rue des Ciseaux.

Ellie poured another glass of the Evian and sat back on the couch. She was hungry, but there was no food in the apartment and she didn't have the energy to go out. She sat for a few minutes not thinking, afraid to be with herself.

The dream seemed obvious. Joel had treated her like meat; he had butchered her sense of trust. She didn't know how to be with that kind of betrayal, that kind of lie. As an alcoholic, she was no stranger to the double life, to pretending to be something she wasn't. But this was so far beyond hiding a bottle of wine or acting sober when she was drunk. She thought again of the trauma counselor's urging that she should feel angry with Joel, perhaps outraged the way Sandy and Arlen were or grimly determined to get to the bottom of it the way Hansen was. But all she could feel was sick, sick and foolish. What kind of fool was she that she had trusted Joel? What kind of person was she that he would do this to her? These questions wouldn't go away.

"I never liked Joel," Sandy had told her the second week after the rape.

"But it was your idea that I go out with him," Ellie said.

"It was my idea that you go out with him once. You'd been complaining about no social life, nothing interesting to do, and I knew from Arlen that Joel was looking for a date for that big-deal fundraiser. I saw it as a chance for you to have a dress-up night on the town. I saw him as a guy for you to go out with, not a guy for you to get involved with."

"Then why didn't you stop me?"

Sandy shook her head. "I tried a couple of times. I told you to go slow, to find out more about him, but you were already determined to make something of it. I knew better than to try to talk you out of it. That never works."

Sandy was right. She hadn't listened. She had wanted a man in her life and Joel had seemed like a good choice. Smart, professional, single. And he had been the kind of cool and detached that always made her want to pursue. How ironic was that? She had chased after a psychopath. No wonder she felt foolish.

Ellie glanced at the clock in the bedroom. It was just after nine, and muffled sounds of revelry from the restaurants below her came through the glass. She should get something to eat but her appetite had gone. She dredged up the energy for a shower and then went back to bed.

32

Capriano didn't call Hansen until well into the next week after the interview with Arlen Gerstead. Hansen had been busy with a knifing that had occurred in a strip mall convenience store and there had been several more arsons so he just had to let Ellie's case stay in Capriano's hands.

Capriano didn't waste time with a greeting. "Nothing from the sex clubs," he said when Hansen answered the phone.

Hansen sighed. "Nothing, huh?"

"I showed the pictures around, but Joel wasn't a regular at either of the two public clubs. One bartender said he might have come around months before but he couldn't be sure. No Tiffany as a dancer. No Asian girls at all. It's almost as if Gerstead had made it all up."

"But the places exist?"

"Oh yeah, they're both there and well known to a buddy I have who works vice. And he says neither place traffics in boys or men. That's what the club managers told me as well—strictly for straight customers."

"And the place in Squirrel Hill?"

"Nothing there at all. I took the directions Gerstead gave us and found a house that matched the description, but when I rang the bell, a security guard came out to the gate and said that the owners were away in someplace in Southeast Asia and wouldn't be back for months. Said he knew nothing about any kind of parties. And I definitely don't have enough to get a warrant for the place."

"A dead end then." Hansen felt especially weary.

"Maybe not. My buddy in vice had heard of these parties. Apparently they move around, never in the same location more than once or twice."

"But Gerstead described that nurse and the fake hospital room. That's an elaborate setup to be temporary."

"Not if you've got super-rich clients willing to pay through the nose. You can set up anything in a few hours."

"I suppose that's true."

Both men were silent then for a moment.

"What's next?" said Hansen. "Do you think Gerstead has told us all he knows? Seems to me he's kind of parsing out information."

"Maybe, but I don't think he knows the second man. I just don't. I think we are going to have to wait until something happens or Ellie McKay remembers something. Or maybe Vice will turn up something on the next party. I'll call you if anything comes up."

Hansen didn't like it, but he knew Capriano was right. What else could they investigate at this point with Richardson dead and Ellie in France? He put the official file away in the office and went back to work. He still hadn't remembered to mention the Gerstead boy staying at Ellie's—or that Ellie had left the country—although he couldn't see how it was connected to the case.

33

The late September sun was coming up later, but Al and Beemus still got up at four to have their toast in the dark, their moments of prayer, human and canine, on the porch swing together. Al needed more quiet time than ever.

He was trying hard to give Ellie the space she needed. He was deeply disappointed that she had not moved to the ranch yet. He did not see how they would get used to each other, find ease with each other, if they didn't spend more time together. At the same time, he had a full life of responsibilities with the land and the animals that waited for no one to sort anything out.

He considered trying to find out what had happened to Ellie before she came to Farmington. He'd used a detective once before and knew that they had ways to find out almost anything. The same man would surely be happy to take his money again. He also realized that if it had been a criminal assault, there'd be information on the Internet. But that seemed distasteful. Ellie had a right to her privacy, a right to her hurts and sorrows, just like he did. He trusted that she would tell him when she was ready. The trick was to make her stay until then.

He threw the dregs of his coffee out into the yard and went in for a second cup. He had a half hour until the foreman would show up for work.

Jim Broadacre had been a big disappointment. He was a hapless fool, nothing like his predecessor in wisdom or thoughtfulness. He had not had Al's vote for pastor when Jack Merchison retired. Al had preferred the woman, a bit young maybe, but livelier, more open to change. But the congregation hadn't been ready for a woman, and Broadacre had a local connection. His son-in-law was assistant manager at the Sears. Al didn't know who else to talk to about Ellie. His dad was dead. Jack too. Gracie was out of the question. He knew lots of folks in Farmington. Hell, he knew most of the town. But that was different. That was neighbor helping neighbor, or nodding at somebody from church, or joshing with a waitress at Arlene's on West Street. He didn't think any of them would understand why he'd married a stranger, a woman passing through town whom he'd met in a bar. He didn't need to be told he was a fool.

He wondered if he and Stevie would have been close when the boy got to be a man. If they'd have had the kind of understanding and knowing he'd had with his dad. The old familiar ache for the boy throbbed deep in his chest. Maybe he could have talked to his son about Ellie. Maybe not.

Al was pretty sure he could fall in love with Ellie. The chemistry was there. He believed she had a good heart. He could love her, perhaps deeply, and they could be good company for each other. His proposal had not been a whim, although it might have looked like that. He had been seeking and waiting for the right one to come along. And Ellie had. But he couldn't seem to find a way to show her that. And . . . he couldn't seem to find a way to lift off the burden, whatever it was, that weighed on her soul.

34

Ellie felt at loose ends in Paris although she tried to establish a routine. She walked each morning for an hour if it didn't rain. She went to a different museum each day, to a movie each afternoon. She took long naps and read some of the newest fiction. Because her housing was cheap, her travel funds were generous, so she took side trips to Giverny to Monet's gardens and out to Versailles again. She became friends with the woman in the apartment below and she reconnected with a couple she knew in the suburbs, but all these people worked and had full lives and she found herself too much alone.

That loneliness and the dream from the first night had brought thoughts of Danny back. Danny with his easy ways. His soft brown hair and blue eyes. Life with him had been easy, it seemed now: lots of sex and laughter, lots of good conversation and good food and even better whiskey. He wasn't Irish, but he may as well have been. He was enamored of the Irish struggle and the Irish poets, whom he quoted at the oddest moments. He was a romantic and Ellie loved that about him.

When she met Danny, Ellie was in her forties and her biological clock was ticking. Not the baby clock—she was past that and her students were children enough for her—but the partner clock. She wanted to share the rest of her life with a partner in a deep romantic commitment, and when Danny chose her, told her he loved her on a misty late evening walk on a covered bridge, she fell deep and hard. *This was it*, she had thought.

They were a good match—all their friends thought so. They both loved literature and movies and music, cats and wine-tastings. They traveled well together. And for a decade, it had worked. Then things fell apart. When Ellie was honest with herself, she knew she'd had a serious problem with alcohol before she met Danny, but his self-image as a connoisseur of single malts and vintage Cabernets and his unspoken insistence that she share that passion set her up for more misery.

Truth be told, she was glad Danny drank. It was a relief not to have to hide her drinking from him, to bask in his unconcern for quantity or frequency. Even when the blackouts began to happen regularly, he said nothing. But they terrified Ellie. So did the increasing severity of her hangovers. She tried cutting back, but to no avail—the need to drink was just too strong. So she decided to stop, telling Danny she had concerns for her liver. He scoffed at that, told her she was a lightweight drinker with nothing to worry about, but he certainly wouldn't force her to drink with him.

For a month she was able to abstain, able to watch him pour bottle after bottle of wine in his own glass at dinner, able to smell the whiskey on his breath when he came to bed late into the night. Then the pressure, subtle at first, began. He wanted her to drink with him. He missed eating out with a fine bottle, he said, missed inviting friends over for cards and whiskey and the jokes and laughter that came when they'd all had a few.

Ellie held out. But then Danny began going out in the evenings, coming back after she was asleep, and then sometimes not showing up until breakfast, and she knew she had a choice to make.

She chose to drink again but held tightly to drinking very little. For a brief while, things were okay. Then Danny took to going out again anyway. And she let go of moderation and the hangovers weren't any better and the blackouts came quicker and finally she got a DUI and her teaching contract was not renewed and the whole house of pretense fell in around her. After spending time in a treatment center, she left Danny and moved to Pennsylvania. But . . . she hadn't stopped loving him. So one night, sitting on the chocolate velour sofa, she gathered her courage and sent the email she'd been fantasizing about since she'd moved into the little apartment on the Rue des Ciseaux.

"I'm in Paris," it said. "I'm lonely. I'll send you a ticket. Will you come?" The next morning, there was a message in her inbox. "Air France Flight 490, Friday 08:30."

*

Ellie refused to pay $75 for a cab out to the airport so she retraced the bus–train–bus route that Michelle had shown her. It was early morning and the commuter train was mostly empty heading away from the inner city.

Knowing Danny was coming at the end of the week, knowing she wouldn't be alone for a while, had changed things for her. She'd wandered the neighborhood with more purpose, scouting out places where they might eat, plays and films they might see. Danny had never been to Paris as far as she knew, and he might want to do all the tourist spots. The Thursday before he was due to arrive, she cleaned the apartment, got fresh flowers from a market vendor, stocked the refrigerator with food and white wine, and made sure there was a bottle of scotch. Buying the liquor made her uncomfortable for a moment, but it wasn't for her, she told herself, but for Danny. Just because it was there didn't mean she had to drink any.

On the train, she reread Sandy's last email.

Arlen was interviewed by the police again. They kept him several hours. He said they just wanted his opinion on where the case was going. That doesn't make sense to me. What could he know? What help could he be? He didn't know Joel as well as you did, and they aren't talking to you anymore. Detective Hansen was there too. Why would he drive all the way from Gettysburg just to listen to Arlen's ideas? I don't get it.

Roger seems to have settled in at your place, though I don't know how much he is there. I've called several evenings and he's been out. I think he's driving over to Akron to see Carol some and probably to connect with his mom and his brothers. Maybe he wants to get back with Carol. I hope so. She's such a sweet girl. I hope he isn't dating someone new in Pittsburgh.

I miss you, Ellie. Lunch on campus isn't any fun without you. I sure wish none of this had happened to us. Keep in touch, Sandy.

Ellie felt a small wave of indignation. *This didn't happen to you, Sandy. It happened to me.* But she let it go. She thought about Arlen and a rush of uneasiness touched her. They had suspected him before. Did they still? It was clear he wasn't the man in the hotel room. It wasn't his DNA. So what part could he have played? She didn't know why the police would want to talk with him again or why Hansen would come all that way. Had he come to see her? Maybe she should have emailed him that she was leaving.

She looked up to see that the train was one stop away from her station. She turned her focus to Danny's arrival.

The airport was surprisingly crowded for eight on a Friday morning. She wove between the many colors of people and roller-bags and backpacks to a spot where she could see the arrival times. Flight 490 was delayed. With customs and immigration, that meant she wouldn't see him until sometime after ten. She took her book to a café and ordered tea and a croissant and pretended to read. But after forty-five minutes, she was too nervous to sit there, so she gave up her table to a handsome African couple in Kente cloth dashikis and started to pace.

Suddenly this all seemed foolish. She hadn't seen Danny in four years or even talked to him on the phone. In those last years together, they'd only gotten along when they were both drinking and, even then, not all that well. He liked women too much to not have moved on to someone else. But maybe not. Maybe he still loved her, maybe he wanted to be with her again and had just been waiting for her to make the first move. Why else would he have responded so promptly to her invitation, been willing to drop everything and come meet her in Paris. How romantic was that! They'd been good for each other for a long time. Maybe they were fated to be together and the whole experience with Joel was just the universe's way of bringing them back together.

Reassured, she spent the last forty-five minutes shopping for perfume and a new scarf before heading to the customs waiting area.

There were lots of arrivals. Families, businessmen, a group of older women in red hats who looked for all the world like a gaggle of geese. A Japanese tour of couples, newlyweds, she guessed. Then ten-fifteen came. Then, ten-thirty. She checked the monitor. Flight 490 had arrived at nine-fifteen. At eleven, she stood in line at Air France. At eleven-fifteen, she reached the counter.

No, Daniel Lewis had not been on Flight 490. Yes, he had had a reservation. No, he was not scheduled on a later flight. Did she want to make him a new reservation?

No, Ellie shook her head, no.

Something dark descended on her then. It perched on her chest, wrapped itself around her heart, settled into her throat. It helped her into a cab, it paid the driver, it offered her a hand up the twisty stone steps to #4, 6 Rue des Ciseaux. It put the perfume and new scarf on the table. It helped her off with her coat and her shoes. It found her a glass and a corkscrew and it settled beside her on the velour sofa. What else are best friends for?

35

"There's been a similar rape."

Hansen looked up to see Capriano at his desk. It had been most of a month since the two men had spoken. Hansen stood and shook Capriano's hand. He grabbed his heavy jacket from the row of coats along the wall and the two men headed out without another word.

There was a bakery three doors down from the station and they pushed into the November wind to reach it. The air inside was heavy with baking yeast and sugar, and the window by their booth was dripping with condensation. Both men ordered black coffee but the waitress brought a plate of mini-glazed doughnuts and chunks of maple bar with the mugs. "Specialties of the house, gentlemen," she said.

Capriano groaned. "This will do nothing for my girlish figure." He reached for a doughnut.

Hansen smiled. "Discipline, Larry, discipline."

Then the waitress walked away and the two men grew serious.

"Tell me," said Hansen.

"The woman was an elementary school teacher from Sewickley named Amanda Carlyle. Found drugged, raped, tortured in a three-hundred-dollar room at the Hyatt Regency."

"Was?"

"Dead when they found her."

"You weren't on the scene?"

"No, I've been in Philadelphia. On my way back now, that's why I stopped by." He paused. "Here's the kicker. The room was registered to Joel Richardson."

Hansen frowned. "A copy cat using the details from the press?"

Capriano shook his head. "The credit card was Richardson's."

Hansen reached out with his paper napkin and cleared a circle on the steamy window so he could look out. He didn't say anything for a while.

"Anything that doesn't fit our case?"

"So far, only that the woman was much younger. Thirty-four."

"How'd she die?"

"They're not sure. She'd been choked—bruising on her neck—but they won't know until the autopsy."

"You've got a serial on your hands," Hansen said. "I don't envy you."

"Well, the McKay case will get more attention now. Have you seen her recently?"

"No, she's gone to Europe. Her college pushed her to get away so the publicity would die down."

"Got contact information?"

Hansen shook his head. "I can get it, either from the school or from the Gersteads, I suspect. Do you want it?"

Capriano shrugged. "Only to ask her if she knew Amanda Carlyle. If there's some link there. Could you ask her? And find out if she's remembered anything more, now that time has gone by."

Hansen nodded. "By the way, I met Gerstead's son, one of them anyway. He's house-sitting for Ellie McKay while she's away."

"Chip off the old block?"

"No, he was a nice kid. Friendly, helpful. I liked him."

"Not a suspect then?" Capriano took the last of the mini-glazed.

"Well, everyone's a suspect, but no, I don't think so, convenient as that would be." Hansen looked out the window again. "Anything I can do to help?"

"Not at this point. Well, yes, one thing." He stuffed the last dough-nut in this mouth. "Don't bring me here again."

36

Thanksgiving Day dawned clear and sunny in Paris. The late fall had been unseasonably dry and Ellie had been grateful both for the warmth and the sun. Grocery shopping in the rain without a car wasn't much fun, and she needed several things for the pumpkin pie she was taking to dinner.

It was eleven-thirty when she left the apartment. She got up later each day as the winter sun took its time arriving. And she was back to the old slowness in her routines of journal and tea and shower. She didn't care. There was nothing to hurry for.

She stopped and knocked at #2 to see if Maryann needed anything from the épicerie but there was no answer. Checked her own mailbox. Empty as usual. Then she pushed open the heavy wooden door and blinked into the sun.

The early lunch crowd was filling the outdoor tables at Chez Panisse and she could hear the familiar sound of chairs on the cobblestones and voices ringing out with drink orders. Her favorite waiter, Carlito, hurried past her with a brief smile and a tray of green and gold aperitifs, and she watched his slender figure move toward the tables.

That's when she saw him. Rumpled brown suit. Graying blond hair a little too short on the sides and a little too long over the forehead. He looked older, sadder, but he smiled when he caught her eye and he got up and held out a chair for her.

She said nothing for a moment, just looked him in the eyes. He smiled, almost shyly. Then she laughed, walked over, and sat down. "Hello, Detective."

"Doug."

"Hello, Doug."

When she came back from doing the shopping, he was sound asleep on her bed, his suit jacket neatly folded next to him. She watched him sleep for a moment, saw that the lines of his face had eased smooth. Then she closed the French doors, poured a glass of wine, and made pie.

At five, as the dark crept on, she woke him. He startled from wherever he'd been dreaming, grabbing her arm.

"It's okay," she said. "It's Ellie. You're all right."

He lay back, breathing hard. "Weird dreams," he said.

"Jet lag."

"Yeah, maybe, but old demons, too." He yawned and stretched and pulled himself up against the headboard.

Ellie could feel the heat of sleep coming off his body. It was soothing, comforting somehow. She knew something was coming between them and she didn't know if she should hurry it up.

"What time is it?" Hansen yawned again.

"A little after five."

"A.m. or p.m.?"

"Afternoon. You've been asleep about four hours. If you want to get over the jet lag quickly, you need to get up now."

"Okay. What time's your dinner?"

"Seven. But we don't have to go."

"No, that's fine. As long as they speak English."

She smiled at him. "They do."

While he showered, she changed into a cherry-red silk sweater and her dressier black pants. Earrings and a bracelet. The scarf she'd bought at the airport weeks before when Danny hadn't come. Then she poured more wine and sat and watched the lights of the city.

"Suit or jeans?" Hansen called from the other room.

For some odd reason, she found his question endearing. "Doesn't matter," she said. "Jeans are fine." She hesitated a moment, then said, "Do you want a drink? I've got white wine and bourbon."

"Bourbon, neat."

She took the glass in to him. He stood shaving at the bathroom mirror, his chest bare. He looked over at her and she realized after a moment that she was blushing. That made him grin and she blushed even more. "Your drink, sir," was all she could manage to say. She put it down on the sink and hurried out.

Maryann drove them to the party, which was across town, somewhere on the edges of Montmartre. She and Hansen sat in front and talked rock and roll. Maryann, who was eighty or more, was an expert on British bands of the Seventies and Eighties, as Andy Summers of the Police was her nephew. Hansen had been a Rolling Stones follower in his youth and they carried on a conversation of concerts and albums with minutiae that made Ellie's head spin.

There were fourteen at the table, mostly British and American expats, a couple of long-term tourists like Ellie, and three American students, including Ellie's friend Michelle and her boyfriend, who was from Indiana. Lenny was good-looking, a smooth face, a strong jaw, and beautiful blue eyes. His hair was Paris-long and had an easy, affable manner, and Ellie could see why Michelle was smitten. Even though he was too old for her—he had to be close to thirty—she was also glad Michelle had found an American boyfriend. She knew from years of experience that relationships with French guys were doomed from the start.

There was most of a traditional Thanksgiving feast, but the wine and political conversation were strictly European. When the conversation turned to George W. Bush and why Americans had elected an idiot for two full terms, Ellie could see that Hansen was ready to go. Maryann wasn't ready to leave so they went on their own.

They walked out into a clear night turning cold. The nearest Métro station was a few blocks away, and Ellie put her arm through his. Neither said much. When they'd found seats in the train, Hansen turned to her. "Does the name Amanda Carlyle mean anything to you?"

"Is this about the case?"

"Yes, it's a name Capriano passed on to me."

"No," she shook her head. "I had a student named Mandy some years back." She thought a moment. "Mandy Simmons. She'd be twenty-three or twenty-four by now."

"No," said Hansen. "That's not her."

They were quiet a minute. Then Hansen said, "Had you met Lenny before?"

"No. Michelle mentioned him when I first arrived. I wasn't surprised to see him. I think she's pretty serious about him. I liked him. Did you?"

"Hmmm, no. He seemed a little too smooth to me."

"What's wrong with smooth? We women like smooth." She smiled at him, put a little flirt into it.

"I know women do. I just find that smooth men aren't always so genuine."

Ellie looked at him. "Well, after my experience with Joel, I'd have to say I agree." She thought a moment. "Are you worried for Michelle?"

"No, nothing like that. You asked me what I thought of him and that's what I think. How'd she meet him?"

"Mutual friend. Some boy she knew from high school had met Lenny at Ball State. Gave Lenny her address in Paris when he said he was coming to Europe on business. You know, the usual way people meet people."

"But not us." He looked at her.

"No, not us," she said.

The train rumbled to a stop at Saint-Germain-des-Prés and they got off. Out of breath from climbing two long flights up out of the ground, they walked in silence down the long pedestrian block of Rue des Ciseaux. It was after ten and the outdoor tables were deserted, though the street was full of people going and coming from inside the restaurants.

"This is a lively place," said Hansen, putting his arm around her and pulling her close.

Ellie smiled. "I like the noise. I find it comforting."

They passed her door and walked on a block to the river. A glittering bateau mouche glided by with Big Band music wafting toward them. They could see the dancers on board. Hansen moved so that he stood behind her, warming her back with his body, his hands on either side of hers on the railing that ran the length of the river bank. She leaned back into him and they stood that way for a few minutes.

Then she turned inside the circle of his arms. "Is Amanda Carlyle connected to Joel in some way?" Fear coursed through her veins in spite of the Valium.

"Shhh," he said, pulling her closer. He touched her lips with his, at first gently, then more deeply. His arms tightened around her, and she hung on for dear life.

Ellie woke at four-fifteen. The apartment was dark, the street quiet below. She was thirsty and her head ached. Hansen lay with his back to the wall, his right arm slung over her loosely, lightly. She moved it and got up. Pulling her robe off the hook on the bathroom door, she went into the kitchen and fixed a glass of cold Perrier with a big splash of bourbon, then sat on the sofa.

The night had not gone well. As long as she and Hansen had stood at the river and kissed like teenagers, she'd been fine. She'd even opened her coat to his hands and felt her knees go weak. But once they'd returned to the apartment and he'd taken his clothes off and stood there clearly wanting her, she'd frozen up. Between gravity and the months of ice cream and pastry therapy, she was already uncomfortable with her body. And she didn't have a fancy negligee to slip into and prolong the mystery, perhaps indefinitely.

Truth was, she was ashamed of the scars, the marks of her ill-fated pursuit of Joel. She hadn't just walked into his trap, she'd made herself available by pursuing him. Some of the scars she couldn't see without two mirrors—the slowly fading stripes on the backs of her legs, on her shoulders. But the cigarette burns on her thighs and belly, the finger marks on her throat. No amount of make-up or clothing made them disappear. The dermatologist she'd seen said they would fade, but that they were so deep and her skin so sufficiently aging, that scars would remain. Joel's legacy to her.

But she might have gotten over her shyness, her embarrassment, with a joke or an impetuous sexy move. But Hansen didn't make one and she couldn't. Instead he slipped between the sheets and waited for her to join him. The moment had been serious between them and that hadn't worked. For without his hands on her skin, she no longer wanted to do this. And she didn't know how to say so. So she turned out all the lights, took two quick slugs of bourbon, undressed in the living room, and got into bed with him.

In the end, it had been pretty simple, and maybe that was for the best. He had kissed her, she had kissed him back. There'd been touching and, at another time, she might have liked it. When he entered her, he'd been gentle, careful, respectful. She'd helped him, he'd helped her. But she didn't climax and she didn't pretend to. When he had, he pulled away and then spooned her with his warm body, and he had drifted off.

Now he was deep asleep and she was alone again. She thought, not for the first time, about Mia Farrow in *Rosemary's Baby*, about having sex with the Devil. Joel had come to seem that to her, an evil force who had tricked her into trusting him and having sex with him, and then had done unspeakable things without her knowledge or permission.

She had not thought of Joel while Hansen made love to her. She had been spared that. But she had not been able to relax, to open herself up and trust, even though her mind believed that she was safe with Hansen, that he wouldn't hurt her. She didn't see how she could ever do that again and maybe not just because of Joel.

If she told herself the truth, sex hadn't been all that good with Joel either. Once she got sober, she realized that in all the relationships and with all the lovers—and there had been quite a few, especially in her thirties—alcohol had been there. Except for a couple of fumbling attempts in college, her sexual self and her alcoholic self were one. She realized now that Joel's indifference to sex had been a relief. He didn't expect much and she found a lot of ways to avoid it.

Now with Hansen, she had alcohol again as a lubricant, but it didn't seem to make any difference. She felt timid in bed, timid and scared, and what kind of man wanted a woman like that? Especially a woman with an aging and mutilated body.

37

Hansen stayed with Ellie in Paris for ten days. He got up early most days and went out by himself. He felt it important to give her space in that little apartment. Early on, he offered to get a hotel room, but she wouldn't have it, and they settled into routines that seemed to work for them both.

On the third day, he found a message from Capriano on his cell phone, so he took himself down to the Seine and called him back. Again, Capriano bypassed the pleasantries, not even saying hello. "The credit card in Richardson's name is new. Applied for a month after his death. It's linked to his bank account, which remains open and active. Richardson isn't getting his salary anymore, of course, but he has investments and they dump in a tidy sum every month."

"Why is his bank account still open? The guy's dead."

"Yeah, but there's no next of kin to close it, no one handling any of those details. And someone—I assume it's our killer—is withdrawing money from ATMs from that account on Richardson's debit card. Because all the records are electronic, the bank doesn't really pay attention."

Hansen thought about this for a minute. "The second man has his computer."

"Yes, like we thought before. That would give him access to the bank account, especially if Richardson had given him passwords or had an obvious password to someone who knew him."

"What about the ATM security tapes?" asked Hansen.

"He's using homeless guys and women to stand in front of the camera and put in the code and take the cash. We found a couple of them and talked to them, but the descriptions didn't match. One guy said he was hired by a blonde woman in a pantsuit, another said it was an overweight deliveryman in a uniform with Bud on the pocket. Maybe he uses disguises, maybe he uses his friends or pays somebody. Anyway, the tapes are no help."

Capriano paused, too, then said, "Have you connected with Ellie McKay?"

"Yes, she doesn't know Amanda Carlyle."

"Did the death freak her out?"

"I didn't tell her that. Just asked if she knew her."

"Has she remembered anything more?"

"Nothing she mentioned." Hansen stepped off the path to let two joggers go by. "What did the coroner find with Carlyle?"

"Asphyxiation through regurgitation. It also appeared she'd been strangled and revived a couple of times hours before."

Hansen gave a deep sigh. "A piece of work, this guy."

"Yeah," said Capriano.

"Same drugs?"

"Yes on the rohypnol but there was also Ambien in her system and a ton of booze. Coroner thinks he may have left her tied up the way he did McKay and she died on her own, choking in her sleep."

"Same kind of marks on the body?"

"Yes."

"Larry, is there anything else we can see as a signature? Anything this guy left behind?"

"Only the use of Joel Richardson's name. That's the only thing I can see so far."

Hansen waited a moment, then said, "I don't think he got careless, do you?"

"With the name, you mean?"

"Yeah."

"No, I don't."

"He's screwing with us, isn't he?"

"Yes," said Capriano. "Yes, indeed. . . . Hey, before I forget, I'll be by that way day after tomorrow. Shall I stop if I have any news?"

"No," said Hansen. "I won't be in the office. I'm headed out on vacation. Going to the shore for a few days with my girls. I'll call you when I get back." He hated lying, especially to a friend.

Hansen hung up then. He strolled on back to the Rue des Ciseaux, stopping to buy the little apple tarts Ellie liked and a chocolate croissant for himself. The food here was just too damn good.

She wasn't there when he got back to the apartment. She also took off for hours during the day, but he didn't know what she did. And he didn't feel comfortable asking. There was a lot of her, in fact, that was a mystery to him. The drinking for one thing. He could have sworn she'd said she didn't drink any more, but they had wine for lunch and dinner most days and a whiskey before bedtime. He wasn't sure how much they were drinking, as she kept the refrigerator and cupboards stocked with food and drink.

Then there were the pills in the cabinet in the bathroom. Two big bottles of Valium and a variety of samples, from Arlen Gerstead no doubt. He wanted to ask her if her doctor knew about all of them. He was concerned that she'd have some kind of reaction to mixing them or that maybe she was planning something with them.

Ellie had been through a lot. Being with her, he realized he hadn't ever given much thought to the victims of violence and what they went through. The violence made him sick, it made him mad, it made him want to get the guys who had done it. But he had never thought about the moment-to-moment life of the victim after the mugging, after the rape, after the attempted murder. He wondered if Ellie wished she was dead, wished that Joel had killed her.

The truth was he didn't know how to help her, didn't know how to knit the contradictions together into a woman he could fall in love with. During the day, she was affectionate with him, touching him when she passed by, kissing him often, holding his hand as they walked down the street. But when he wanted more, wanted to make love to her, she turned cool, went somewhere else when they were in bed together. She didn't push him away, didn't say no. He could have dealt with that. But this cool acquiescence he didn't understand.

Then as the days passed, she seemed to soften. They spent more time together. She took him to the Eiffel Tower and Notre Dame, to the home of Victor Hugo and the Holocaust museum. She had a wealth of information and she told him stories that made him wish he'd paid attention in his history classes. He saw that there were two Ellies—the vulnerable woman who had been brutalized by a sick man and his even sicker companion and then this competent, often funny college professor. And although he found himself a little intimidated by her intellect, she made no big deal about this disparity between them.

"Everybody has their own kind of smart," she said when he mentioned how much she knew. "I may be book-smart, but you are definitely street-smart. What's more, you're heart-smart, and that means a lot to me."

Heart-smart. No one had ever called him that before. His wife would have scoffed. His brand of romance had never appealed to Claire and that had hurt him deeply. He knew himself to be a sensitive guy, an understanding man. He felt glad that Ellie could see it.

᠁

"I'm going back tomorrow."

Ellie looked up at him from her journal. She wrote each morning at the table in the living room while Hansen showered and shaved. A strange cloud seemed to pass over her face, but she just nodded and turned back to her writing.

He stood there a moment longer. He was too unsure of his feelings to make some kind of promise to her. A possibility was definitely there, for him anyway. He liked her, he desired her, but was that enough? Although he hated to admit it, Richardson was there with them, too. He didn't think he could erase Richardson for her and, until that happened, wasn't this some kind of weird rebound relationship?

They had sex again that night. The last several nights, Ellie had initiated it and the potential for something good seemed to increase. But the moment he entered her, she went away. He could see it in her eyes, hear it in her breath. He was glad she didn't pretend, that would have broken his heart, but he couldn't satisfy her and he didn't know what to do.

This time, when he had come and they had parted, he could feel her wound-up beside him. Before, the holding back had eased after. This time it didn't.

"I'm sorry," she said finally. "I'm sure this is disappointing to you."

"No," he lied. "It's okay."

"No, it's not. But I can't do anything else right now. I don't know if this will make any sense, but I need it to be ordinary, what happens between us, dull and ordinary. I couldn't handle the earth moving or rockets going off. When we do this, I'm supposed to be in my body, but I just can't be. I wish I could. You can't know how much I wish I could. How much I wish I'd never met Joel."

He felt a hot flash of anger at Richardson, at fate. Then he kissed her hand, which he had taken in his. "I wouldn't know you then."

She laughed, a short, bitter sound. But when she spoke, her voice was softer. "I am glad to know you, Doug. I'm so glad you came to Paris. I will treasure these days. But it isn't enough. I wish I could say that it is, but it isn't."

"You could come back with me, spend your sabbatical in Gettysburg." He hadn't meant to say this.

"I'm not sure I can ever go back to Gettysburg."

The anger flashed in him again. Here was Richardson manipulating his life from beyond the grave.

"When will you come back to Pittsburgh?" He made his voice neutral this time.

"In the spring," she said. "March or April. I've been working a little. Getting some ideas for some writing I could do. I'll go back to that after you leave."

"Can we stay in touch?"

"Yes, of course. You can call me anytime or email. I care about you. I wish I could care more."

He pulled her close and they lay like that a long time. But when he woke in the night, her place in the bed was cold and the lamp glowed from the living room.

♟

She wouldn't let him take a cab to the airport. Instead they took a long route on buses and trains. He hadn't wanted her to come with him that far. It was a waste of time and he wasn't sure how they would part. But it felt right somehow to have her company for a couple more hours.

They checked in his bags and got coffee and one of the best chocolate croissants he'd had. "Can you ship these to me?" he said.

Her face, which had been closed all morning, cleared and she laughed. "There are excellent French bakeries in the States. I'll bet you can find a good croissant in Philadelphia."

They talked a while about her research. He didn't understand much of it. Something about photography and the novel of the nineteenth century. There were original documents she wanted to look at that were only available at the National Library. He smiled at her enthusiasm and the reverence with which she spoke of handling these newspapers and books that were 150 years old. Yet that didn't seem enough to him as "something to do." He was glad to be going back to his job. He needed the structure, the purpose. This was the longest vacation he had taken since his daughters were in grade school and it was beginning to wear on him. He wanted to meet with Capriano and find the second man.

He glanced at his watch. Twenty minutes until boarding. The butterflies were beginning to circle in his stomach. He didn't like flying, didn't like being cooped up in a big metal can for hours. He finished the cappuccino and finger-licked the crumbs from his plate.

"Go ahead," Ellie said, laughing again. "You know you want another one."

He bought two, asked for a plastic bag to keep the butter smears out of his pocket. The girl looked at him as if he were crazy but handed him a grocery sack.

Ellie had gathered up his book and his reading glasses and put them in the little cloth bag she'd given him. He went over to her, took the bag from her and put it on the table, then put his arms around her and kissed her. "Go now," he said quietly. "It'll be easier for us both."

He pulled back to look in her face and saw that her eyes were full of tears. "I don't know what will become of . . ." she said but he stopped her words with his mouth, picked up the bag, and headed to the security gate. When he looked back, she had gone.

38

"It will never last. You know that, don't you?"

The woman who slid in across from Ellie in the back booth at Muddy Waters the morning after her return from Chama Valley had amazing red hair. It was the kind of hair that didn't look real but most certainly was. It was also thick and a little bit curly. Ellie had always envied women with hair like that.

Jean jacket, black t-shirt, a large chunk of polished turquoise on a thick silver chain over her small breasts. The woman sat casually across from her, her arm slung over the back of the booth. Girlfriend to girlfriend. Except for the look on her face.

Ellie said nothing. Almost no one knew her in Farmington. She could count those who did on ten fingers: Al, Mona, the desk clerks at the Residence Inn, the rancheros, the dean at the college. She certainly didn't know this person. So she waited.

The redhead waved away the approaching waitress, looked out the window, and then turned back to Ellie. "You think you can waltz in here and insinuate yourself in our lives. It doesn't work that way. You don't know anything about us and how we live here. We have history, and you, you're not part of that." The woman's voice was low, threatening in a way that vibrated along Ellie's spine.

"Are you . . . have you been going through my things?" Ellie asked.

"Yeah, right. As if I have time to follow you around." Then the woman reached over and picked up Ellie's tea. She looked her in the eye, spat in the cup, then put it back where it had been. "I feel sorry for you. I'll bet you think he's just a regular guy. A good man. Well, he'll leave you, too."

She slid out of the booth and leaned down over Ellie's shoulder. "Ask him what really happened to Annie."

39

"The woman who runs the sex parties has agreed to meet with us." Capriano's voice came clear and strong over the connection. "Any chance you can come this way?"

Hansen sighed. Since his return from France two weeks before, he had put Ellie and the case in a back pocket of his mind. His disappointment with what had happened between them was profound. He thought he had gone to Paris open to something that could occur, but he knew now that he had planned to fall in love, to commit his future to Ellie, to come back with a woman in his life again. Instead he was more alone than ever.

"You there, Doug?"

"Yeah, I'm here. When were you thinking of seeing her?"

"Tomorrow afternoon about three."

"Let me think a minute." Hansen had been busy. The arsons were ongoing, and an old man had died in one of the fires. The chief was pressing for an arrest. "Yeah, I'll be there. Meet you at the station at two-thirty."

❧

Marilyn Tomei was a very handsome woman in her mid-forties. Hansen guessed she had been a model before she became a madam.

She met them in the penthouse suite of Pittsburgh Towers. Even though the furnishings were elegant and expensive, it was clear she did not live there. It was clear from the five-star hotel furnishings that no one did.

A linebacker bodyguard opened the door to them. He stood back at the sign of the badges and the woman rose off the couch and extended her hand. Her smile was warm, welcoming, and all together professional. "Coffee?" she said. "Something cold?"

The detectives declined. They all sat then around the glass-and-chrome coffee table. Hansen glanced at the one book on the table, a photo display of antique motorcycles.

Capriano spoke first. "We appreciate your meeting with us. As my colleague told you, we're investigating a rape and suicide of two Pittsburgh residents. We believe the suicide, Joel Richardson, was a client of yours."

"I have no clients, detective. I don't need to work for a living. But I do entertain a great deal. Perhaps I met Mr. Richardson socially, although the name doesn't ring a bell." She smiled that same smile. Hansen wondered if it took a conscious effort to be so agreeable.

He pulled out photos, a professional head shot of Joel Richardson that the hospital had given them and the mug shot of Arlen Gerstead. He handed the Richardson photo to the woman.

"Yes, I have met this man several times. But the name he gave me was Chad, Joel Chad. He's a doctor, I believe. And I haven't seen him for a number of months."

"That's Joel Richardson," Capriano said.

The woman smiled. "I don't ask men for their identification when they introduce themselves."

"Why would you?" Capriano smiled as well. "Richardson killed himself last September after the rape and torture of his girlfriend by another man. We're trying to find out information that will lead us to the second man."

Distaste crossed the woman's face. "As I told you, I only meet men socially and I had only a passing acquaintance with Joel Chad. He came to a few parties I gave over the spring and summer."

"Did Richardson, or Chad, bring other men with him? Perhaps a younger man, a lover maybe?"

40

Ellie woke to the cold, gray light of Paris winter edging its way around the half-open curtains and sending its dim fingers into the corners of the apartment. It was ten-thirty or eleven, she guessed. She'd unplugged the clock in early December. Mario snored softly beside her, curled up like a small boy.

The day of Hansen's departure had been the last clear day for months. The warm, dry fall was followed by the descent of a cold, bitter fog over all of northern Europe. It hung on through the holidays and well into February, wreaking havoc with flights, traffic accidents, and a proliferation of bar fights, which were all reported on the télé.

Ellie couldn't have cared less. As long as the college's checks got deposited into her account and the supermarché continued to sell cheap wine, she was fine. She'd relearned how much easier and cheaper it was to stay drunk in Paris than in Pittsburgh.

She went into the kitchen and put on the kettle. She resisted the urge for a glass of wine even though she knew it would make her feel better. She needed to return some materials to the library today and if she started drinking now, she might never leave the apartment. If she made tea and toast, she could rouse Mario and get him gone before she needed to shower and leave herself.

She made a first cup for herself and moved around the massage table to the dining area, where she pulled out her journal.

155

She'd been writing every day since Hansen had left, keeping track of her consumption of food and alcohol, the occasional social event, but mostly the long days of nothing. She had not, however, kept track in the journal of her appointments with Mario.

"You'll like him," Marie-Noël had said as she cut Ellie's hair. "He does Thai, he does Swedish. He also does *massage érotique*. Some of my clients find him very talented."

Ellie wasn't interested in the *érotique* but her lower back needed attention. At the next haircut, Marie-Noël introduced her to Mario. He wasn't the young gigolo she'd imagined, but a slight Italian man of about forty. He gave her several sessions of Swedish massage for her back and then one night stayed for dinner, to practice his English he said. It got late, they had both drunk a lot, and he spent the night in her bed. Ellie didn't want sex; she just didn't want to be so alone. And so they fell into a routine of massage and the night on Wednesdays. She paid him handsomely for the massage, but he wouldn't take money for the night together and was insulted when she tried.

"You are a beautiful woman," he said, "and a lonely one. I make you a gift of my time."

He gave her another gift as well. "Who did this to you?" he exclaimed when he saw the scars. Ellie had shook her head and remained silent. The next time he came, he brought special herbal creams and gently rubbed them into the scars. "Je suis belle," he would say. "Répétez." *I am beautiful. Say it with me.*

Ellie could not see that the scars faded any but she began to look at herself in the mirror when she got out of the shower. She had not done that since Gettysburg.

As the cold, rainy winter in Paris dragged on, Ellie slipped deeper into a drug-enhanced hibernation. The days took on a repetition that was both comforting and deadening. She slept late, put in a few half-hearted hours at the library once or twice a week, went to a movie most afternoons, then was awake a good part of the night, often writing in her journal at three or four. She read a lot but retained little, telling herself it was still good practice with the language.

She and Mario had become lovers, although *lovers* wasn't the right word. By the time Mario arrived for the Wednesday evening massage and English lessons, Ellie would already be drunk and she would just get drunker until the conversation and ensuing sex was a blur, experienced in snatches as she faded in and out. In her earlier years of drinking, the blackouts had frightened her. Now she welcomed their oblivion.

41

Hansen drove to Pittsburgh one Thursday morning late in February. Capriano had wanted to delay the interview with Sandy Gerstead for some weeks while he pursued several leads. He wasn't working the case full time, far from it, but he kept at it. Hansen admired him for it. For Capriano, it was pure police work, pure pride in his job, not the complicated mess Hansen had found himself in with Ellie.

When the Greensburg exit came up, Hansen made a quick decision and pulled off the turnpike. He could take the surface roads into Pittsburgh and go by Ellie's place. Maybe she had come back.

The silver Mazda was in the driveway, the same car the boy had been unloading. Ellie's red Honda was still on the street. Hansen wondered if the kid was driving it some to keep the battery going. The dirty heaped snow in front and behind the Honda meant probably not. He thought about going to the door, seeing if the kid knew when Ellie would be back. Then he stopped himself. Best not to go there again. It hadn't worked out well the first time and nothing had changed that he could see.

He started to drive on, then stopped. Something nagged at him, something little and sharp in the back of his mind. He put the car in reverse and jotted down the Mazda's plate number. He called it in and then headed into the city.

✿

Capriano was on the phone when Hansen got to the station. Hansen sat down in the chair next to the desk; he was in no hurry. The detectives' room was pretty quiet. Most desks were empty: a man here, a woman there, on the phone, doing paper work. The room had a lethargy about it that Hansen recognized from his own station when there wasn't a crisis in swing.

"Sorry about that," Capriano said, putting the phone down. "Our dishwasher is on the blink and major appliances are my jurisdiction."

"Any news?"

"We've been trying to trace the pentobarbital, but with no luck. We'd need a vial with numbers and he hasn't left us one. It's commonly used by veterinarians for euthanasia. It's controlled for vets, but it's also apparently easy to get in Mexico or on the street."

"Do you think he got it from Richardson himself?"

"Maybe, but Richardson would have to have signed for it, and there's no record of that. Of course that doesn't mean that there aren't falsified records at his ER but we don't have enough evidence to pursue that."

Hansen nodded. "Mrs. Gerstead here?"

Capriano nodded.

"Lawyer?"

Capriano shook his head.

"Husband?"

Capriano shook his head again. "I told her she might be more comfortable if she came without him." He handed Hansen a manila envelope.

Hansen looked through the contents, glancing up from time to time at the other man, who nodded each time he did.

"She know any of this?"

"I doubt it." Capriano stood. "Need coffee or water?"

"No, I'm fine. Let's go talk to her."

✿

Sandy Gerstead looked up when the two detectives entered the interview room. She didn't smile. Hansen saw that she held her purse in her lap. The gesture was old-fashioned, something his mom would have done. It told him a lot.

"Thanks for coming in, Mrs. Gerstead." Capriano's smile was warm and casual. "You remember Detective Hansen."

"Of course." She held out her hand to Hansen. "You were very kind to Ellie in that awful week right after . . ."

Hansen smiled and shook her hand. "Hello, Sandy," he said, then pulled a chair a little to one side again and gave the floor to Capriano.

"We're still on the case, Mrs. Gerstead. We're still trying to figure out what happened to Dr. Richardson and Dr. McKay."

"I don't have any new information to give you, Detective. I haven't remembered anything else. To be honest, I've tried to forget that weekend."

"How's Ellie doing, Sandy?" Hansen spoke up.

"She's still in France. But beyond that, I don't really know. She doesn't email me and I got tired of leaving messages and her not calling me back. I guess she's just busy with research. She has friends there, too." The woman looked sad, lost somehow. Hansen knew how she felt.

"We want to make it safe for Dr. McKay to come home," said Capriano, "so we're trying to tie up as many loose ends as possible."

"Okay," said Sandy, "but I don't know how I can help."

"Well, some things have come to our attention about your husband and Dr. Richardson that make us wonder if Mr. Gerstead knows more than he's telling us. And that makes us wonder if you know more than you've told us. Maybe you know something about the two of them and are afraid to say anything."

Sandy frowned. "What sort of things have come to your attention?"

"Did Arlen tell you that he and Joel frequented sex clubs here in town?"

"What do you mean, 'sex clubs'? You mean like strippers? That's ridiculous."

Capriano went on. "We have witnesses that place your husband and Joel in several different locations frequented by prostitutes."

"That doesn't mean anything." Her voice was defensive but she looked stricken with shame.

"Arlen was a good customer at these places," Capriano said.

"I don't believe you."

Hansen saw her knuckles whiten as she gripped the purse. He hated this part of the job.

Capriano shifted direction. "Have you and your husband recently come into some money? An inheritance maybe or does one of you gamble a little?"

Sandy Gerstead shook her head. "No, we live on our salaries. I work, Arlen works. Neither one of us gambles. We don't even buy lottery tickets. I think they're a waste of good money. Why? What's going on?"

"One of the sex clubs is, how I shall put this, 'high class.' It's expensive to join, expensive to attend. We're talking a thousand dollars an evening."

"Well, Joel had a lot of money. I know that. Maybe he paid for Arlen. If Arlen even went to those places and I'm sure he didn't. He isn't that kind of man." There were tears in her eyes.

Hansen saw the sympathy in Capriano's eyes. He was relieved to see the other man's discomfort with what they were doing.

"Sandy, we know this is painful to hear. But we're trying to sort this all out. Your husband has continued to go to this club since Dr. Richardson died, at least three times that we know of," Hansen said.

"That's not possible. We don't have that kind of money." Loyalty and disgust battled in her eyes.

Hansen got up and took a bottle of water from a small table in the corner and placed it in front of her. She looked at it as if it were a snake about to bite her.

"Mrs. Gerstead," said Capriano, "did you know that your husband is using an apartment here in the city?"

"It must have to do with his work. He's a sales representative for a big pharmaceutical company."

"We don't think so. He rented this apartment in November, gave his name as Joel Richardson when he signed the lease. We've been watching this apartment for some time. Do you know this woman?" Capriano handed her several photos. One of Arlen Gerstead and a young, curvaceous blonde, the couple was holding hands. In a second photo, the blonde, dressed as a nurse, was about to enter a white Toyota Avalon. "That's your husband's car, isn't it?"

Sandy Gerstead nodded. "I don't know anything about this," she said, her voice small and tight. The stricken look of shame seemed welded to her face now.

Capriano kept it up. "Where would your husband get this kind of money? Is he selling drugs? Are you two selling drugs?"

"No," the woman's voice rose, became shrill, exasperated. "I don't know what Arlen is up to. He goes to work, I go to work. We come home, we spend time together. He's good to me. We love each other. I don't know anything about this. You know I don't." She looked directly at Hansen. "You know I don't," she said again.

Hansen could only nod at her. *Maybe*, he thought, *she'll see it's an apology.*

✹

"We've just destroyed a marriage, Larry," said Hansen. The two men stood at the curb a block down from the station.

"No, Doug, Arlen Gerstead destroyed his marriage. I'm not taking responsibility for this."

"Yeah, you're right, but it was still ugly."

Capriano nodded. "Let's just hope it does what we need it to."

✹

On the way home, Hansen checked his messages. The Mazda in Ellie's driveway was registered to a Jason L. Dirrelich. Address in one of the boroughs that Hansen was unfamiliar with. Friend of the kid, no doubt.

42

"Gracie Armand," said Mona. "It was most likely Gracie. She's Al's sister-in-law, or rather, former sister-in-law. He hasn't introduced you yet?"

Ellie sat across from the therapist. She shook her head. "I haven't met anyone in Al's life except the rancheros and the foreman. She's Annie's sister, then."

"Yes." Mona paused, then said, "There's been talk for a year or so that they were keeping company although nothing public or official."

"So she's jealous?"

"Maybe. I don't know her except in passing, so I have no idea what her relationship is with Al or what they promised each other."

"Do you know what happened to Annie?"

"No, it was before I came here. Al has been a widower as long as I've known him. Have you asked him what happened to her?"

"No, I assumed she died of illness. We haven't told each other all that much about our pasts." Ellie hesitated a moment and said, "I'm feeling really paranoid. I feel like I'm being watched, like somebody's going through my things at the hotel. This morning when I came back, the door was ajar."

"Had the maid been there?"

"Maybe but I didn't see her cart anywhere. I wondered if this woman, if Gracie, would do that."

Mona shook her head. "I don't know, Ellie. It seems an odd thing for a grown woman to do. She's confronted you directly so it seems unlikely she would sneak around. Have you told Al any of this?"

"No. He'll just pressure me to move out to the ranch with him, and I'm just not ready to do that."

"What are you waiting for, Ellie? Are you not wanting to be with Al?"

"Yes, I'm pretty sure I am. But I know I have to tell him about Joel and I can't, not yet."

"But do you feel unsafe at the hotel?"

"No, I guess not. I'm just oversensitive to everything."

"Well, a lot has happened to you."

Mona was silent then. Ellie didn't know what to say next so she just sipped tea from her mug and looked out the window.

Finally Mona asked about the trip to Chama Valley, and Ellie told her of Sofia's refusal to help her and how she needed to decide what she wanted.

"Doesn't sound so much like a refusal as a postponement. That happens sometimes. Did her reasoning make sense to you?" Mona asked.

"Yes," Ellie said and she could hear her own petulance. It made her smile, and Mona smiled too.

"What *do* you want, Ellie?"

"I want all this not to have happened. I want my life back, my body back—no scars, no rape."

Mona nodded. "What else do you want that you can't have?"

"I want to never have met Joel Richardson."

"I know. That would be wonderful, wouldn't it?" When Ellie didn't respond, she said, "What's under all this, Ellie? What do you want that's under all this?"

Ellie looked out at the rich evening light glowing on the street. "I want to feel safe." She felt five years old.

"We all have a right to that," said Mona. "A right to feel safe in our bodies, in our homes, in our world. And people—men—have violated that safety for you."

They sat in silence with that for a few minutes.

Then Mona said, "What do you think it will take to feel safe?"

Ellie shook her head. "I don't know."

"Hmm, I think you do, Ellie. I think in your body, in your soul, you know whom and what you trust."

"I don't."

"The child in you doesn't perhaps. But the adult self has more skills."

Ellie felt the petulance wash over her again. Why couldn't Mona just tell her the answer? Why couldn't somebody fix this for her?

"Did you trust Joel Richardson when you met him?"

"I didn't have any reason not to trust him."

"That wasn't my question. Think again."

"Yes . . . No . . . I didn't ever think about it. He looked good. He was charming, witty, intellectual. He had style. We had good conversations. He treated me well."

"Tell me more about that. What do you mean 'he treated you well'?"

Ellie hesitated. Her mind wanted to go blank. She wanted Mona to stop pushing her. Finally she said, "There didn't seem to be anything wrong with how he treated me."

Mona didn't say anything, as if she were waiting again for Ellie to go on but she didn't want to. Wasn't it time for the session to be over? Ellie glanced at her watch. She'd been there forty-five minutes. Mona wasn't going to let her off the hook.

"You're trying to get me to take responsibility for what Joel did to me, aren't you? Own my part?"

"No, I'm not. Even though that twelve-step idea is often useful, it is not helpful for someone who has been brutalized by another. No one asks for that. What I am suggesting is that you never figured out whether Joel was trustworthy. You didn't check with your inner wisdom, your intuition, your Higher Self, whatever you'd like to call it."

"No." Ellie was surprised at the relief she felt in seeing this. "And I should have."

"I wouldn't say 'should.' But 'could have' seems appropriate. Checking in with yourself is a way to move forward into feeling safe more of the time."

"How do I that? I don't have a clue."

"Oh, but of course you do. Is there any place you feel safe here in Farmington?"

"Well, I feel pretty safe here." She didn't know why, but she trusted Mona.

"Good. Where do you feel that in your body? Close your eyes and try to find that feeling."

Ellie sank back again into the cushions. She closed her eyes and scanned her body. "In my chest," she said after a few minutes. "Around my heart and in my stomach."

"That's it. When we can learn to check in with ourselves about people or situations, we can access our boundaries more easily, choose what is safe for us."

Mona was quiet then again. After a moment, she said, "We need to stop."

Ellie opened her eyes and looked at Mona. "What do I do about Al and what the sister-in-law said?"

"What do you want to do?"

"I want to know what can hurt me."

"That sounds absolutely right. Then ask him."

43

With the coming of the equinox, with the first greening of the trees, the famous Paris light brightened and a small piece of hope unveiled itself. Ellie began walking again, long walks that were less exploration of the city than a way to stay out of her apartment. She drank less and less, using the Valium to soften the edges of withdrawal from the months of too much wine and whiskey. She went half-heartedly to a few AA meetings. Nothing clicked, but she remembered there was a way out and she paced herself as best she could with both drugs and drink. Eventually the drinking stopped. The Valium was more complicated, but she cut back. A new tenant was due to arrive in the apartment at Rue des Ciseaux, so on April 1, she headed home.

Ellie was weary as the plane landed in Pittsburgh. It had been noon all day as she crossed the time zones following the sun in its midday arc. It was one-thirty in the afternoon when she got to New York, five-thirty when she got to Pittsburgh. She'd been awake for twenty hours.

As she stood waiting in the aisle, packed in with the others who were impatient to get out of the cramped space, she thought about Hansen. She had emailed him two days earlier with her flight times. "In case you're around," she'd written. "I'd like to reconnect."

There had been no answer—they hadn't communicated at all since December when he had left Paris—but she could hope, couldn't she?

But he wasn't there. Sandy was.

Her old friend stood off to one side. She smiled when Ellie caught her eye, but it was a sad smile. Ellie felt guilty. She had been a lousy correspondent while she'd been away. She hadn't told Sandy about Hansen's visit, or her relationship with Mario, or any of the long nights of numbing out and searching her soul. She felt she'd aged years, but she didn't know how to explain all that happened, and she didn't see how she and Sandy could get back the easy, comfortable friendship they'd had before all this had happened.

Sandy too looked older, she thought, and weary. She'd have to ask about that.

The two women hugged, Ellie hanging on an extra moment as if in apology. Then they went to the baggage claim. The conversation stayed light: Ellie chatted about the flight, the marginal food, the snoring priest who'd kept falling onto her shoulder. Sandy laughed; it seemed genuine and Ellie felt hopeful.

The bags were already there and so they trundled them out to the parking lot. Ellie was struck by the heat and humidity, already too high for early April. How could people not believe in global warming? She stripped off her jacket and threw it in the back as Sandy pulled out into traffic and they began the forty-five minutes to Greensburg.

Ellie relaxed. It felt good to see Sandy, to have a woman she could talk to again. She'd been lonely for that. She'd been lonely for everything that was part of a normal life. Maybe they could get some of it back.

"How's Arlen? I expected he'd drive tonight. Is he working?"

Sandy stared straight ahead at the highway. "I threw him out." Her voice was small and pinched.

"You threw him out?" Ellie's mind, tired as it was, began to race. Was there some new development in the case? Had Arlen been there that night after all? She reined herself back in, wanting to be a good friend. "What's happened?"

"He's having an affair. With a young blonde with big tits. Such a cliché!"

"Arlen?" Ellie could hear the disbelief in her own voice. "Arlen?"

Sandy shrugged. "The detectives showed me pictures. He has an apartment in the city and I guess he's living there with her. She can't be more than thirty."

"Do you know her?"

Sandy shook her head. "No. I assume she's somebody he met through work."

"I can't wrap my head around this," said Ellie. "Arlen just doesn't seem the type. You guys were so good together." She didn't say that Arlen wasn't the kind of guy that most women found attractive.

"That's what I thought. I thought he really loved me."

"Men and their dicks," Ellie said. "He doesn't love her. It's just a sex thing."

Sandy shrugged again. "It doesn't matter. He's been cheating on me and I just couldn't have that. So I told him to get out."

"When did this happen?"

"Two weeks ago."

Ellie touched her friend's shoulder. "I'm so sorry I wasn't here for you."

Sandy looked over at her and nodded. "It's been tough without you these past months. Though I know you needed to go. Did it do what you needed it to do?"

Ellie's turn to shrug. "I don't know. Time went by. And nobody there knew or cared." She thought about Hansen and wondered if she should say something. Later maybe. "Maybe that's all I can ask for," she said aloud.

There was silence then for a mile or two. Then Ellie spoke. "Do you think you two can get over this? Maybe counseling?"

"I don't know. The whole Gettysburg thing was hard for us, too. And Arlen hanging out with Joel. The detectives told me Arlen had been to sex clubs with Joel."

"You mean like strip joints, like the Bada Bing in *The Sopranos*?"

"I don't know. I didn't ask for any details. But definitely with hookers."

"This just gets uglier and uglier, doesn't it?" Ellie felt sick.

Sandy nodded. They had come to the exit on the turnpike and Ellie saw the familiar streets she had driven the last eight years.

"Are you okay for money?" Ellie asked as they drove past the entrance to the college. "Is Arlen paying his part of your bills?"

"So far. Though I don't know where he's getting the money for the apartment."

"Maybe the blonde is paying for the apartment." Ellie knew how preposterous that was as she said it. Young blondes didn't pay for apartments for older men who looked like Arlen.

"Yeah, right," said Sandy. "But it isn't coming out of his check. That's still being direct deposited into our account and Arlen is just taking out spending money. I've wondered if Joel left him money in his will."

"They weren't those kind of friends."

Sandy looked over at her with the same sad smile she'd given her at the airport. "Ellie, I don't think we know what kind of friends they were."

44

Ellie spent the next weeks focused on Sandy, offering her the companionship and reassurance that Sandy had given to her after Gettysburg. They ate lunch together on campus and spent evenings playing cards, walking in the early spring loveliness of Ellie's neighborhood, talking. Sandy had seen a lawyer to find out about divorce or a legal separation or whatever would most protect her from what she called "Arlen's insanity." Ellie played the sounding board.

Ellie also spent time in her office. She had a cordial welcome home from the dean and was offered an early summer school class to begin mid-May, teaching English grammar to new Korean nursing students. Ellie loved working with the international students and their eagerness to please, so different from the half-hearted interest shown to foreign language by the western Pennsylvania kids. The events of the fall seemed forgotten.

She was glad to be back with her cats. Roger Gerstead had kept the apartment up pretty well, and Sandy had overseen a thorough cleaning including a smudging with sage before she returned, so she felt comfortable there. She began to feel a bit of the normalcy she had wanted when she returned from Paris.

✿

Late on May 10, a Sunday evening, Ellie thought she heard a knock on the door. It was nearly ten and she was brushing her teeth. Sandy had gone home minutes earlier and Ellie wondered if she'd forgotten something.

"Sandy, is that you?"

There was no answer but the knock came again, louder now, so she went down the four stairs to the landing and opened the door as far as the chain would allow. Doug Hansen stood there.

Ellie's heart leapt, just a little. She smiled and closed the door, undid the chain, and opened the door wide. But he didn't smile and he didn't take her in his arms. He didn't even make a move to come in. She suddenly felt cold and afraid.

"Ellie," he said. "Is Sandy Gerstead here?"

She shook her head. "She just left. Maybe five minutes ago. Has something happened?"

He nodded. "Her husband's body was found this evening."

Fear washed over her. "Was it an accident?"

He shook his head.

"She didn't do it. She couldn't have. She was with me all afternoon."

He moved in closer to her on the landing and touched her shoulder. "Ellie, we don't suspect her. We need to notify her."

She moved toward him then and he held her, but she felt little comfort even in the familiarity of his arms.

After a moment, he followed her up into the kitchen. She said nothing, held up the kettle, and looked at him.

He shook his head. "Would she have gone straight home?"

"Yes," Ellie said, "of course. Why wouldn't she?"

"Ellie, relax. I know this is hard."

She stopped and turned around and looked at him. She took a deep breath and blew it out. "You're right. I just thought that this was starting to be over. I just wanted it to be over."

He nodded at her, sympathy written plain on his face. "How has it been to be back?"

"Okay," she said. "I start teaching again next month. Summer school. One of my favorite classes. I'm ready for things to be normal, every day. Why can't it just be over?"

Hansen shrugged. "Things don't always work that way. I'm sorry."

She turned back to the counter, gripped the edge. "I wanted you to come to the airport." She didn't turn around.

"I know. It didn't seem like the right idea."

"Too late, isn't it?" She turned then and looked at him.

He looked back at her. "It's not that exactly." He paused and in those few seconds his phone rang. He saw who it was and stepped out on the landing. When he came back, his expression was grim. "She's there now—at her house. Do you want to come and be with her?"

"Yes, of course." Ellie went into the bedroom and got dressed.

♁

Capriano and his partner Jackson were waiting in their car outside the house. Capriano nodded at Ellie and at Hansen and the three of then went to the door. The house was dark downstairs, though lights were on in two of the windows of the upper story. It took Sandy Gerstead several minutes to answer the doorbell.

She stood there, the entry light on behind her. She was still dressed—jeans and a soft white blouse. Her face was pink and she smelled of soap and toothpaste.

"Something's happened to Arlen," she said when she saw the detectives. Her voice was flat, dead almost.

Ellie moved straight to her and wrapped her in a hug.

Somehow over the next few minutes, they settled into the living room. The two detectives in easy chairs, Ellie and Sandy on the couch across the coffee table from them. Ellie had brought in a tray of glasses filled with water although no one touched them.

Capriano spoke directly to the new widow. "I'm sorry to have to tell you that your husband is dead. His body was found a couple of hours ago."

Sandy nodded, looked at her hands, then across at the mantle where her wedding picture stood.

"Was she with him? That blonde. Is she dead, too?" she asked.

"Yes," said Capriano and he looked at Hansen. "They're both dead."

"Was it an overdose?" Sandy asked. "Bad drugs? I knew his job would get him into trouble."

"No," said Capriano. "We're not sure, but we don't think it was drugs, not specifically."

Hansen saw the murder scene in his mind and he shivered. Gettysburg again, down to the last detail. The blonde call-girl, for that's what she was, tied to the bed with gold cords. Another cord around her neck, twisted so tight it bit into her flesh. The body streaked with welts and burns. Gerstead in a wingback chair, his head tipped back, the needle in his arm. He wore a white physician's jacket and clipped to the pocket was Joel Richardson's hospital ID. There was no sign of struggle.

Hansen hoped Capriano wouldn't share these details. He didn't want Ellie to hear any of this.

Capriano didn't. He went through the usual interview questions. When had Sandy last heard from her husband? What had the women done all day? Had they separated for any length of time? Had either of whom talked to Arlen over the course of the day? Did they know who he might have been meeting?

The two women weren't any more helpful than Hansen expected. Sandy said she hadn't talked to Gerstead in three days. They'd been separated for several weeks. He'd taken all his clothes and effects, she assumed to the apartment. He'd called her at work on Thursday to ask if he could come by and get his tools and some of his music. She didn't know if he'd been there; she hadn't bothered to check if the things were gone.

"Can you add anything, Dr. McKay?" Capriano had been intently watching Sandy Gerstead. Now he looked at Ellie for the first time.

She shook her head. "I haven't seen Arlen since last fall. I'm sure he knew better than to call me. He knew I'd side with Sandy in this mess."

Hansen knew that that was true, and he could see that both women were reeling from the information. He also remembered that Ellie didn't know that this was the third incident. She would still be believing her experience was the only one. He stood. "Any more questions for right now, Larry? I'm sure Mrs. Gerstead has calls she needs to make."

"We'll need someone to verify identification of the body," Capriano said.

"Sandy doesn't need to do that," said Ellie. "One of his sons can do it."

"Roger?" said Hansen.

Ellie looked at him and nodded.

"I went by your place right after you went to France. I met Roger Gerstead then."

"He was house-sitting for me," Ellie told Capriano.

"Do you have a number for him?" Capriano asked.

Ellie pulled out her cell phone, found the number, and wrote it on a slip of paper from her wallet.

The two men stood then. The silence seemed awkward to Hansen, like a date gone bad, no one knowing what to do next. He spoke up. "Ellie, do you need your car?"

"Yes, but I don't want to leave Sandy alone."

"How long will it take?" Capriano said.

"Twenty minutes at most," said Hansen. "It's not far."

"Jackson and I will stay then. Just make it quick."

Hansen nodded. Ellie hugged Sandy, who sat like a statue, and she and Hansen went out the door.

"Is there something you're not telling me?" Ellie asked as they drove away.

Hansen looked straight ahead at the road. How much would keep her safe? How much would terrify her? Was there any middle ground? Then he shrugged and decided to tell her the truth, or most of it, anyway.

"There have been other incidents."

"Other incidents? What does that mean?"

Hansen looked over at her, at the confusion on her face, a confusion that was morphing into panic.

"A woman was found dead in February in a hotel in the city. The circumstances were similar to what happened to you."

"Was her boyfriend killed, too?"

Hansen shook his head. "No, she was alone at the scene. And her death may have been accidental."

"Accidental?" Ellie put her hand on his arm.

"Asphyxiation through overdose. She had a lot of drugs in her system."

"Prescriptions?"

"No, street drugs."

"Did she know Joel or Arlen?" Ellie's voice was small, almost child-like.

"No, we found no connection at all."

Ellie was quiet a long moment. Then she said, "You said incidents. Plural."

"Arlen."

"What about Arlen?"

"It was all similar to Gettysburg. They were found in a hotel. Arlen was in a chair with pentobarbital. The girl in the bed, like you."

Her hand slipped away from his arm. The car felt as though all the air had been sucked right out of it. He looked over at her. Her face had gone blank. He watched to see if she was breathing and was relieved to see her chest rise and fall. He wanted to put his arms around her and reassure her that it would be all right, but that wasn't the truth. He couldn't guarantee anything.

"How did the girl die, the girl with Arlen?"

"The same way. Asphyxiated."

"He choked her like he choked me?"

"No, she died some hours later, hours after the assault. Vomited and it got into her lungs."

"Accidental."

Hansen heard the bitterness in Ellie's voice, but there was nothing he could say.

They had come to her street and her red Honda Civic sat to the right. Hansen was conscious of the time and yet he couldn't leave her like this. He took a deep breath "Do you need to go inside?"

She nodded. She didn't look at him.

"I'll come with you."

They walked up the street and then up the outside stairs. The house was quiet and dark except for the two porch lights, one over the door on the long front porch, one over Ellie's door. He reflexively went in first, checked the rooms, but he knew that the killer wouldn't be there. That wasn't what this was about.

Ellie gathered her things from the bathroom and the bedroom, stuffing them into a cloth bag. She fed the two cats. She said nothing and she still didn't look at him. When she was ready to go, she looked at him and nodded. And they went out.

Once in her car, she rolled down the window.

"I'll follow you over," he said.

"You don't need to do that."

"Yes, I do. Ellie, I . . ." he paused. "There seems so much to talk about and I don't know what to say."

She looked up at him with a sad smile. "Bad timing, Doug. We've had bad timing. And . . ." she gave a little bitter laugh, "bad karma."

"I guess."

She hesitated and he hoped she felt as reluctant to part as he did.

"Are we in danger, Doug? Sandy and I?"

"I don't know," he said. "I don't think so. But it would be best if you and Sandy stayed together at night. Capriano and I will talk to the locals and get a patrol to come by her house."

"Actually, I'm going to try to talk Sandy into coming here to stay with me. I've got cats and she doesn't. And maybe it would be better for her to get out of that house."

"Just let Capriano know that when you get back over there." He was silent a moment. "We're going to get him, Ellie. I know it."

She smiled that same sad smile and rolled up her window. He drove right behind her to the Gerstead house and waited until she had gone inside. Then he started the long drive back to Gettysburg.

45

Ellie put off talking to Al for a few days after her session with Mona. The feeling of being watched faded, and things stayed in place in her room. Only one thing spooked her: Coming down the hall to her room after dinner one night, she thought she saw gold cords on the carpet outside her room. There were two of them, and her throat seized up in fear. But when she put her glasses on and got closer, she saw that they were ordinary pieces of rope, beige, harmless. Only the light in the hallway had made them look familiar. She chided herself for interpreting everything as scary and wished Sandy were there to laugh with her. She knew that some of this was a result of nothing much to do, no purpose, no structure, and no one to confide in. She knew Al would love to be that one person, but something held her back.

Ellie had always shied away from marriage. When she was younger, her circle of friends didn't believe in any of the old institutions. They believed in careers for women, free love, sexual experimentation. Having kids and a family was for later, much later, and then it was only one option among many. And without kids, there was no need for marriage. It was a philosophy that resonated with something in Ellie, who felt a need to be attached and free at the same time. That had been fine with the men in her life, the early lovers, then Danny, then Joel.

But the violation of her body and her spirit had changed how she was with herself. She thought about Al's words the night they had met. "Can someone else come along? Be there to pick up the pieces. Bring you back home to yourself." It hadn't worked with Hansen, or maybe she hadn't been ready yet. She knew that if she asked Al about Annie—and Gracie—that it would only be fair to answer his questions about her past, if he asked them. She also knew that the only point in having these conversations was to get closer to each other, to become husband and wife. The big question was if she was ready now.

46

Hansen didn't see Ellie again until the funeral for Arlen Gerstead. When he arrived, the fifty or sixty mourners were being urged to take the front rows of the large gothic chapel buried in the heart of the campus. In the back, under the massive pipe organ, sat several rows of ancient nuns. Ellie and Sandy Gerstead sat in the front. Both women wore black, the dresses similar enough that Hansen couldn't tell them apart. Behind them sat the son Roger and a stout, gray-haired woman in a very tight navy blue suit. Gerstead's first wife, he assumed. They looked tired and strained. Hansen wondered where the other son was. Ellie had said there were two boys. Toward the back sat Ellie's student-friend Michelle and the boyfriend from Paris. The girl looked different. Older, tired. The first deaths of people we know will do that. The guy looked the same, though his hair was short now and darker than Hansen remembered. He was sorry to see they were still together. He wouldn't want one of his girls to be going out with Lenny.

The chapel was impressive. Hansen's own religious experience had been meager and Lutheran. This was old-style Catholic with vaulted ceilings, gleaming hardwood pews and floors, rich stained glass with a preponderance of blue. The air was heavy with incense. He wondered idly if Ellie was Catholic, if Gerstead had been, or if the chapel had been chosen because both women worked on campus.

There was no casket. He knew from Capriano that the body had been cremated once the autopsy was done. Gerstead had died of an overdose of pentobarbital and Valium, but there was nothing to indicate that the second man had had a hand in his death. Just like with Joel Richardson, the only prints on the syringe were Gerstead's. But this copy-cat suicide cast strong doubt on what had happened to Richardson. Often with serial events, the more it happened, the more they knew. But not this time.

Hansen walked up the side aisle and crossed in front of Ellie so she would see him. She looked good, better than he expected. He'd noticed earlier that she had put on some weight and she carried it nicely. She smiled at him, a real smile of warmth and greeting, and he felt his earlier desire for her well up. Bad timing, she had said. That's for sure. But could they overcome it? Did he want to?

He nodded at Jackson, Capriano's partner, but saw no sign of his friend. It was only in the movies that the police hoped to catch the killer at the funeral. Jackson's appearance was a courtesy to the family, a visual memo that they were still on the case. And his own appearance? Ellie was his friend. They had been lovers. He wanted her to know that he was there for her.

He took a seat a dozen rows back from the front, several empty pews between him and the mourners. The priest went through the unfamiliar ritual and people rose and sat and kneeled and sat, Ellie and Sandy among them, and Hansen watched.

Several people got up and spoke platitudes about Arlen Gerstead. One was a former boss, another a fellow salesman. Roger Gerstead got up and spoke for the family. He thanked people for coming, he spoke warmly of his father in the vague way of the young. Hansen didn't really listen. He hadn't liked Arlen Gerstead one bit.

The whole service took about thirty-five minutes. There was a small reception in an adjoining room. Cookies, fruit juice, coffee. The large photo of Arlen that had stood on an easel in the front of the chapel now stood by the trash can. Hansen couldn't help but note the symbolism.

Roger Gerstead and his mother stood to one side while most of the others greeted and consoled Sandy. Ellie stood close to her friend, anchoring her, it seemed. Michelle spoke to the two older women. Lenny wasn't with her and Hansen didn't see him anywhere.

Then Hansen saw an opening and approached the two women. He spoke briefly to Sandy, then asked Ellie if they might talk a moment. She nodded and they moved to the far end of the room.

"How are you two holding up?"

Ellie tilted her head at the question. "Well, I'd say a little better each day. She was pretty upset at first. She hadn't really come to grips with the separation, Arlen's affair, that whole mess. And then suddenly for him to be dead. Just like Joel. It all seems so complicated, so messy. Who are these men that we know so little about?"

"I wish I knew, Ellie. I wish I could explain it all to you." He touched her shoulder and felt her move a little closer to him. He wanted to embrace her.

She sighed. "I'm not glad Arlen is dead, but I must say it's been helpful to have someone else to worry about, and nice to be able to be there for Sandy after she was so good to me. I was pretty uncommunicative when I was in France, really mired in my own misery, and I'm glad to be able to do something for her. It helps to try to get us both back to normal."

He nodded and held himself back from touching her again.

"I'm back at work finally, teaching a class up here. Trying to keep some structure going. That feels therapeutic too."

"I can relate. Work is really important."

She smiled at him again. "I should get back."

"Ellie, one question. I thought Arlen had two sons."

She frowned. "He does. He did. Twins. But only Roger came today."

"Bad blood?"

"What? Oh, with Arlen? I don't know. You'd have to ask Sandy. I know they were both unhappy when Arlen divorced their mom, even though it was her idea. She had another man at the time. They all live in Ohio." She turned to leave.

"One more thing. Is the other son named Jason?"

"No. His name is Michael."

"Have you ever met him?"

"Once. A few years back at a graduation party for Roger. Michael was there briefly. He never warmed up to Sandy as stepmother although she and Roger get along fine."

"Then, did you ever hear Arlen speak of a Jason Dirrelich?" He spelled the last name for her.

She shook her head.

"Okay, Ellie. Take care of yourself."

He watched her move across the room, stopping to talk briefly with two or three small groups of people. Then she rejoined Sandy and he was alone again.

47

Then somehow, life went back to normal. Ellie spent some of each day on campus, teaching her class and taking care of the endless personal and professional paperwork that had piled up during her absence. She had her apartment cleaned and her bedroom painted. She got a new mattress and springs. She felt in a hurry to move on now.

Sandy stayed with her another week after the funeral, then moved home to get the house ready to sell. The same reporters who had plagued Ellie now plagued the Gerstead property for a week, but then the shooting of a black kid fleeing a robbery in Squirrel Hill took all the juice out of the Gerstead scandal and things quieted down.

Ellie thought about Hansen. She went over their conversations word for word, looking for an opening, a way back to the potential that had come off him in waves in Paris, but it hadn't been there. Clearly, he cared about her and wanted her to be well. But he didn't want to be with her and she couldn't blame him. She felt downhearted.

In mid-June, Sandy went to upstate New York to visit her ancient father. "I hate to leave you, Ellie," she said. "But I need to go and I need to get out of town. Maybe that damn house will sell while I'm gone." She'd already found a condo closer to Pittsburgh, which she

184

wanted to buy and was trying to talk Ellie into getting one in the same complex.

"That's okay. Now that I'm working, I'm doing much better. And I think this must be all over." She needed to believe that. That the killer had been after Joel and Arlen and now that they were dead, it was over. "You go and have the best time you can."

Sandy rolled her eyes at the thought and both women laughed.

48

As it turned out, Hansen and Capriano were of the same mind. In their weekly phone conversations about the three cases, they had come to the decision that Richardson and Gerstead were the targets, that the women—Ellie, the Carlyle woman, the nurse-prostitute—had been collateral damage. Not all the evidence pointed that way, but enough of it did for the idea to be feasible.

"What do you think about the other Gerstead boy? Do you think he's good for it?" Hansen asked on a Tuesday in late June. He heard Capriano slurp, coffee probably as it was just past ten in the morning.

"We did some checking, Doug. He has a solid alibi for the whole weekend of Arlen's murder. He works at a halfway-house in Akron for disabled adults and he was on duty the whole weekend, sleeps there and everything."

"He couldn't have slipped away while people were asleep?"

"Doesn't seem feasible. First, Akron is quite a drive, as you well know. And there are three caregivers at the home at all times, and two have to be awake and on duty at a time. It's just too far and too many hours to be gone. Besides, there would have been a DNA connection with Arlen's blood."

"Yeah, that's right. Arlen would have been a partial match if it was his kid."

"Do you have some need for this to be oedipal?"

Hansen could hear the chuckle under Capriano's words.

"No," he said, "I just want a good suspect."

"Me too."

"Do you think there could be more than one killer?"

"I don't think so. There're too many details that are the same in each incident. The guy had to have been at the first one to stage the other two."

"I know. I'm just fishing. I want this guy off the streets."

Capriano slurped again. "Are you still seeing Ellie McKay?"

"I'm not seeing her, Larry."

Capriano looked him in the eye. "I know you went to Paris last Thanksgiving."

"I did. And I saw her there. But nothing came of it. Nothing."

"Hmmm. Okay, if you say so. She's a good-looking woman. And smart too."

"Both those things, but we aren't seeing each other. However, that doesn't preclude me from wanting to get whoever raped her behind bars."

"Of course not. I was just asking." He paused and then cleared his throat. "My captain wants you to step back from this now. What with the last three deaths squarely in our jurisdiction, he wants Jackson and me to be full-tilt on this. It's not that we don't appreciate your help and we'll certainly keep you posted with the outcome, but it isn't going to be a joint case anymore. Your captain agrees. Sounds like he wants your attention on cases there."

Hansen felt a surge of anger. Then another surge. But he kept his mouth shut and pushed the feelings down.

Capriano spoke into the awkward silence. "It's nothing personal. Your work has helped get us this far but we've got to take it now."

"I know. Just keep me informed then."

"Sure. Take it easy." And Capriano was gone.

49

The summer lurched by in full-blown heat and humidity. Capriano and Jackson worked the case in the time between gang fights and hit-and-runs and drug busts and bar brawls. There were other murders but none were of ordinary citizens—none were the kind of murders that get big press, and most were quickly solved. The second man seemed to have vanished with the death of Arlen Gerstead.

Hansen went back to the lesser routines of small-town police work: robberies, burglaries, DUIs. He missed the work with Capriano, but he felt too old to move to a big city and start over. He worked his garden, went camping for a week with each of his girls. He felt old and tired much of the time. He thought about Ellie, missed her, missed the possibility of romance and companionship he had hoped would happen with her. But he didn't try to see her. He let that go.

Sandy moved to Pittsburgh but couldn't convince Ellie to do the same. Ellie liked her apartment, liked being close to campus. What's more, she didn't really associate it with Joel, since they had spent most of their time together in the city at his place. She missed having Sandy close but saw her on campus every work day and often spent Saturday night with her in the city.

For a while they had talked about Arlen and Joel and what they knew, but that grew too tiresome and too painful. Sandy seemed to

188

focus solely on Arlen's betrayal of their marriage vows of fidelity and that annoyed Ellie, who saw the issues as so much larger. She and Joel hadn't agreed to be monogamous, and she didn't care if he had been bisexual or had slept with the second man, as Hansen had suggested. That wasn't the betrayal that she felt deep within her heart. No, it was the fact that she had been a pawn in their game. She had not been a person to them, and they had not considered her at all, except as an object to be used however they wanted.

Ellie was not naïve. You didn't get a PhD in French literature without reading the Marquis de Sade. You didn't live sixty years of a life with your eyes open to the world without knowing that people played sex games, innocent and not, without knowing that some women and some men liked being tied up and some liked being peed on. She also knew that women got raped all the time, maybe every five minutes, by soldiers and grocery delivery boys and frat brothers and even drunken husbands. But that was not what had happened to her.

She and Danny had done their share of timid sexual experimentation. They had tied each other up with silk scarves and had sex in an airplane bathroom and fondled each other in a restaurant one time. They had even swapped partners one drunken evening in Houston, but it had been more interesting to him than it had been to her and he had quickly agreed to not doing it again.

But none of this had prepared her for Joel's indifference and his disrespect. These words were too timid for what he had done—and let be done—to her but she couldn't find other words, not in speaking about it to the trauma counselor, not in writing about it in her journal. The counselor encouraged her to own her experience, to use "abused" and "tortured" and "betrayed," but even those bigger words couldn't explain the inner hand that squeezed her chest and belly and throat when she thought of Joel and now of Arlen, too. They couldn't explain the tears that came unbidden in the produce aisle or, worse, in the classroom. They couldn't explain the dreams that seemed unrelated in content but that carried a sense of dread and death.

So Ellie threw herself into school. She took on some additional responsibilities advising international students, planned a new course on African women's literature, volunteered for committees that a year ago she would have avoided at any cost. She needed work to ground her. She volunteered at the local animal shelter, joined a choir. Anything to stay busy, to stay connected to others.

Twice she dreamed of Hansen and Paris. She wondered if she should call him but she, too, let that go. They had had chances to reconnect and it hadn't happened. She couldn't chase him down, not with how little she had to offer.

50

Ellie drove out to the ranch to see Al as the evening was falling. The late September heat still wafted off the pavement, but there was a small breeze, so she turned off the air-conditioner and opened her windows. The drive out to the ranch had become familiar. The ranch wasn't home—she still couldn't quite imagine that, but it was comfortable to drive down the long entrance and come up to the big low house with its veranda and to have Al and Beemus waiting for her in the porch swing.

She put her hand on her husband's shoulder in greeting. He touched it with his own and then she sat down beside him in the rocker that he'd gotten her as a wedding gift.

"Gracie came to see me," she said.

Al reached down to pet the dog. "I was afraid she might."

"I wish you'd told me that. I wished you'd told me about her."

"I'm sorry. I should have."

"She tried to frighten me away."

Al frowned. "What? Did she threaten you? She's hot-tempered but I don't think she'd hurt you."

"Actually she implied that I should be afraid of you."

"That doesn't make any sense. I've never hurt her. I told you I don't hit women or animals." He got up and paced the porch, finally making a full circle of the house. When he came back, he was carrying two glasses of ice and lemonade. He handed her one, then sat down. "What else did she say?"

"To ask you what really happened to Annie."

He sighed. "That seems fair enough."

And so, as the dusk turned to dark and the day's heat turned to desert chill, he told her the long story. How Annie had nearly died of grief when Stevie drowned. How in the months following, she had begged him to make another child with her, another son. How he had at first refused, too mired in his own sorrow to want to touch her. Then they had tried and tried and tried, and sex between them became not love, not pleasure, but desperation. Twice Annie thought she was pregnant. Twice it turned out not to be true. Early menopause had come instead of another child.

Al had the ranch, the cattle, the crops, the hired hands. This saved him. Annie teetered on the edge for several years, then found herself in a church-run grief support group. When someone died, she was there for the spouse, the parents, the children, the friends, the neighbors. She took an apartment in town so she could be on call 24/7. They lived mostly apart for a number of years.

"Then one day, my pastor came to see me. He was retired by then. Jack was a great guy. A dad to me after mine died. We sat and talked on this porch one long Sunday afternoon, and he told me I needed to start courting my wife again, that people who loved each other could overcome their difficulties.

"So Annie and I started seeing each other again—dating, I guess you'd say. We went to dinner and the movies and walked a lot together in town. I learned who she had become over those years and I guess I let her see who I was by then, too. There wasn't any passion left and that made me sad. But bit by bit we got our affection back for each other. And that seemed good. So she moved back to the ranch and we had eight more good years together."

Al tipped the lemonade glass on end. It was empty and Ellie said, "I'll get us some water. Stay put."

She took her time, used the bathroom, brushed through her hair. She wanted to give him space for all those memories.

She brought a shawl out and a blanket with her. Al didn't want either one so she wrapped herself in both. She couldn't understand why he wasn't cold, why men so often weren't cold.

Al sat swinging and petting Beemus and for a moment Ellie wondered if he'd even seen her come back out. Finally she said, "So you and Annie had eight more good years before she died."

Al gave a deep sigh. "Not exactly," he said.

"We had eight more good years. At least they seemed good to me. One summer, disease went through the herd, but we had the money for the vet and we saved most of it. Annie was right there by me. She went on doing some kind of volunteer work in town, but she'd stopped focusing on that group of survivors. For a while she took some classes at the college. Then she started working with babies at the hospital and I hoped that would satisfy the grandbaby need that women get. I didn't know how else to help her with that. Life went on. You know how it does." Al looked over at Ellie for confirmation.

She nodded and smiled at him.

"At the end, Annie seemed really happy. We went to bed together more often, talked of doing some traveling. The last day, she spent making pies. I heard her singing in the kitchen." He looked out into the night. "The next day she was gone."

"Heart attack?"

"Heart attack? No, she was gone, just gone. Took her clothes, that was all. Left me a Dear John letter. Blue envelope on the kitchen table. The stuff she always used for condolences. Said she'd met someone, wanted a chance at a different life."

His words took Ellie by surprise. Not just the content, that Annie had run off with someone, but the sorrow in Al's telling of it. There was no bitterness, no anger, just grief, deep grief. She reached out and touched his hand but he didn't respond.

"At first, I was . . ." he said after a bit. "I don't know what I was. Shocked, stunned, baffled. Angry. I felt so foolish. How could I not have seen this coming? It wasn't me who was making her happy. It was some other guy. I tore up the place looking for clues."

He got up in agitation at the memories and went out into the yard. Ellie watched the old dog hesitate: follow or stay? She felt the same way. In the end, she stayed where she was and, after a time, Al came back to her.

The rest of the story wasn't long. Al had done what he could to find her, then hired a detective. The other man was an English teacher at the college, younger than Annie by fifteen years. They had gone to San Francisco. Al flew out and met with Annie but the meeting hadn't gone well.

"She was in love, she said." Al's voice was steady in the darkness but Ellie could hear an old bitterness. "Through with the ranch and the winters and the dust. She wanted to be a city person. Go to museums and plays."

Ellie felt a wave of sympathy for this other woman, a wave that touched on her own doubt.

Al went on. "I couldn't blame her. I couldn't offer her that. I'm a rancher, born and bred to it. She gave me her rings back, and I told her she was free. Then I came home."

Ellie waited to see if he would say more, but he just went on rubbing Beemus behind the ears and the only sound was the dog groaning in pleasure.

"Did you see her again?" she asked after a bit.

"Oh, yeah. We divorced that next year, but the teacher wouldn't marry her. Didn't believe in it. Apparently didn't believe in faithfulness either. She came back to Farmington for a while, lived in town with Gracie. We saw each other some but she didn't seem to want what I had to offer and I didn't want a reluctant wife." He stood up and stretched and this time Beemus got up with him. The old dog tottered down the steps and then around the corner. Al moved over to the stairs to wait for him.

Ellie was tempted to go to Al, to console him. It was a painful story. But there had to be more to the story, to Gracie's words. She moved over to the porch swing. "Come sit here with me, Al. Tell me the rest. I need to know why Gracie felt she had to warn me about you."

51

Oscar was sitting on Ellie's chest when she woke up. The mid-August Pennsylvania sky was heavy with white-gray humidity, the summer fog of heat and wretchedness. She glanced at the clock and saw that it was nearly eight-thirty. No wonder Oscar was all over her. He was hungry. *And what happened to the alarm that chimed promptly at seven each morning?* she wondered. She felt groggy from too long in bed.

She let Nellie in through the front door, fed both cats, then used the bathroom. If she hurried, there'd be time for tea and breakfast before she headed off for her Saturday drawing class. She made the tea, some peanut butter toast, and a dish of yogurt and banana. The edginess of being late and the residual sluggishness from the half-Valium she still took each night battled for her wits. The tea helped. So did the food. Her head began to clear.

She pulled on the old black cotton slacks and sweatshirt she used for the studio, got the fishing tackle box full of pastels out of the closet, and went out to her car. She saw that there was a sheet of paper face down on the windshield. Her heart leapt for a second. Had Hansen left her a note? But no, he'd have come to the door if he'd wanted to see her. She pulled the paper off and saw that it was a circular for an end-of-summer plant sale at the grocery store two blocks over. She put it in her car and headed off.

The drawing was something new for her. Even with months gone by now since Arlen's death, she felt the same driving need to stay busy, busy with her hands, busy with her mind. And slowly it was working. She and Sandy seldom talked about Arlen or Joel or anything that had happened. It began to seem another lifetime. She still had dreams, but they had faded in intensity, and every once in a while, she didn't think about any of it for a whole day.

She stayed two hours at the drawing studio, then left the class early. None of the sketches she'd done pleased her or engaged her. The music was too raucous, too energetic. It incited her restlessness rather than distracting her. She didn't make her apologies to the instructor as she left, just nodded at him after she'd cleaned up her workspace and gathered her things. She stopped at the grocery store on her way back. The sun had come out and the plant sale was in full swing. She added a big pot with tiny maroon mums to her cart.

Fall was coming on early, and the big trees on her street were all starting to turn. The first sprays of yellow and russet softened the old elms and she felt inspired to get her camera out when she got home. She could take the print with her the next week to class. Maybe using that subject would take her deeper into the drawing.

She went in and put the ice cream away, then went back down to the car and wrestled the pot up the stairs, stopping every two or three steps to set it down. It must have weighed thirty pounds and was awkward to grasp. She cursed herself for not buying two smaller pots. But when it was in place on her little landing, it looked so cheerful, she was glad she'd gone to the trouble.

Winded and sweaty from the effort, she stripped her clothes off in the central hallway and got into the shower. She let the water run on her head and shoulders a long time, then, still drying off, she went into the bedroom. As she rummaged for something to put on, her eye caught something bright in the mirror on the closet door. She felt her breath catch in her throat.

There, dangling from the bedposts, were four braided gold cords.

52

"This is Detective Hansen. Leave a message."

It was the sixth time Ellie had called and she hung up when she heard his voice. There was nothing to say that she hadn't already said. If he was getting his messages, then he knew what was going on and he wasn't calling her back. That seemed unlikely. Surely he would call her back. But what kind of detective didn't get his phone messages?

Ellie'd been on the road for two hours now. During the first moments of terror, when she'd believed the second man might be in her apartment, she'd felt paralyzed. It had been all she could do to pull on her clothes to make herself less vulnerable. Then she'd screwed up her courage and gone downstairs to find her landlord. Taylor was in his living room, just off the front porch. She could see the football game on TV when he came to the door.

She didn't say much, said she thought an intruder had come into her place and might still be there. Taylor took the look on her face seriously. He disappeared briefly and then he came back with a baseball bat and preceded her up the stairs. There was really no place to hide on the first floor—the rooms all opened out onto the central landing and only the bathroom and bedroom had doors on them. The bedroom had the only closet big enough to hide in and he certainly wasn't there. Ellie stayed below while Taylor went up into the third floor, but he found nothing. The rooms there had no closets and no one was lurking in the funky second bathroom where she kept the litter box.

"I didn't find any damage or any sign that someone's broken in or gone out one of the attic windows," he said as he came back down. "Is anything missing?"

"I'm not sure," said Ellie. "I was mostly afraid he was here."

"Maybe we should call the police. I can do that if you like."

"No, I'll call them from my friend Sandy's house. I mostly just want to get out of here. It feels kind of creepy here."

The younger man shrugged. "Okay, well, I'm just downstairs if you need me." And he took his bat and went out the door.

Ellie locked the door behind him. She didn't let her mind go to implications. She just got busy. She brought down two roller bags from the attic and packed as quickly as she could. Then she put the cats in their carriers, gathered up their food and litter and a spare litter box, and put it all in the car. She didn't bother to lock the door on her way out.

Sandy wasn't home and, in a way, it was a relief. She couldn't count on Sandy to be an ally at this moment. Her own grief and loss stood between them. She let herself in with the key Sandy had given her to the new condo, and she carried in the cats and the food and the litter and left a note saying that she just had to get away and would let Sandy know where she was in a day or two.

Then she got in the car and headed to Gettysburg, to Hansen. It was the only safe place she could think of.

🐾

It was almost six and getting dark when she pulled up in front of the brick building that housed the Gettysburg police. There were two police cars out in front and lights on, but no one on the street. Hansen had not called her back.

She locked the car and got out. She was stiff from the hours of sitting hunched over the wheel, watching her rearview mirror to see if she was being followed. She had stopped only once—at a rest area to get a cola and a chocolate bar from a machine. She'd needed the sugar and caffeine to stay sharp. She hadn't eaten since breakfast.

She hadn't been to the station before. The year before, the detectives had talked to her at the hotel, at the hospital, at the B&B. There had been no reason for her to come here. She pushed the glass door open and stepped up to the counter. The officer on duty was black and wore his belt low beneath a ponderous gut. "What can I do for you, ma'am?"

"I'm looking for Detective Doug Hansen. It's urgent. I've been calling his number but he must not be on duty."

"He's not. Can I help you?"

"I don't have a home number. Can you give it to me?"

"I can't do that, ma'am. We don't give out personal information on our officers."

"Perhaps you could call him for me. He'll want to know I'm here. I'm Ellie McKay. He knows me." Ellie tried to keep the desperation out of her voice, to sound calm and sane.

The officer shook his head. "Sorry, I can't do that. But I can let you speak to another detective. In fact, Detective Hansen's partner is on duty. Would you like to speak to him?"

Ellie felt like she would cry. "Okay," she said. "Okay."

"Why don't you have a seat over there?" he said, motioning to a cushioned bench that ran along the wall across from the counter. "I'll call him and ask him to come right down."

Ellie nodded, found a tissue in her purse for her nose and eyes, and sat down on the bench. Ten awful minutes crawled by, and she felt she would jump out of her skin.

Finally the door opened and Skopowlski stood in front of her, extending his hand. "Dr. McKay, what can I do for you?"

The man was only vaguely familiar and Ellie realized she could probably not have picked him out of a crowd. All of her attention had been on Hansen during that week the year before, and Skopowlski had never come to see her in Pittsburgh when Hansen did.

She stood up now and shook his hand. "I'm looking for Doug . . . Detective Hansen. I've been trying to reach him on his cell phone but he's not answering."

Skopowlski nodded. "Is this about your case? The Pittsburgh police are handling that now."

"Yes . . . no. I . . . I need to see Doug, to talk with him. It's about the case, but it's also personal. He and I . . ." Ellie didn't know what to say. She didn't want to tell the partner something he wasn't supposed to know.

"If it's about the case, perhaps I can help you." Skopowlski's expression was neutral, professional.

"No, I would rather talk with Doug." Ellie could feel the tears starting again.

"I'm sorry, Dr. McKay. Doug isn't available. He's not actually here in town. He's in Canada with his family."

"Is he coming back soon? It's important that I talk to him."

"No, he's not. As a matter of fact, he's on medical leave."

"Is he all right? What's happened?"

Skopowlski frowned. "He was shot during a mugging in Montreal. He's recuperating from surgery." Skopowlski paused. "So, I'm really the only person who can help you."

🟋

Skopowlski led Ellie to an office at the back of the room where she told him about finding the gold cords in her bedroom, about packing up and getting out of there. She felt him soften a little toward her. She suspected he disapproved of her relationship with Doug, whatever he knew of it, but he was nothing but courteous when he heard what had happened.

Skopowlski called Capriano and he interviewed Ellie as well on speaker phone. But she had nothing more to say other than what she had told Skopowlski. She hadn't seen anyone lurking about, hadn't felt she was being watched or followed. No one had a key to her apartment except the landlord and Sandy Gerstead.

"What about the Gerstead boy, the one who house-sat for you?" asked Capriano.

"I had the locks changed after Arlen died. Sandy and I both did. It just seemed the safest thing to do."

"Is there a hide-a-key on the property?"

"Not for my door. The spare I have is in my desk at school."

"Was there a window open?" Skopowlski broke in.

"No," said Ellie. "It was cold that morning and everything was closed and locked. And it would take a ladder to get to the second story anyway."

"I'm afraid that's not much of a deterrent," said Skopowlski. Somehow his comment made her feel stupid.

"Dr. McKay, we'll need your permission to search your apartment. I'd like to see if he left us, or rather you, any other calling cards. Are you headed back to Greensburg tonight?"

Ellie paused. She looked at Skopowlski, whose expression was noncommittal.

"Dr. McKay, are you there?" Capriano spoke again.

"Yes, no, I'm not sure when I'll be back. I can't . . . I just can't be there now."

Capriano sighed. "Okay. Can you call your landlord and give him a heads-up that we'll be coming out tonight?"

Ellie exhaled in relief. She had been afraid that he would insist. "Yes, I can do that."

"And can you stay in Gettysburg tonight? Can I reach you by phone there?"

Ellie agreed to that too and gave him her cell number.

As soon as Capriano was off the line, Skopowlski stood up from the table and Ellie felt dismissed.

"I took your number down and I'll be in touch from this end, if anything happens." Skopowlski moved out into the squad room, leading the way.

"Okay," said Ellie. "Tell me, do you know where Doug is? I'd like to send flowers."

The detective moved over to his desk and checked a note pad and wrote something down. "This is the number I have for him."

Ellie thanked him and then there seemed nothing more to say and she left. Skopowlski did not walk her out.

She took one of the main streets heading north out of town and drove until she came to a twenty-four-hour restaurant. She ordered soup and a grilled cheese sandwich, but when it came, she found she had little appetite for it and she ate a few bites of soup and half the sandwich and let the rest grow cold. As she paid her bill, she asked if there were a motel nearby.

"Days Inn up a few blocks," said the cashier, so she drove up the road and checked in for the night. She busied herself with unpacking her toothbrush and taking a long hot shower and getting into her pajamas but then there was nothing more to do. She turned on the TV for company, but she found the noise too irritating, so she turned it off and sat in silence on the bed.

She was deeply anxious despite the Valium she had taken after her shower. The terror she had felt on seeing the cords was gone, and for some reason, she did not believe she had been followed, either to Sandy's to drop off the cats or out of town. There was no sense of that. But she did not understand what this man wanted with her. He'd had a chance to kill her in Gettysburg and he hadn't done it. Well, maybe Joel had stopped him. Maybe Joel had still been in charge. Why now? Why had he come now? And what did he want?

She felt terribly, achingly alone. Even though her romance with Hansen had not survived Paris, she had counted on him being there. He was no longer her lover, but he was surely her friend and he was a good detective. She had felt safe with him still concerned about the case, safe in a way she didn't with Capriano or Skopowlski. And now he was in trouble.

She went out to the car and got the road atlas she always carried in the back seat. Montreal wasn't too far to drive. It would give her something to do, somewhere to go. And who knows? Maybe she and Doug could reconnect.

The phone rang a long time with no answering machine pick-up. She redialed and this time a voice heavy with Québécois inflexion answered. Ellie spoke in French, asking for Hansen.

"I'm sorry," the woman said, still in English, "Monsieur Hansen cannot use the telephone."

"I know that," said Ellie, trying her French again. "I want to see how he is doing."

"Are you a relative?"

"Yes," she said without hesitation. "I'm his sister."

"Then I'll let you speak to his wife." And the woman put the phone down.

"This is Claire Hansen," a deep, throaty, and equally accented voice came on the line. "Who is this? My husband doesn't have a sister. "

"I'm sorry. I just wanted to get some information. My name is Ellen McKay. Dr. Ellen McKay. I'm a friend of Doug's from Pennsylvania. I'm calling to find out how he is."

There was a long pause. Then the woman sighed. "Doug seems to be doing okay. The operation went well but his recovery may be slow."

Ellie wasn't sure what to say next. "His partner told me he was mugged. Did they catch the man?"

"Well, he wasn't mugged. He was trying to help a couple that was being robbed on the street and one of the robbers shot him. I don't know any more than that." She pronounced the word *row-bear*, like the French Robert.

"Merci, Madame. Vous êtes très gentille."

The woman on the line paused again. Ellie wondered if she had been surprised by her use of French and got ready to explain about her career and her PhD, but the woman spoke again to her in English.

"Are you Doug's lover? Are you the woman from Paris?"

Ellie was taken aback by the other woman's directness. "No. I mean yes, he came to Paris to see me last year, but no, we are just friends. Last year I was . . . hurt. . . Doug was the detective on my case and we got to be friends."

"I know the story," Claire Hansen said. She sounded weary, though her tone was cool, neutral. "I know who you are."

Ellie decided to shift gears. "I'm so sorry about Doug. I'd like to stay in touch. Can I call you again to see how he's doing?"

The Canadian sighed and then said, "I'll take your number and give it to him when he is better."

"He has my number," said Ellie.

"Then I'm sure he will call you if it's important to him," the woman said and the line went dead.

Again, Ellie felt dismissed. She couldn't quite figure out why she was in the wrong in all this. She got up and got ready for bed. It was just past eight, but she couldn't imagine being awake any longer and feeling this way.

♋

The phone woke her out of a deep dream of being pulled further and further down into a suffocating blackness. She felt relieved to see the streak of neon shining in the split of the curtain. The phone went to voicemail before she could reach it, but it rang again right away.

It was Capriano. He apologized for waking her though she saw that it wasn't even nine-thirty. She struggled to wake up and listen to him.

"We found nothing more in your apartment. No other sign that he'd been there. We dusted for prints but don't have results yet. I assume we'll find yours, the Gersteads, Doug Hansen's." He paused.

"And Roger Gerstead's," Ellie said. "You'll find his, too."

"Anybody else?"

"Well, Roger could have had someone over. He stayed there for months."

"Do you know him well?"

"Not really. I'd met him a half-dozen times at Arlen's and Sandy's. Mostly at the holidays or Arlen's birthday. He seemed like a nice kid and he needed a place to stay and I needed a house-sitter. It was actually Sandy's idea. It seemed like a nice coincidence and he took good care of my cats and my place so I had no complaints." She hesitated a moment. "You don't suspect him?"

"No . . . no," said Capriano. "But we're looking for any connection we can find. You never met any of his friends? No one ever came looking for him after you came back?"

"No . . . well, wait. A couple of weeks after I got home, some young people showed up on a Saturday night. Must have been around eight-thirty. Two girls and a guy. They were already pretty well sloshed and they were looking for Roger. The two young women were very pretty, and all dressed up—makeup, expensive clothes—like fashion models. But the guy didn't look like he belonged with them at all.

His hair was long, unwashed. Jeans, jean jacket, all that needed washing, too. He had a mustache, a big silver belt buckle. Kind of biker or hippy-looking. He looked vaguely familiar, but I couldn't place him. I wondered later if he'd been a student at the college or someone I knew from Paris."

"You get any names?"

"No, even if they'd said them, it's been months. I wouldn't remember. I just remember what an odd combination they were."

"Did they come into your place?"

It was Ellie's turn to pause. "Yes," she said finally. "The guy asked to use the bathroom. I didn't intend to let them in but he pushed his way in and went straight to the bathroom. We could hear him peeing from the landing. Then he came right out, thanked me, and they left. Oh God, was that him?"

"I don't know," said Capriano. "Could have been nobody."

Neither of them said anything for a few minutes. Then Capriano said, "I don't know how safe you are in your place right now. You might want to stay somewhere else. With a friend."

"Do you think I'll be safe with Sandy Gerstead?"

He waited, then said, "I can't tell you that. We just don't know enough."

"Okay then," said Ellie.

"I'm sorry," said Capriano.

"Me too," said Ellie. She sat there a moment with the phone in her hand. Then she put it in her purse, packed her stuff back up into the car, and headed out into the night.

53

Ellie drove south, out of Pennsylvania and into Maryland. She drove until a little past midnight. By then, the adrenaline of the two conversations had worn off and the fatigue had set in, and she knew she couldn't drive all night. In addition, there'd been no one else on the road except truckers for a half-hour so she felt safely alone. She pulled off at a Holiday Inn and took an upstairs room. She dumped her suitcase and headed to the bar before it closed. The place was deserted except for two couples in a corner having a quiet conversation. She sat at the bar and drank a double rye on the rocks pretty quickly and went back to her room. That and the Valium she took helped her sleep all night.

When she woke at eight, she was groggy. A shower helped, breakfast in the café, too. Before she checked out of her room, she called Sandy. The number rang and rang and then rang through to voicemail. In a way, Ellie was relieved to just leave a message.

"Hi Sandy. I'm sorry to just dump the cats on you like this but I think you're safer there without me. I hope so anyway. I'm heading south. Don't know where or how long I'll be gone. I'll send you money for their care. Or maybe Roger could house-sit for me again. If you could talk to the dean and explain, I'd really appreciate it. Somehow I think my life in Pittsburgh is over. If I get settled some place, I'll send for the cats."

She paused a moment. "I'm sorry I can't be there for you. I just need to take care of myself. I'm too scared to stay there. Take care of yourself. I'll miss you."

On her way to the car, she threw her cell phone into a dumpster. She'd pick up a pay-as-you-go somewhere down the road.

The fact that she had deserted Sandy nagged at her. She had lots of hours in the car to mull that over. Should she have told Sandy about the gold cords? About the killer—for that's surely who it must have been—finding her house? Was the killer after her or after them both? Would Sandy be safer knowing that or safer not knowing? Maybe Capriano had already told her, already searched Sandy's house for more evidence. Maybe Sandy wasn't answering because she, too, had left.

She thought of Hansen and sent him a prayer. If she had come back to the States with him in December, if she had moved to Gettysburg with him, he might not have been in Montreal. And the killer might not have come after her. But then he might have come after Sandy. It was all too complicated.

She forced her mind back to the road, back to the Leonard Cohen CD that was playing, back to the present.

She drove across West Virginia into Kentucky, then across the corner of Tennessee and Arkansas into Texas. She drove for four days, stopping at rest stops every few hours, stopping at chain restaurants for soup and sandwiches, stopping in motels with lounges where she could get a drink or two and the bartender wouldn't let anyone hit on her. She'd never realized there were so many lonely middle-aged men out looking. Was it sex? Love? Comfort of some kind they wanted? A couple of times she was tempted. The men were clean, well-dressed, eager but not too pushy. Not too young and not too old. It was something to think about, not sleeping alone, someone to protect her if the killer came in the night. But she couldn't bring herself to do it. What if . . . just what if the one she chose was the killer? And then that began to have its appeal, too. If she said yes and it was the killer, she wouldn't have to be afraid anymore.

That kind of thinking was madness and she knew it. But she felt crazy some of the time. There were many moments in the last year when she'd felt unhinged, that the solid ground that had been beneath her feet all these decades had been swept away.

The young rape counselor she'd seen right after Gettysburg hadn't been much help, but one thing she'd said had stayed with Ellie: "You may find it hard to trust the decisions you make for a while. This happens to women who are raped by men they thought were safe."

This had resonated with her. She had trusted Joel. Assumed he was a regular guy, a professional, normal. And he had had a dark secret, a terrible secret. Not only had he not cared what happened to her, but he had also paid to have it done. She couldn't get over that.

That sense of distrust had stood between her and Hansen when he came to Paris. Of course, he wasn't the rapist. But he had secrets. Of course he did. He was too old not to. And she didn't want those secrets to hurt her.

On the fifth afternoon of driving, she got to Dallas. Since Tennessee, she'd acknowledged that she had a destination, that she was going to Danny. There were other old friends in the address book: in Virginia, in South Carolina, in Florida. Former colleagues and classmates. But they were all women, all more innocent bystanders like Sandy, whom she had unwittingly involved in this. Well, no, that wasn't right. Arlen was at the center of this. Arlen, who had introduced her to Joel. Arlen, who had gotten himself killed and through Joel put both her and Sandy in danger.

She had known Arlen and Sandy for eight years. She and Sandy had been close almost that whole time. She would have trusted Arlen with her life. And he had turned out to be twisted as well. What was it about these men and their ways of using and abusing women? How could a woman know she was safe? Whom could she trust?

Could she trust Danny? She thought so. He was no saint, but he was who he said he was. He was an alcoholic with no intention of quitting, a man who loved women—all women. In the ten years they'd been together, he'd been unfaithful to Ellie a dozen times, but honest and open about it every single time. He hated deception. So she knew that she could trust him to tell the truth. If he couldn't be there for her, he would say so.

♆

Danny picked up on the third ring, the whiskey and smoke still there in his voice. He didn't seem surprised to hear from her though all those years had gone by.

"I'm coming through Houston, Danny," Ellie said after they'd exchanged "how are you" and "it's a long story." "In fact, I'm in Dallas. Wondering if you might have room for me for a few days."

While the hesitation was there, it lasted only a few seconds. "I'll have to clear the decks," he said, "but I'm happy to do that. Are you okay?"

"Like I said, it's a long story."

"Okay, then," he said. "Bring plenty of bourbon. And hey, Ellie? I'm sorry about Paris."

♆

As she turned off Westheimer and wound her way up to Stratford Avenue, there were signs of change but not much. The Baby Giant had become a 7-Eleven. The laundromat was a nail salon. A few of the old beauties along the short four blocks had been fixed up: new paint, new roofs, redone foundations. At the same time, the wretched bungalows that sat between them were more rundown than ever. She pulled up in front of 203, the little house back from the street where she and Danny had been happy and then unhappy and then miserable for way too long before she'd left and moved north.

It felt odd to stand at that familiar door and hear the same doorbell. It felt even odder to see the Danny who opened the door. A Danny whose dark curls had gone gray, whose mustache had descended into a soul patch and goatee, equally gray. He'd grown stouter through the middle though it looked like he still worked out. There was something to be said for vanity.

Of course he was taking her in too: The pale skin, the extra pounds, maybe thirty by this point. She'd given up the makeup when she left him. She'd given up the chic clothes and the constant dieting to stay thin enough to keep him. The extra pounds had crept on the last few years and especially since Paris. Her hair was still dark by design, but her famous brows were now salt and pepper, and she knew the stress of the last twelve months showed in her skin. *So what?* she thought. *I'm not here to seduce him. I'm here because I don't know where else to go to be safe.*

The hug they shared was both genuine and awkward and, to recover, she thrust the brown paper peace offering at him. He grinned then and it was the old Danny, and she felt better as she followed him inside.

54

Ellie was flooded with memories as she stepped into the house. Their house. Danny wasn't much into the look of his environment. He just wanted it comfortable, comfortable and familiar. And familiar it was. She'd left him most of the furniture and it was all arranged as before. The monstrous purple sofa across from the little fireplace, the leather recliner he'd found in a thrift store, the crowing rooster lamps his mother had left him, claiming they were worth a fortune.

On every table top there was an ashtray. Although the house smelled of smoke, they were all clean, it was one thing he was fastidious about. But she had forgotten the smoking or chosen not to think about it. She wasn't sure she could stay here even if he asked her.

He'd moved on into the kitchen and she could hear him talking to her. She followed him then and watched him pull down the Waterford crystal highball glasses he was so proud of and fill them with ice and then bourbon over it. He chatted about the weather and the writing job he was working on for a foundation in Seattle, how work had slowed but that he was doing okay. She realized he might well be as nervous as she was after all these years.

They took the drinks into the living room. It was dim in the late afternoon, shaded as it was by old oak trees and the two larger houses on either side. A big orange tom wandered in, yawning and stretching.

"That's Lawrence," Danny said. "He found me about four years ago."

"He's handsome," said Ellie. "I meant to write and tell you how sorry I was to hear about Chester. I appreciated your letting me know."

Danny smiled sadly. "He was a great cat."

"He was." Ellie took a deep sip of the bourbon. She began to relax. "How have you been, Danny?"

"Good enough. Pretty much the same as always." He paused. "Is this a social visit, El? Things sounded more serious than that when you called."

She sighed. How much to tell? And how to tell it? "No, it's not. I mean no, it's not a social visit. And yes, things are serious. I don't quite know how to explain it all."

"Are you in trouble?"

"Yes. I mean no. I'm not on the lam if that's what you're thinking. I guess you still don't read the papers much."

He shook his head.

"Last fall, the man I was dating paid another man to rape and hurt me while he watched. Then he killed himself." She looked down at her hands, then over at Danny. His eyes were huge and the disbelief that first appeared turned to a deep scowl.

"Oh, Ellie. My God, that's horrendous! Are you all right?"

"Physically, yes. I have scars . . . burns and other scars . . . but that part has healed up." She willed him to come and sit by her on the sofa, to hold her, but he sat in the recliner, anger crossing his face, clenching and unclenching the fist that didn't hold the drink.

"Did they catch the guy?"

"No," she said and the tightness in her throat that she'd been experiencing these last days welled up again. After a moment, she told him as much of the story as she could bear. How she met Joel, Arlen's connection, his death, and finally the gold cords in her apartment in Greensburg and her decision to leave town. She did not mention Hansen. She did not mention the police at all.

Danny asked questions. At first, it seemed that he wanted to know about her, but then it began to feel more like an interview. She saw that he had stepped over into writer mode, his old newspaper training coming out. *Of course*, she thought, *he's seeing this as a novel*. Suddenly she didn't feel like saying much more.

"Do you think he might have followed you here?" Danny asked as he stood up. He came over and got her glass and took it to the kitchen and refilled it. "Are you in danger right now?"

She felt put off by his question. Did he need the drama for himself? "I don't know," she said finally. "I wasn't aware of seeing the same car on the road anywhere."

"That's good," he said. And she felt a little easier.

"How can I help you, Ellie? What can I do?"

"I don't know, Danny. I couldn't stay there. I don't know where to go or what to do. Maybe I could stay here a few days to sort things out." She looked at him for the first time in a few minutes.

He nodded. "Let me make a call."

"You've got somebody?"

He nodded again. "Yeah, Melissa. She has her own place, but we're together most of the time. I'll talk to her."

"I can stay somewhere else. I can just move on. I don't want to be a complication for you."

"That's okay, Ellie. We'll sort it out." And he went out to the porch to make his call.

Ellie used the bathroom. It was familiar, too, though there was a new shower and better lighting. She glanced into the second bedroom, which had been their guest room and was now clearly Danny's office. A card table held a lamp and a laptop, and there were a couple of filing cabinets and stacks of paper everywhere. In the bigger bedroom, although not bigger by much, she saw that Danny still had the water bed. The platform frame they'd had built by a craftsman in Dallas filled up the whole room as before.

The bourbon was flowing in her veins by now. They'd each had three strong ones and she hadn't eaten since breakfast. But she wasn't drunk, just relaxed and sleepy. She kicked off her shoes and lay down, pulling the edge of the comforter around her in the air-conditioned room. She was out in less than a minute.

🌑

She woke to sounds of Danny in the kitchen, the smell of meat and garlic heavy in the air. Although she wasn't hungry, it was a great relief not to be alone.

They ate in the living room, the silence mostly comfortable between them. When she'd asked him about Melissa, he'd just said "all worked out" and that had been that. Later they talked of old friends in the city and in Austin, where they'd been fond of the music scene, Danny catching her up on their doings. Some of it she already knew, but she let him believe it was all news to her. He smoked a joint, but she shook her head when he handed it to her, deciding bourbon was enough. They listened to music. It was a lot like old times, except that everything had changed.

When they went to bed sometime in the wee hours, she was loose enough with whiskey to let him touch her and have sex with her. He was so familiar to her, the way he smelled, the way his hands felt, that she was sure it would be all right. And it was, or as close to all right as she thought she could get right then.

They stayed together the next three days. The gallons of bourbon she had brought lasted that long. Each day Danny was up by six and he worked all morning and Ellie read or slept. About two, the work-day would be over. Danny would walk to the 7-Eleven for beer and she would fix sandwiches and they would start drinking and playing cards or board games. They watched old movies on Netflix and some of the stand-up comics he found funny. It did Ellie good to laugh and forget for a while.

They went to bed late, past midnight, and each night Danny made love to her in the old way. She felt very little. There was no desire, no yearning except to be held and feel safe, and she was willing to let him in so she could have that. Her dreams were few and confused. Joel's face flitted by, Sandy's as well, but there was no story, no situation in them for her to fear.

On Friday at lunch, Danny announced that Melissa was coming back that night for the weekend. "I can't put her off any longer, Ellie," he said. "And I don't want to lose her."

"Of course," she said. "I can leave this afternoon." But her throat closed up in fear and her mind raced.

"Have you decided where you'll go next?"

The casualness of his question irritated her. She had put off thinking about the future all week. She had rested in the moment and in the safety of being there with him. When would she have solved all the complications? She took a deep breath. It was her problem, not Danny's. And that was what was so terrifying. It was all her problem. Hansen hadn't fixed it. Capriano hadn't fixed it. Danny couldn't fix it.

"New Mexico," she said finally. She'd always wanted to visit Santa Fe and Taos.

"Got friends there?" Danny said. "One of your grad school buddies?"

"Yes," she lied. "A couple I knew in France. They live in Albuquerque."

"Good," he said. "I wouldn't want you to be alone."

Ellie packed up and left within the hour. She didn't want to get caught in the nightmare of the late Friday afternoon exodus from the inner city. That saved her an emotional parting from Danny. A quick kiss and her bags in the car and she could let the tears flow on her own as she hit the beltway and angled southwest. San Antonio seemed a good destination.

55

It was dinnertime when Ellie got to San Antonio, but she wasn't much interested in food. She checked in to the Holiday Inn near the airport, as it was just off the freeway. She was momentarily tempted to stay down at the fancier hotel near the River Walk, but she didn't have the energy to find it. She wasn't about to play tourist anyway.

She took a shower and lay on the bed for a while, flipping channels on the TV. She had hoped for the oblivion of sleep, but she was too restless, so she got dressed and went down to the lounge. It was just after seven.

⚘

The hallway door woke her as it closed. The bedside clock glowed 2:52. Enough light seeped in from the edges of the heavy curtains to see the covers in disarray, her clothes in a heap on the floor. Her mouth was dry and her lips sore. Bourbon wafted up at her from the glass on the table.

She closed her eyes and tried to find the evening. Zeke? Zach? A short man with ruddy cheeks and styled hair. A good suit, even a vest—an unusual sight in an airport hotel bar. He sold heavy equipment to the Saudis, he'd said. He came to her table late, after spending a couple of hours chatting up a blonde in a well-filled sweater set. Ellie didn't care that she wasn't first choice. Anything seemed better than being alone.

She got up now and used the bathroom, scrubbed him off her face with a cold washcloth and soap, brushed him out of her mouth. There was still plenty of ice in the bucket and the man had left the bottle. She was grateful for small favors. She poured a stiff drink and then stood at the tall windows with the heavy curtains closed behind her. She felt safe, invisible.

There were many lights—the airport, the freeway—traffic even now deep in the night. She tried to watch the moving lights, to clear her mind of all thoughts, but Joel and Arlen hung like floaters in the eye of her mind, dark, shapeless specters whose decisions had stolen her life from her. She wasn't afraid. There was enough liquor in her to keep all that at bay. What she felt was adrift, the boat rudderless, the ocean vast. This was something no Zeke or Zach could touch, much as she wanted him to. She stood there a long time, enough to refill the glass twice. Then she slept without dreaming until noon.

She stayed in San Antonio for three days. She drank Bloody Marys with lunch and slept in the afternoons. She read mystery novels that she had bought in the gift shop. She watched movies on pay-per-view. Each night a Zeke or a Zach would put her to bed.

On the fourth morning, she checked out. She made reservations for herself at Holiday Inns in Del Rio, Alpine, El Paso, Truth or Consequences, Albuquerque. The days blurred into one another. She drove to the towns in the afternoons, took a shower, found a bar. Some nights there was a man, a man her age or a little younger, a man who would buy her lots of drinks and then take her to bed. Some nights she drank alone. She had stopped worrying about the killer, stopped worrying about how much she drank. She had given all of that over to fate.

※

In Santa Fe, she found a branch of her bank, paid her credit card bills, closed her liquid accounts, and put the money in traveler's checks. She didn't want to be tied to Pennsylvania anymore. There was nothing there for her.

Slowly, strangely, something in Ellie began to come alive again. The town was friendly, slow-paced, restful. The skies were blue, the air crisp in the mornings, scented in the heat of the afternoon. *Languid* was the word that came to her. She treated herself to a massage at a spa, thinking that maybe she should soak some of the alcohol out of her system. The masseuse said nothing about the welted scars on her back and the burn marks on her thighs, just treated her kindly and gently. Ellie went back twice more to feel the warmth of those hands.

One morning she signed up for a walking tour of Santa Fe art and architecture. It was a guided tour and there were mostly gray-haired couples. Some were happy, maybe newlyweds, and she felt a pang of envy. Would she ever be half of a couple again? Her last desire for that had led her to Joel. Despair wrapped its slobbery fingers around her heart and a wrenching dizziness made her sit down on a street bench.

"Hello, are you all right?"

The concern belonged to a woman in her late thirties, a Dutch bob of shiny brown hair framing a pretty face. A little girl of four or five, clearly her daughter, clutched one of the loops on the mother's cargo pants. The little girl wore a tie-dye tutu and hot pink tights.

"Yes, thank you," said Ellie. "Just an unpleasant thought." She saw that the group tour had disappeared into the art museum.

"Can I get you some water? Do you need anything?" The young woman sat down on the bench next to her and the little girl climbed into her mother's lap.

"No, thanks. I've got water." And as if she needed to prove it, Ellie took out a green bottle from her bag and took a long swallow.

The woman sat back as if she had all the time in the world and the little girl snuggled in. "If you don't mind," she said, "we'll just rest here a moment with you. Lu always likes a bit of a rest when we've been gallivanting around town, don't you, honey?"

The child nodded and put her thumb in her mouth, then pulled it out as if she remembered she was too big for that now.

After a long moment, the woman spoke again. "I'm Janet and this is Lu, Lulubelle, Lucy, Lucinda, and Lucky Lulu."

The girl giggled in delight.

"We live here in Santa Fe. Are you visiting?"

"Yes," said Ellie. "I'm traveling for a while and just came from Texas where I saw an old friend."

"I've never been to Texas," said Janet. "But you don't sound like you're from there."

"No, I'm from the Northwest but I was living most recently in Pittsburgh. I was a teacher there."

"I thought about being a teacher," Janet said, "but I had some other jobs . Then, we had Lu and now I work part time. I'm really a writer." She stroked the little girl's hair and the child closed her eyes. "Are you on sabbatical?"

"Sort of. Just taking some time to sort things out."

"Santa Fe is a good place for that. Lots of people come here wanting a change. We did—my husband and I and Lu and our dog." She smiled and it was a very happy smile. It made Ellie feel happy too. She realized she hadn't seen or felt anyone's happiness in a long time.

The tour group came out in a straggly bunch. Ellie watched the leader try to gather them together.

"Are you with the tour?" asked Janet. "I've thought about doing that someday but it doesn't look like it would be much fun for Lu."

"Probably not," said Ellie. "It's pretty serious. Lots of facts." She looked at her watch and saw that it was close to one. She wondered if she should invite her Good Samaritan to lunch, but Janet looked at her watch too and said it was time to go. She handed the sleeping child to Ellie, stood up, and then took her daughter as if she weighed nothing at all. She gave Ellie another happy smile.

"Enjoy your stay. I hope you find what you are looking for." And she moved off down the street, her arms full of love.

Ellie sat a while longer still. She let the tour go on without her. She breathed deeply, more relaxed than she'd been in a long time.

She walked back toward the B&B. She found a small café and had a bowl of tortilla soup and read the local paper. When the café closed up at two-thirty, she moved on, looking in gallery windows. The stylized browns and golds of the landscapes were not nearly as interesting to her as the real thing she had been driving through. Maybe these were all intended for buyers in the north, expensive souvenirs of a different topography. In one window, a beautiful tuxedo cat that looked like Nellie was cleaning itself between two paintings. These were different kinds of landscapes, green and lush. The paintings were signed in a small, neat hand: Jake Logan. She didn't know the name but she liked his work.

The glow of good feeling didn't last all day. By evening she was restless, haunted again, and she went down to the bar on the corner. But she didn't respond when men looked her way and she came back early.

The next day she went back to the museum on the off-chance that she would run into Janet and Lu, but they didn't come and she realized how foolish that thought had been. She spent another couple of hours wandering the galleries and shops but what she wanted wasn't for sale in any of them. The anxious, itchy feeling was back in full force by mid-afternoon and she checked out and headed northwest to Farmington.

56

It took Hansen some weeks to get back to Pennsylvania. The surgery, the deep fatigue that followed, took a toll. Being with Claire had also added to the strain. Even though he had been grateful for a place to recuperate, all the reasons they weren't together had come back in a flood. Before the shooting, he'd already figured out that their daughters had connived to get the parents together in Montreal in hopes of reconciliation. It hadn't worked and he had spent the weeks in her house feeling very much the unwelcome guest. And Claire had screened his calls and parceled out information so that he didn't find out Ellie was on the road until nearly a month after she had left Greensburg.

Driving home through Toronto and down in Pennsylvania, he stopped at Ellie's apartment. It was mid-afternoon and no one responded to his knock. He tried the apartment below. The landlord wasn't there but his wife was. She said that Ellie had been spooked by something—she didn't know what—and gone away. The place had been empty for weeks. A woman named Sandy Gerstead had come and given them a check for four months' rent. They looked in once in a while to be sure the place was okay, but there'd been no word from Ellie.

Was there mail piling up? he'd asked.

No, the woman said.

He found Sandy Gerstead at the college library. She smiled at him when he knocked on her office doorpost. It was a sad smile.

Hansen saw that she had aged, the skin on her jaw and neck loose, deep lines around her mouth, her hair gray where before it had been streaked with blonde. She'd gone into the neglect that happened with grief and trauma. He'd seen that all too often. He wondered if that had happened to Ellie.

After an exchange of greetings that meant nothing to either of them, he asked if she had heard from Ellie.

"Not a word in six weeks." She sighed. "She emailed me twice after she had left town. Once to tell me that you had been shot and that she felt she had nowhere to go."

Hansen nodded though he felt sick inside. "And the second email?"

"A few days later. Another brief message. She was getting as far away as she could."

"Did you keep the emails? Can I read them?"

She shook her head. "No, sorry, I didn't see any point." After a moment she said, "I don't blame her, you know. For the silence. I think she might blame me."

"For what?" he said, but he already knew.

"For Joel," she said. "I introduced them. Or Arlen did. How could she not blame me?"

Hansen kept his opinion to himself.

Sandy went on. "I assume you haven't found the guy."

"No, we're still looking," he paused. "Are you safe here?"

"I guess. A colleague from the library has moved into my place. I feel better with him there."

"That's good." He paused again. "I'm going to find her, Sandy."

"I hope you do. Tell her I miss her."

The campus was deserted. It was late afternoon on a Thursday. Unfamiliar with the layout, Hansen had parked a ways down the hill so he walked back to his car, the heat dripping off his face and the humidity heavy as fog around him.

He sat in his car and let the air conditioner run. He felt unsure of his next move. He should go back to Gettysburg. He was due to start work on Monday and the department needed him. The weeks of his medical leave had left them short-handed, and he knew the chief was getting pressure to retire him and replace him. He could stop that from happening by getting on the turnpike and heading east. But he hated unsolved cases. They made him feel like a failure. He also hated unresolved relationships. He wanted things clean and square between him and those he cared about. Ellie represented both to him, and that made him very unhappy.

He knew what he had to do. He started the car and got on the turnpike.

57

Ellie woke early. The light was soft, day just coming on, and the pale gold walls glowed with the dawn. The air through the open windows was still desert-cool. She was lying on her side, and for a moment she watched the breeze dance the curtains to and fro. Faint sounds of a guitar wafted in as well—one of the rancheros perhaps.

She could feel the sheets against her skin all the length of her body, and for an instant, panic rose up within her. Then she remembered the night and Al's gentleness and her breathing slowed again. She turned over and reached out to touch him but he was gone. She knew he was always up before it was light, a habit he said he didn't think he could change. It was all right. She was glad to be alone, to have time to think and feel her way into all that happened between them.

They had sat talking late into the night. Beemus had settled in between them, his head resting on Al's thigh.

At first Al said there wasn't much left to the story, but with Ellie's coaxing, he told her the rest. How he and Annie had talked of getting back together, but she wouldn't move to the ranch and he wouldn't move to town.

"I can't believe she even thought I'd move. She knew me better than that." He scratched the dog's ears. "That went on for two years. I began to grow weary of the whole thing. And as I said, I didn't want a reluctant wife. I wanted a partner, somebody to love and to love me."

At the same time, he heard rumors that Annie was seeing other men in town—their insurance guy, their dentist. He didn't know if this was true. Annie denied it, but the men wouldn't look him in the eye when they ran into each other.

"In a way, it wasn't any of my business. We were divorced. She was free to do what she wanted. But Farmington is a small town. Everybody knows your business, and I didn't like knowing people were talking about her, about us and our personal lives." He looked out into the night, then back at Ellie, and he smiled sadly.

"Then Annie got cancer. At first, it didn't seem too bad, her chances looked good. But when they did the surgery to take her breasts, they found it had spread." He sighed. "She refused chemo. Somewhere in there, during her illness, she found religion. There was a crackpot preacher in a little church in a storefront near the barrio. He was saving people from hell. And she fell for it all. She said this was God's punishment for her breaking her marriage vows, for being an adulteress. Can you imagine? In this day and age?"

Ellie reached out and took his hand in both of hers. She wasn't sure what to say.

"Gracie and I fought about all this. She felt it was up to me to convince Annie to take the chemo, to stay alive. Wanted me to marry Annie again. She felt I was abandoning her sister. But there didn't seem anything I could do. I talked to Annie, several times. Did one of those intervention things with Gracie and some of her friends, but she wouldn't listen. She moved in with Gracie as it got bad. I went most days to see her, but after a while, I just stayed outside and Gracie would come out and give me the news."

He got up then and moved to the edge of the porch. He stood looking out, but his body was turned toward Ellie, including her somehow. "It took another month. She didn't want me there. I would have been there. I would have done that for her. But Gracie asked me to respect Annie's wishes and I agreed. Afterward, I realized I should have insisted. We were together a lot of years, Annie and me. We shared a whole life. I should have been there at the end."

"It's hard either way," said Ellie. She felt her heart soften in her chest toward this man.

Al looked over at her and nodded. "We scattered her ashes here, on the land, Gracie and me. I refused to let that preacher anywhere near her. Over the next year, Gracie and I buried the hatchet. And then we started spending time together. I was lonely. I think she was too. But it wasn't serious for me. One Larroquette sister was enough. But I think Gracie had plans. And now I've spoiled those for her. I think she's pretty angry with me. Not much I can do about that."

He came back over and sat down. He put his arms around Ellie and pulled her close. "That's it. That's the whole sordid story. Now you know all my secrets."

She leaned into her husband then and relaxed. Another wave of sympathy, of compassion washed over her. She felt a tenderness for him that hadn't been there since he'd told her about the boy. Here was a man who had suffered, had doubted himself, had struggled. A man who was willing to share his past. Could she do that, too?

Al moved back a little and looked into her eyes. She wished she were younger, not so she would look better, but so that she could see him more clearly. But she smiled and he kissed her and she kissed him back. And they got up and went into the bedroom, Beemus tottering behind.

The tenderness stayed with them into the night. It was there as Al lit the candles, as he undressed his wife and she undressed him, as they lay on the bed together. The kisses were gentle, the touching from each of them soft and encouraging. He let her lead the way, let her take her time, and she was grateful. The fear came once, then again, the ghosts murmuring at the edges of the room, but she turned away from them all and back to Al.

And when they had released each other and Al had pulled the green velour blanket up over them to ward off the desert chill, she told him of Joel and of Gettysburg and of the gold cords and of running away. But she kept Hansen to herself.

58

"Doug Hansen, back from the dead!" From across the tavern, Capriano looked wider than the last time Hansen had seen him. It wasn't a criticism. In fact, he was a little jealous. The other man at least wasn't wasting away the way he was. Two surgeries and recuperation had cost him much of his muscle tone. He was just now starting to get his appetite and his strength back.

Capriano grinned and shook his hand before settling into the booth. "Didn't know if you were back on the job yet or not. Heard it was pretty bad."

Hansen shrugged but said nothing. He was tired of the details, tired of conversations about a hole in his lungs and spleen repair. He hadn't even known he had a spleen before he got shot. "I'm okay now," he said, but only because Capriano was waiting for a reply. "I'll be back on active duty next week."

"Well, I'm glad you called. Saved me the trouble. There's been a development." He set several files on the table. "A Texas case from some weeks back has cross-referenced with ours. A rape-suicide."

"Enough like ours to come to your attention."

"More than enough. It just took a while for their test results to come in and then come through the system. A couple, man in his late fifties, woman in her forties. She was tortured and raped, man dead of pentobarbital. She survived but barely. She was strangled repeatedly and has brain damage from lack of oxygen. She hasn't been able to tell them anything. But here's the kicker that led them to us. Joel Richardson's DNA was found at the scene."

"You're kidding me. How is that possible?"

"My thoughts exactly. How is that possible?"

"What kind of DNA?"

"Sperm. Richardson's sperm."

"In the woman?" None of this made any sense to Hansen.

"No, the perp wore a condom. The sperm was smeared on the sheets."

"So this guy is carrying Richardson's jism around with him?"

"Yup. Turns out you can keep it in your freezer. It probably won't get anybody pregnant but it'll keep."

He paused to let Hansen think about this. Finally, he said, "Are you ready for the next piece?"

Hansen nodded, though he was afraid to hear it.

"The male vic was one Danny Lewis, a freelance writer of some sort in Houston. The woman was his girlfriend, Melissa Vasquez, a computer programmer. No record on either one of them but it turns out that Lewis was Ellie McKay's live-in back in the late '90s." He paused. "And that's not all. McKay's prints were all over the apartment."

"And Ellie herself?" he asked.

Capriano shrugged and shook his head. "Nada. None of the neighbors remember seeing her, none of the local merchants could ID her picture. Nothing."

There was no real relief in that information for Hansen. He spoke his next thought. "Our perp is tracking her."

"Hell, yes, he is," said Capriano, frowning. "What I think is that she went to visit Lewis. After the cords showed up in her apartment, she was pretty spooked. Did Skopowlski tell you she'd gone to Gettysburg looking for you?"

Hansen nodded.

Capriano went on. "My guess is that when she got to Houston, there was the other girlfriend and so maybe she only stayed a little while . . . hours even." He shuffled through one of the files looking for some detail.

"Four days," said Hansen.

"Four days what?"

"Four days is how long she was there."

"What do you know I don't know?"

"There's a four-day gap in her credit card use between Dallas and San Antonio. I didn't know what it was before, but now I'd say she stayed with this guy. What was his name?"

"Lewis."

"She stayed with Lewis."

"How long have you been working on this, Doug?" Capriano smiled and shook his head.

"Well, recuperation is pretty boring." He grinned. "And a guy I used to work with moved to the FBI in DC. They have some program that lets them track people's credit cards without a warrant. He gave me a little grief since we don't have a suspect, but he owed me a favor and was willing to check out what he could."

Capriano frowned. "I don't much like going around the system like that."

"Usually I don't either, but I need to help her."

Capriano sighed. "How do you think the killer is tracking her? And don't tell me he has a friend in the FBI."

"I don't know. But he seems pretty resourceful. Maybe there are ways to hack into her accounts. One of the credit cards is with her bank. Its activity would show up on her online banking stuff."

"Do you know where Ellie is now?"

Hansen shook his head. "The credit card use stopped in Santa Fe. That was four weeks ago. She also closed her bank accounts then."

Capriano frowned. "What happened in Santa Fe?"

"I don't know. Nothing according to local police. They have no record of her staying there after one night. She just vanishes."

He thought a moment. "When exactly were the Houston murders?"

"Before that." Capriano checked the file. "About five week ago." He paused. "He killed Lewis and the girlfriend right after she left Houston."

Hansen nodded. "Do you think he has her?" He tried hard to sound like a detective.

"You mean 'had'? I don't think he would keep her long. Not this long. But her body hasn't shown up as far as we know. And he's not into burying them. My guess is he's still looking—or he's biding his time. Waiting for some phase of the moon or some whim."

"What are the odds he'll give up?" Hansen knew this was a stupid question and Capriano's answer confirmed it.

"A psychopath like this guy? No way."

59

Hansen checked into the Holiday Inn in Santa Fe a little more than six weeks after Ellie had done so. He had driven what he could figure out of her route, following her nightly charges to the credit cards. None of the hotel clerks remembered her. None of the bartenders remembered her either. Each time he had shown them her picture, but as one girl said, "She looks like anybody."

In Houston, he'd connected with the police first thing. He'd cajoled Capriano into calling ahead and introducing him as a consultant to the Pittsburgh PD. They both knew that would have more clout than his Gettysburg badge. Besides, his chief was none too happy with his request for additional medical leave.

But the Houston police had little to tell him. A detective named Frank Spears had been assigned to the case. A big man in his late fifties, Spears looked as heavy and slow as his Louisiana accent.

"We got nothing," he said when Hansen explained what he was there for. "It's pretty clear the killer wore gloves and a condom when he raped the woman. To be honest, none of the setup made any sense to us until we connected it with your case. The woman tied to the bed, the white coat on the dead guy, the needle in his arm. He wasn't a medical person, nor was she. At first we thought they were playing some kind of game that went south, but her friends swore that couldn't be it and she was so full of drugs . . ."

"Rohypnol."

Spears nodded. "Yup. Then when Caprese called . . ."

"Capriano."

"Yeah, that's the guy. Then we knew what we had, but where to go? Killer's not local and the connection, this Dr. McKay, she's not local either. And Caprese said that she's not a viable suspect."

"No, she was the victim in the first case."

"And so the killer is looking for her?"

"That's what we think."

"Can she identify him?"

"No," said Hansen. "She was drugged, too. Doesn't remember any of it."

"Then what's he want with her?"

Hansen was silent for a long moment. Then he spoke, "I'd say he is toying with her. Hunter and prey. Cat and mouse. I think it's a game."

Spears grimaced. "I hate these cases."

"Me too."

After that, there wasn't much more to say. They talked about the white coat. Spears had checked with local hospitals but it was generic. "Could have been stolen," he said. "DeBakey Med Center loses a few dozen a year. They don't track them. And it could have been purchased online."

Hansen just nodded at this.

Spears asked if he wanted to visit the crime scene but Hansen knew it wouldn't tell him anything new. He did ask about Lewis's computer, whether there'd been email from Ellie to Lewis before or since the murder. But there was nothing.

He drove on to San Antonio, where finally a desk clerk recognized her. But there was nothing to learn there. He kept following the credit cards north and west until he got to Santa Fe, until he got to where she vanished.

He slept hard that first night and couldn't drag himself out of bed until late into the afternoon. The truth was he was exhausted. He'd been driving himself hard and his stamina was still low. He got up, showered, and shaved. But that seemed to take all he had. After a rest, he went downstairs for dinner. He asked the desk clerks and the restaurant staff about Ellie, but no one remembered her. He went back to bed.

The next day he felt better and he slowly widened his circle out from the hotel, showing her picture to shopkeepers and wait staff in the blocks around the Holiday Inn. Nothing. Then, in the middle of that second afternoon, he came upon the branch of Ellie's bank and he remembered that activity on her checking account had stopped on the same day as the credit cards. He'd assumed something had happened to her, that she hadn't been able to use it. Now he wondered if she'd made some decision, some move to try and keep the killer from tracking her.

The tellers at the bank couldn't help him, so he waited for twenty minutes for a banker. That man was equally of no help, even when he showed his badge. So he asked for a manager and eventually they discovered another banker, a young woman this time, who remembered talking to Ellie.

"Yes, she was very pleasant. Said she was traveling and needed traveler's checks. I convinced her not to close her account, which was what she wanted to do. I was proud of myself for keeping a customer." She looked at her manager, who smiled at her and nodded.

"It was a lot of money she wanted to convert, but then, retired people travel a lot, don't they?" She looked at Hansen this time.

He agreed. He asked a few more questions but there wasn't much more. Traveler's checks didn't come back to the bank that had sold them. They went to the issuer for accounting. He could contact American Express but he'd probably need a court order, the manager said.

Hansen felt stymied. Ellie had cash, lots of cash, and her trail could have continued to Canada or Hawaii or anywhere. And there'd be no money trail. But there was a better chance that she was alive.

Then as he was leaving the bank, the young woman banker called after him. Said Ellie had asked her about a B&B close by where she might get a room for a few days. She had recommended two places. Hansen wrote them down. At least he had someplace to start now.

60

When the phone rang, Hansen was deep in a dream: He had Arlen Gerstead by the throat in an interview room. The man weighed nothing and Hansen shook him like a rag doll. Traveler's checks flew around the room and Gerstead laughed and laughed.

The ringing stopped and then started up again. He looked at the clock: 1:15. A long streak of afternoon sun lay on the floor. He swung his legs over the side of the bed and picked up his phone.

"She's married." It was Capriano.

"Who's married?" Hansen was having trouble shaking off the dream. He hadn't meant to sleep, had meant to just wait for Capriano's call, but the fatigue and the ache in his side where the bullets had been had obviously done him in.

"Ellie McKay. That's why we've lost track of her."

"That's not possible."

"My friend, it is possible. I am holding a marriage license from Flagstaff, Arizona. She got married four weeks ago. Changed her name. She's now Ellie Robison."

Hansen fought his confusion. "How are we just finding this out? Marriages are in the system."

"Yeah, but somebody has to enter it into the system and it looks like they're a tad bit behind in Flagstaff."

"Is there a Flagstaff address?"

"No, a PO box in Farmington, New Mexico, not far from where you are."

"And the husband?"

"Al Robison, a rancher. Lived there all his life. Sixty-four. Widower. No record. Upstanding citizen. All-around nice guy."

"He's not our killer then."

"No. Local police say he has a busy life on the ranch, no foreman. Seldom leaves town and has been seen every few days for months."

"They know about the wedding?"

"Yup. Seems everybody knows everybody's business in Farmington. Met her in a bar, married her six days later."

Again Hansen tried to hang on to his detective self. "When did the license appear in the records?"

"Yesterday. Why?"

"Did you get the message I left you?"

"No. I've been out. Murder-suicide near Pitt. Haven't checked since noon."

"I found a B&B where Ellie stayed here in Santa Fe. The woman who runs it remembered her."

"Did she know where Ellie was headed when she left?"

"North, that's all Ellie had said."

"Farmington's north of you." Capriano said. "Her next stop."

"Just a minute," he said. He got up and went into the bathroom and in thirty seconds had the coffee machine set up and beginning to gurgle.

"What else, Doug?"

"Day before yesterday, a young couple stayed a night at the same B&B. The fellow said a friend had recommended it. Had stayed there recently. He gave Ellie's name."

"A couple?" said Capriano.

"Yeah," said Hansen. "The young woman registered for them. Michelle Rinaldi. I met one of Ellie's students in Paris. Her name was Michelle. I didn't get a last name. However, the description fits. White, tall, slim, long dark hair. She and Ellie were close. It could well be her."

"And the guy? What'd he look like?"

"White, late twenties, early thirties. Short hair, light brown. Clean-shaven. 'A nice-looking couple,' the woman said." He poured himself some coffee and then began to pack his things.

"Sounds like Roger Gerstead."

"That's what I thought, too, but I showed her his picture and she said no. Not even a resemblance. And the girl called him Jazz." He hesitated. "This could be innocent, you know. Could be that Ellie has been in communication with Michelle. Could be kids on a road trip."

"Yeah, and I could be the next mayor of Pittsburgh, but it's not likely. Not after Houston. We know the killer's tracking her." There were a few seconds of silence and then he said, "Hold on, Doug. I need to take this other call." Then he came back on. "I sent Jackson out to talk to Mrs. Gerstead. We're missing some big pieces and somebody knows them. Somebody knows this guy, whoever he is. That somebody may even know how he met Richardson."

"Well, I suspect Arlen did. And you're right, maybe Sandy Gerstead does, too."

"No, not her. I sent Jackson to Akron to talk to the first Mrs. Gerstead. We never really put her in the picture."

"That seems a really long shot. She and Arlen divorced more than twenty years ago."

"Yeah," said Capriano. "But I don't know what else we've got."

Both men were silent for a moment, and Hansen went on packing.

Then Capriano spoke. "How far to Farmington from where you are?"

"I don't know. A ways. There are really big spaces out here. I'm going to leave now. And at least we've got the advantage. We know where Ellie is."

"Don't kid yourself, Doug. If we've got the marriage info, the killer's got it."

"And he's a day ahead of me."

"That, too."

61

Ellie spent two more nights at the Residence Inn although Al wanted her to come back into town, pack up, and move to the ranch the very afternoon after the sweetness of their confessions and their night together. For him, everything seemed settled. For Ellie, it wasn't that simple.

She was fond of Al, that was certain. He was a good man, a solid man. He would treat her well and there would be a life together of steadiness and more certainty than she had ever imagined existed. There was a deep pull in part of her toward that.

It was hard to imagine Farmington as home. She'd always preferred a greener landscape. But Houston and Pittsburgh had both seemed alien at first, and then she had grown comfortable in each. And there would be lots of new things to learn about the ranch and about a farm community, and the curious student in her was intrigued.

And in a sense, what else was there? She couldn't imagine that any amount of pleading would make the dean give her back her job. She had tenure, it was true, but the college would rather buy her out than deal with the scandal. And she was the one who had fled, had broken her current contract. What kind of bargaining position did that leave her in?

And what was in Pennsylvania, anyway? She still cared about Sandy, cared about her a great deal, but Joel and Arlen stood there between them, so many bad memories. It wasn't Sandy's fault but somehow that didn't matter.

She thought about Hansen with a dull ache in her heart. If Paris had been different, if she had been different, maybe something could have happened there. There had been the promise of chemistry between them, something that wasn't there with Al. And Hansen understood what had happened to her, understood in a visceral way that comforted her. Al had been shocked at her story and then kind. It was a genuine kindness, she knew, but one that came from who he was, not what he had experienced. And so even if it wasn't a secret anymore, even if her experience was out in the open, it hadn't bonded them the way it had with Hansen.

She knew she had to let Hansen go from her heart. He had made it clear that nothing more would happen between them and she assumed he was back with his wife. We tend to seek out those who have loved us when we are in trouble. She had done that with Danny, and Hansen would do that with the woman in Montreal. Besides, they had kids together, a long history.

And she was married to Al. It had been an impulsive move on both their parts, but Al seemed so sure of a future together. It was worth a try.

Her decision once made, Ellie got busy. She wrote a letter to the dean of the college and resigned. She called the community college in Farmington and made an appointment to see the dean there again, to offer her services in any way that she could be helpful. She called the shaman and made an appointment for the soul retrieval for the next week. And then she went shopping for a wedding gift for Al.

62

It took Hansen less than ten minutes to check out of the Holiday Inn in Santa Fe and get on the road. It took Capriano less than twenty to call him back.

"There's an Ellie Robison registered at the Residence Inn in Farmington," he said when Hansen picked up the phone.

"She's married to this rancher and she's staying in a Residence Inn?" Hansen didn't like things like this, things he couldn't figure out.

"I don't know," said Capriano. "None of this makes a lot of sense to me. She only knew the guy a few days before she married him. But it's a place to start." He paused. "Do you have some kind of plan, Doug? Are you going to check in with the locals before you ride your high horse out to the ranch?"

"You've been watching too much TV, Larry."

"Quite possibly. But this guy's been getting grown men to sit still while he kills them. I don't want that to happen to you."

"I'll be careful."

"Why am I not reassured?"

"Hey, besides advice, can you check on some things for me?"

"Of course. What do you need?"

"Find out what you can about Michelle Rinaldi. She was a student at the college where Ellie taught. The school should have an address for her and for her folks. Maybe they can identify the boyfriend. When I saw her last, she was with a guy named Lenny. I think he was from Indiana."

"Already on it."

"Oh shit!"

"What is it?"

"The last time I saw Michelle Rinaldi and this Lenny was at Arlen Gerstead's funeral."

They were both silent a moment.

"You've got no last name for this guy?" said Capriano.

"No," said Hansen. "And another thing. I feel so stupid. There's a name I didn't run down. Jason Dirrelich." He spelled it for Capriano. "The car Roger Gerstead was driving while he stayed at Ellie's was registered to a Jason Dirrelich. I just filed it away, intending to follow up and I didn't."

"You think Lenny and Dirrelich are the same guy?" said Capriano.

"I don't know but the B&B owner said that Michelle called her friend Jazz. Jason isn't too far from that. That's what made me think of it."

"Okay, you got it. Let me know when you get to Farmington." And Capriano disconnected.

Hansen turned his attention to the road. He wished Skopowlski were there to do the driving so he could think. But at least the road was clear and dry and there was little traffic.

He knew in his gut that Michelle's boyfriend was the killer, it was just too coincidental. A clever cover—the road trip to visit a favorite professor, the girl as a beard. And showing up in Paris and at the funeral. It all so fit together. He'd come across a few psychopaths in his time. The men were often handsome and always charming. Ted Bundy wasn't the poster boy for these guys for nothing.

He tried to dismiss Ellie from his thoughts. This was about the killer of three men and one woman and a rapist of who knew how many other women. This was about keeping it from happening again. And he hadn't put her in danger, he didn't believe that. But he did believe that everything we do has an effect on everything else. His indecision about his feelings at that moment, crucial or not, had set all the rest of this in play: his trip to Montreal, Ellie's flight, Houston, even probably her marriage to the cowboy. And she was in danger. She didn't know the face of the killer, wouldn't know to escape him when he came for her.

As he cleared the outskirts of Santa Fe, a mileage sign appeared: Farmington 210. Three hours if he was lucky. He'd called to see about a flight but there was nothing until the next morning, and he had no funds or authorization to hire anything private. The killer was a day ahead although he might well take his time. He might well think he had plenty of time. He might well not know that Hansen was tracking him as he had tracked Ellie.

Through the years, Hansen had learned how to be with time. Long stake-outs in the car with an uncommunicative partner, long evenings at home with an uncommunicative wife, he'd learned to go to a quiet place in himself, create an emptiness for something else to move in. He wouldn't have called it a spiritual practice, although that wouldn't have embarrassed him. It was more a survival technique that he had cultivated. He moved himself now into that zone as he drove, not thinking too much, not planning. Just letting the miles go by. He didn't watch the clock.

Miles and miles later, the ringing of his phone brought him back. Capriano.

"What have you got for me, Larry?"

"Not much. Jason Dirrelich is a dead end."

"How so?" He hung onto the peacefulness he had been feeling.

"He's Joel Richardson."

"What?"

"The DMV address is the same apartment that Arlen Gerstead was using, the one where he was killed, the one Richardson had rented. And the driver's license in Dirrelich's name has Richardson's photo. And get this, Jason Dirrelich is an anagram for Joel Richardson."

"Shit," said Hansen. "That's no help. All it tells us is that Richardson knew Roger Gerstead and he loaned the kid a car."

"Maybe not even that. Richardson could have given the car to Arlen, who then gave it to his son."

"So we've got nothing for me to give the locals on this guy." Hansen hated this.

"Nope. No name, no connection, no physical evidence, nothing."

"What about Lenny?"

"What about him? You've got no photo, no last name. I'm not a miracle worker."

"You sure know how to help a guy out, Larry."

"I know. I'm sorry. I'm grasping at straws here."

There was a pause. Then Hansen said, "Anything on Michelle Rinaldi?"

"She got an apartment in Pittsburgh when she came back from Paris. Substitute teaches at a couple of high schools while she looks for a full-time job. Parents live in Greensburg, said she flew to Santa Fe to meet Lenny, whose last name they don't know. How do parents let their daughter go out with someone whose last name they don't know?"

"I don't know, Larry. This sucks. Do you think she's involved in the murders?"

"No, I think she's just part of the game and maybe one of the next victims."

"That's occurred to me too," Hansen said.

Capriano sighed. "I'll be in touch if I get anything." And he was gone.

Hansen drove on. He felt alone, painfully alone. Earlier that morning, he'd been tempted to ask Capriano to fly out and meet him in Farmington, to see this through with him. He respected his friend's experience and intelligence, and he knew that together they could come up with a good plan. But Capriano had other cases. And he couldn't justify medical leave the way Hansen was doing.

Hansen didn't have much of a plan. Find Ellie, save her if possible. Then what? Hand her over to the cowboy husband? That would be the decent thing. Clearly, she'd moved on. But that wasn't what he wanted. Something substantial was there between them. He knew it, and he believed she knew it. He cursed his hesitation when she had come back from Paris, his need to run away to Montreal and what remained of his family. What had he been thinking?

Another road sign. Farmington 25. Anxiety rose up in his throat.

63

Ellie found just the right gift at the jeweler's next to First Cup Coffee House—a heavy sterling silver frame that could sit on Al's desk or the mantle. She thought she'd take a few pictures of Al with Beemus and then frame one, a testament to the man and his love for his dog. She wondered if her cats would get along with Beemus, if maybe Sandy would drive them out and visit for a few days.

She stopped at the front desk on her way to her room to check out. She paid the bill with some of the remaining traveler's checks. She was conscious of the independence of the gesture for Al had been paying her bills. But it seemed important to do this, to close out her single life herself. Then she went to her room and packed her things. She didn't pack carefully, she was only going a few miles.

She left the hotel at five-fifteen with one stop to make—Sweet Basil Thai for yellow curry with chicken and shrimp pad thai, Al's favorites. She had called ahead to order.

64

Hansen spotted the Residence Inn as he came into town from the southeast. It was just past five. He thought about stopping, but he knew he should check in with the local police before he did anything. It wasn't just courtesy; it was a way to protect the case. His anxiety began to ratchet up and the weather didn't help. In the last couple of hours, it had shifted. The clear blue sky with big white clouds was now dark and threatening, and bruised purple thunderheads were moving in from the mountains.

The desk sergeant was a heavy-set young woman with a broad, brown face and amazing dark eyes. WINONA CROSSRIDER said the nameplate. "We've been expecting you," she said when he told her his name and showed his badge. "You're from Pittsburgh, right?"

Hansen nodded. The finer geographic points of his jurisdiction seemed irrelevant.

"You'll be wanting to talk to Chief Madison. He's gone to dinner. Said you should wait. I expect him in a half hour or so."

"Can you tell me where he is?"

She frowned. "He doesn't like to have his meal disturbed." Her voice dropped to a whisper. "He gets together with his wife."

"Is there anyone else I can talk to? I'm in a hurry here. Is there a detective on duty?"

"William Two Horses is our detective. I can call him if you like."

"Please." Hansen moved away from the desk. Against one wall was a row of orange plastic chairs, chairs placed there for anxious parents and less aggressive town drunks. He sat down in one, but was up again in thirty seconds. He went back to the desk. "Do you know Al Robison?"

The woman nodded. "Not personally. But I know who he is."

"Can you give me his address or tell me how to find his ranch?"

"Sure, I guess." And she wrote on a piece of paper and handed it to him. "I put in a call to William. He's on his way back to the station to meet you."

"Thanks," he said. "Tell him that I'm going to the Residence Inn and then out to the Robison ranch. I'll call if I need backup." He glanced at her and saw that her eyes had widened in excitement. "Is there a direct line here?" he asked, taking out his phone. He programmed it in as she recited it. Then he thanked her again and headed out.

"Wait," she called after him. "I think you should wait for William."

He shook his head in response and headed out the door and down the block to his car.

65

Ellie made one additional stop on her way out of town. A block from the Thai place was a florist, and she bought a huge bouquet of flowers to fill the house with color. Then amid the competing smells of phlox and pad thai, she drove out to the ranch. The wind was picking up and a few raindrops spotted her windshield.

She found herself keenly aware of this moment, of its endings and beginnings. The decisions she had made and the letters she had written that morning most likely signaled the end of her career as a professor, perhaps as an intellectual. She wasn't sure what would become of that part of her.

And she was beginning life as a married woman. She was committing her life into the care of another, for better or worse. She would need courage and bravery and determination. The image of a bonneted pioneer woman came to mind, and it made her laugh. The laughter sparked a sense of happy anticipation, and she was glad for it.

She turned into the driveway to the ranch, the house ahead of her, lights on in the gloom of the approaching rain. As she drew near, she saw Al and Beemus in the yard, as if they had anticipated her arrival. She smiled. Then coming down the porch stairs toward her husband and the dog, she saw a young couple. The woman smiled and waved at her, and Ellie grinned with pleasure, not stopping to wonder how they'd found her.

66

There was no one at the front desk at the Residence Inn and no counter-top bell to ding. Hansen stepped behind the counter and opened a door on the right, startling a young man who stood leaning against a desk and eating a sandwich. Tuna fish permeated the air.

The young man jumped up. "You can't come in here, sir!"

Hansen showed him his badge.

"I'll be right out." The kid looked guilt-stricken. In less than a minute, he was in position, all smiles and professionalism. "What can I do for you, sir?"

"I need to know what room Ellie Robison is in."

"She's no longer here. She checked out this afternoon. About two hours ago."

A wave of relief swept over Hansen. It might not be too late.

"What she's driving?"

"We're not allowed to give out that kind of information, sir."

"Do I need to speak to the manager?"

The kid frowned. "At dinner time, I'm the manager, sir."

"Do I need to call the chief of police to get your cooperation?"

The kid blanched and typed into the computer. "Honda Civic, New Mexico plates, UXL683," he said.

Hansen didn't thank him as he left.

.

Back in his car, Hansen willed himself again to slow down. He took deep breaths, slowly exhaling and relaxing his body. He needed to proceed with caution, with clarity. He put the address for the Robison ranch in his GPS, and he checked his gun. As he was driving out of the hotel parking lot, his phone rang. Capriano again. Hansen pulled to the curb.

"There's another kid in the Gerstead family," said Capriano.

"Yeah, we know that. Roger has a twin, Michael. Lives in Ohio. And they all have the same DNA. And it doesn't match."

"No, this is a third kid. The first Mrs. Gerstead, Maureen, already had a six-year-old when she married Arlen. No DNA relation to Arlen. The kid was apparently trouble, a lot of trouble, and when the twins were born, Arlen 'encouraged' her, that's the word she used, to send the boy to live with his father in the sticks outside of Cincinnati. The boy was eight. She went on with her life, raised the twins with Arlen until he left her for Sandy. The last time she saw the boy, he was fourteen. He's now thirty-two."

"Funny that Ellie didn't mention him."

"She probably didn't know about him. Sandy Gerstead didn't. Arlen had never said a word."

"What's his name? Is he in the system?"

"Stanhope. Arthur Leonard Stanhope. Goes by Lenny, I'd guess."

"Bingo," thought Hansen. Michelle's boyfriend.

Capriano went on speaking. "He has a juvenile record but it's sealed."

"Doesn't matter," said Hansen. "We know what's in it."

"Yeah, tortured pets and an early sexual assault."

"The father still alive?"

"No, died of a drug overdose a year ago, pentobarbital. No surprise there, huh?"

"None. Any ties to Arlen?"

"We're looking into it," said Capriano. "I think Arlen and Lenny knew each other all this time. Maybe Arlen was blackmailing Lenny for some of Joel's money. That would explain how he could afford the sex clubs and the apartment."

"Makes sense. Got a DMV photo on Lenny?"

"Sending it to your phone now. We've already had the Santa Fe people show it to the woman at the B&B. It's him. Go to the locals, Doug. You've got what you need now. I'll call ahead and fill them in. How far are you from the station?"

"Hey, I'm almost to the ranch," Hansen lied. "Just send them after me. I can't wait." He closed the phone and put the car in gear. The rain was now coming down in gallon buckets.

67

Hansen had to go slow. The rain had sucked all the light out of the sky even though it wasn't even six o'clock. In places where the pavement was uneven, he felt the car hydroplaning. He was doubly handicapped by not knowing the road or where he was going. He had to rely on the GPS.

So intent was he on the road ahead that he didn't see the flashing lights until they were right behind him, filling the car with red and blue stripes. He pulled over.

The officer didn't come to his window. Instead he opened the passenger door and jack-knifed his long body into the seat beside Hansen. Brown skin, brown hair, brown eyes, brown uniform. Forty maybe, forty-five.

"Detective Two Horses," said Hansen.

The man nodded. "You're an impatient man, Detective Hansen."

"I believe the situation warrants considerable urgency."

"I believe it does. And caution."

Hansen nodded. "What can you tell me about the ranch?"

The Farmington detective described the long driveway, the house, then the barn and bunkhouse considerably further on.

Hansen described the scene they had found each time. The woman on the bed, the man in a chair. He told Two Horses how little they knew of how the killer made it happen, of how he subdued the man and the woman. In the first killing, Ellie had been drugged hours before the brutality and Joel had been an accomplice. But they had no way of knowing if Arlen Gerstead had known who the killer was or if he, too, had participated. And in the Houston murder, Danny Levinson wouldn't have known his assailant. They could only guess if any of this information would be helpful to them in what lay ahead at the ranch.

After listening to what Hansen had to say, Two Horses tried to call his chief but the cell service was too weak. "Guess it's you and me," he said.

"Okay," said Hansen. And they settled on a plan. Hansen would follow the Farmington detective to the ranch. They'd park a bit before the driveway and walk in to the house with Two Horses taking the lead. From there, they'd have to play it by ear.

The rain was already letting up, the clouds scudding north. It wasn't quite dark, but deep patches of ground fog made the driving treacherous. Hansen stayed as close to the other car as he could, trying to keep the taillights in view.

In about ten minutes, Two Horses pulled off the road at a turnout and Hansen did the same. Two Horses took out a pair of rifles and a pair of flashlights and offered one of each to Hansen. Hansen took the flashlight, but he shook his head at the rifle and held up his revolver instead. Two Horses shrugged. Then he headed off down the road, the flashlight beam low and in front. Hansen followed suit.

Slowly Hansen's eyes adjusted to the gloom. Then the men turned off the road and into the gravel drive and his adrenalin really began to kick in.

As they neared the house, he could see the buildings laid out as Two Horses had described. In the far distance to the left were a large barn and a long, low building. Through the fog, he could see that lights were on in the bunkhouse, and a few chords from a guitar came to him on the wind. With his eyes on the bunkhouse, Hansen tripped over a large bundle on the ground, near Ellie's red Honda. On closer inspection, he saw that it was a dog. He bent down and touched it. Still warm, still breathing. Next to the Honda was an older Subaru Outback with Pennsylvania plates. They were here.

He pulled himself up straight and looked for Two Horses. The man had moved toward the house, which was ahead and slightly to the right—two stories, a wraparound porch. A lamp burned downstairs, near the center of the porch. Hallway or front room, he figured. The rest of the downstairs was dark. Upstairs, one room was well lit. One of the windows in the room was open a bit, but he heard nothing, no conversation, no cries for help.

Two Horses signaled to him to wait and he moved around the back of the house. In another minute he was back. "Three doors," he whispered, gesturing front, back, and far side. Hansen nodded to show he had understood. He was loath to let the younger man run this, but he was twenty years older and still weakened from the shooting in Montreal. And he had the wisdom to set his ego aside to see this come out right.

The young detective pulled him back a hundred yards or so into a dense patch of fog. "I didn't see anyone downstairs so it looks like they're on the second floor," his voice just above a whisper. "I suggest we approach them together. You go in the front and cover the bottom of the stairs. I'll go in the back, check out the back of the house, and meet you at the stairs."

"Won't he hear us break in?"

Two Horses looked at him. "Why would we break in? We don't lock our doors here." Then he looked down at Hansen's shoes, knelt down and checked the soles, gave him a thumbs-up when he saw they were rubber. Then he evaporated into the night.

Hansen unlocked the safety on his gun, then walked as quietly as he could to the porch and crept up the stairs. Sure enough, the front door opened easily and there ahead of him was a broad, bannistered staircase. The door to the living room was ajar and the glow of the lamp came out at him. He stepped back into the deepest shadows he could find and willed his breath to slow and be easy.

Three, maybe four minutes passed. He thought he heard movement upstairs, but it was faint, muffled, and he wasn't sure if it wasn't just the blood pounding in his ears. He heard no voices. Two Horses materialized right next to him. He hadn't heard the man enter the house or move through the rooms. One second Hansen was alone, the next second Two Horses was right there.

The man tapped him on the shoulder, then beckoned in the dim light for him to follow up the stairs as he began to move in the same

252

amazing silence. Like a cat, Hansen thought, conscious of his own heavy tread on the steps, the rustle of his pant legs against the bottom of his jacket.

There was a surprisingly wide landing at the top of the stairs, Hansen saw, and a big window through which he could see the fading twilight. An open corridor ran across both sides of the stairwell, two doors on each side. All the doors were closed, although under one he could see light. Two Horses motioned him to stay as he moved silently to the two dark rooms on the right. He opened the first door, stepped gracefully inside, then in a few seconds stepped out again. At the second door, he did the same thing, only he paused inside the room a long moment, then motioned Hansen into the room.

Two Horses had a low-beam flashlight pointed to the floor. In the dim light, Hansen could see Ellie and the girl on the bed. He took it all in a second. Ellie lay face up, the girl on top of her. Both women were naked, their breasts touching, their genitals pressed together, their legs entangled and the four ankles bound together. Ellie's mouth was taped shut and her wrists were tied to the bedpost. The girl's arms appeared to be free, but her head was slumped on Ellie's shoulder. She was clearly drugged.

Ellie was not. Her eyes wide with panic, she looked at him with as much fear and grief as he had ever seen. He moved to her side, put his hand on her cheek in reassurance. "Wait," he mouthed as she began to struggle against her bonds.

At the same time, Two Horses had cut the tape that held the women's ankles and was lifting the girl into his arms as if she weighed nothing. Hansen watched him go, then silently closed the door and began freeing Ellie from the gold cords that held her wrists. As soon as one hand was free, she pulled the tape off her mouth, wincing as she did so. He put his finger to her lips to silence her and she nodded and lay back and let him free the other hand. They clung to each other for a moment. Then he wrapped her in a blanket he found on a chair and led her down the stairs to the porch. He wished he were younger, stronger. That he could carry her down.

In the foggy distance, he could see Two Horses in the yard, next to Ellie's car. He gave Ellie a gentle push in that direction and headed back into the house and up the stairs.

Hansen gripped the gun in both hands. His palms felt sweaty, the way they had when he was a rookie. He crept to the last door on the left, where he saw a glimmer of light underneath the door, and put his hand to the knob. He hesitated, but only to marshal his forces. He had stopped planning when he reached the top of the stairs.

He turned the handle and slowly pushed the door ajar. It was another bedroom and dark, but ahead to the right was another room and light splayed out from it. Hansen tightened his grip on his gun and moved to the open door.

"Come on in, Detective. The party's getting started in here. I'm just about to dispatch Cowboy Al to his Maker. You don't want to miss it."

The bathroom was enormous, a Jacuzzi tub, a glass block shower. In the middle of the floor was an old-fashioned rocking chair and strapped into it was a tall, broad-shouldered man Hansen knew must be Al Robison. His blue shirtsleeve was rolled up and taped in the crook of his arm was a needle, the plunger half-in. His head was slumped over, but Hansen saw his chest rise and fall.

Lenny Stanhope stood beside Robison. He wore sweat pants, athletic socks, running shoes. He was naked from the waist up, his chest and shoulders slim and muscular. They seemed to gleam in the light. He looked the picture of health. Hansen raised his gun, and Stanhope reached down and put his forefinger and thumb on the plunger.

"I'll bet I'm faster, old man," Stanhope said. "Are you sure this is how you want to play it?"

"You don't want to die," said Hansen.

"You don't know what I want," said the kid with a smile that was disconcerting in its friendliness.

Hansen hesitated a moment, then lowered the gun, though he didn't take his finger off the trigger. He watched Lenny's face. It was familiar—he'd met the guy twice before at least, but there was nothing really to remember. Smooth skin, regular features, white teeth. Handsome but in a bland kind of way. An easy face to forget. Only the eyes were off. They were blue, they were cold, they were dead.

Hansen spoke. "How much did you give him?"

"Enough for now." The kid's tone was matter of fact.

"How did you get him in the chair?"

"A little liquid sleepy-bye in his lemonade."

"Same thing you gave the girl?"

The kid nodded. "She got the rohypnol, too."

"And the professor?"

"That naughty girl wouldn't play, wouldn't drink what I fixed for her. I told her it'd be easier, easier to not know, but she wanted to go out awake. Her choice. Funny. She's the only one who's wanted to be awake."

"Why'd you come after her? She didn't know who you were."

The kid shrugged.

"I get it about Joel. He was your lover, wasn't he?"

"I wouldn't call him that. We had sex, lots of it, but love?" He seemed to consider the question carefully, then shook his head. "No, no love. But he played the game well and I admired that."

"Sex games?"

"No." Stanhope rolled his eyes in exasperation. "Geez, man, get your head out of the gutter. No, the game we all play. The game of pretending to be nice, pretending to be good, when we aren't. Like Arlen. Pretending to be a good husband, a good father, but the truth was he was lousy at all of it. And he gives it all up for a prostitute." The same look of loathing crossed his face again. "And you, Detective. You've been pretending to be an upright cop but you've been screwing the victim. Naughty boy! But I guess it's not your fault. Most people don't play the game well."

"And Richardson? Was he good at the game? Teach you everything he knew?"

"Let's just say it was a mutually beneficial relationship."

"So are you Jason Dirrelich? Or was Richardson?"

The kid smiled. "You found the car registration. We both thought that was a nice touch. Joel thought up the anagram, but the car was my idea. What's the old word, a 'red herring,' whatever that is?"

"And Joel's sperm? Another red herring? That was pure genius. Probably his idea. I'm thinking he was the brains of the outfit."

"Trying to piss me off, Detective? Or should I call you Doug?" He shook his head. "It isn't going to work. I've got the upper hand here and we both know it."

Stanhope looked down at the syringe in his hand, and Hansen saw his hand tremble or itch maybe. Then the kid looked back at him. "Shall we get on with it?"

"Just a couple more questions. Just for my own curiosity. We're not in any hurry here, are we? How did you meet Richardson? Through your dad?"

The snort was full of derision. "As if. It's the other way around. I told Joel about Arlen, about the pharmacy connection."

"Then how did you meet Joel?"

"The lovely and talented Madame Tomei. She knows how to connect men of like inclinations."

For the first time, Hansen could see the evil behind the kid's eyes. If he'd been at the top of his game, he'd have seen it in Paris when he first met him. He went back to his questions. "How did you find her? Doctor McKay?"

"Find her? I didn't have to find her. I followed her. To Gettysburg where she must have been looking for you. I even went into the police station there and asked directions. She didn't see me, of course. Then to Houston. Then to a bunch of dinko towns in Texas, where she stayed in a Holiday Inn every time. Women are so stupid. But I like road trips."

"How did you know to follow her here?"

"For a cop, you're not too smart, are you, Detective? I had her credit card numbers—got them in her apartment. I made a copy of Roger's key. You know my brother, excuse me, my step-brother, Roger. It didn't take much time to find Ellie's papers, her strong box. What a joke! Then once I had the passwords, it was easy enough to check in online and see where she was going. You cops always pretend that you know what we're thinking and what we're going to do next. But you're not that smart. If you were, you'd have found me long ago."

Hansen let the insult go by. "Why didn't you just let her go? She couldn't identify you."

"Now, Detective, that's old thinking. There's more to life than not getting caught. But I don't expect you to understand that. So just consider her a loose end I needed to tie up." He grinned. "Just a little joke of the trade. Or consider it part of the game. That's all." There was no hurt, no bitterness in his voice. Just that matter-of-factness.

All the while Hansen kept him talking, he watched the second bathroom door behind Stanhope. He figured it led to the hallway or perhaps the other bedroom. He realized he was waiting for Two Horses to come in, take this guy by surprise. But nothing happened.

"So what do we do now, Arthur?"

The kid laughed, a mean, ugly sound. "Lenny," he said. "Or Jazz. I like Jazz. Sounds kind of cool, doesn't it?"

Hansen saw the kid's fingers twitch again. *Eager to kill*, he thought. Then from the bedroom behind him, Hansen heard a noise, a creak in the floorboards. He turned his head to the sound and when he turned back, the plunger had gone all the way into the syringe in Robison's arm and the kid was through the door behind him.

He had no time to think, no time to decide. He started after the kid. The small room was dark but not quite. He could just see the shape of the kid moving to the window. He lunged after him, grabbed his arm, and then felt him slip, literally, out of his grasp, leaving Hansen with an empty, oily hand. *The gleaming muscles*, Hansen thought.

In a flash, the kid had the window open and was out of reach. Hansen was right behind him, but from the window, he could see the boy roll off the porch roof and sprint away into the fog. No clear shot. No sense in the chase either. He was carrying thirty pounds and thirty years that the kid didn't have, and none of the agility, speed, and stamina that he did.

As he turned back to Al Robison, he heard a rifle shot. Then another. *Two Horses*, he thought. He prayed the kid was down. Dead would be fine with him.

He hurried back to the bathroom. He was relieved to find Robison still breathing. He opened his phone and dialed 911.

"An ambulance is already on its way, sir," the operator told him, and he heard the siren in the distance.

EPILOGUE

Ellie lay on the floor, dense carpeting and a warm woven throw rug beneath her, a blanket imprinted with the length of the body of a wolf tucked in around her. Her eyes were closed. She could feel the heat from Brown Bear Woman, who lay next to her. She had aligned her body with Ellie's, only a few inches between them. From a speaker somewhere, a rhythmic drumming filled the air. The shaman's breath was loud for a few minutes, deep, shuddering exhales, muscles twitching, settling, then peaceful and quiet.

Ellie's mind drifted. A hummingbird crossed her vision. Then she saw a bear, and in the flat of its paw, the hummingbird danced. The images were so unexpected that she wondered if the shaman had put something into her tea. But she felt clear, and calmer than she had in a long time. She relaxed and drifted again.

Joel's face rose up in her mind. "Forgive whatever you can," the shaman had said before they set out on the journey. She felt the old pain well up, the hurt, the anger, and then she wished it gone. She brought Arlen's face to her mind as well and did the same. She didn't want them to come with her into her new life. In her mind, she buried them, blessed their spirits, wished them peace.

Ellie worried vaguely about the time. Had they been lying here a half hour? An hour? She took a deep breath. It didn't matter. He would wait. This was important.

Danny next. That was much harder. Once upon a time, she had loved him dearly. And because of that, she had drawn him into the circle of death that Joel had drawn around her. She lay there a few minutes, asking Danny's forgiveness, accepting what she had done. She knew there was more work to do there, to forgive herself. And she knew she was willing to do the work.

Her left palm began to itch. She wondered if this were a sign that the shaman was successful, or unsuccessful, or if her palm just itched. She watched her analytical self in action for a moment or two, then turned back to her breath. The hummingbird came again. Danced across her vision. She sensed the bear behind her, strong, solid, protective. She slept.

Five minutes or an hour passed. She didn't know. But then she heard the shaman's breathing shift. As if on cue, the drumming intensified, then slowed, and the woman moved away from her and sat up. She spoke in a low, soothing voice and asked permission to reunite Ellie with the part of her soul that had been damaged. When Ellie nodded, the woman cupped her hands at Ellie's heart and blew into her chest. She repeated this at the top of Ellie's head. She urged Ellie to rest and assimilate it all. She moved away. The drumming had stopped, the room was quiet.

Ellie lay still another long while. She felt warm and sleepy. She felt at peace.

ℒ

When Ellie stepped out onto the porch and into the sunlight, he got out of the car. She looked different, he thought. Lighter, clearer somehow. As she came towards him, she smiled. At first the look was shy, almost sheepish, then it broadened, opened. She was happy, and Hansen knew that they were going to be all right.

Acknowledgments

This book was written with support from a loving community of women writers and creatives during Writing Fridays in Portland, Oregon, and writing retreats at Aldermarsh on Whidbey Island, Washington. My thanks especially to Diane Sorensen, Bridget Benton, Jan Underwood, and Pamela Stringer. Thanks also to my sisters and thoughtful beta readers, Kerry Fall and Melanie St. John; to my editor Nicole Frail at Skyhorse, who's made the process so easy; and to my kind and persistent agent, Andrea Somberg at the Harvey Klinger agency, who really championed my story.

READER'S GUIDE TO *FOG OF DEAD SOULS*

A Conversation with the Author

How did you come to write *Fog*?

JK: Like my first novel, this book started from a writing prompt, a sentence from poet Gary Snyder: "I walked into a bar in Farmington, New Mexico." In the ten-minute writing I did using that prompt, a sixty-year-old woman desperately in need of a drink showed up. I wrote about four paragraphs and moved on to other prompts. But I couldn't get Ellie out of my mind and when I finished my first novel, *The Color of Longing*, I knew I would write about her.

To be honest, I had no idea what I was in for and no plans to write a thriller. It was just what happened. Once I introduced Ellie to the cowboy, I had to figure out why she was traveling, and a series of images went through my mind: the Gettysburg battlefields, which I had found a creepy, creepy place even after a century and a half; a fancy hotel room and a dead boyfriend; a handsome older detective; a mysterious psychopath. And they worked themselves into the novel piece by piece. It was quite a ride and I didn't know how the story was going to turn out until I wrote the ending.

What makes this an unusual story?

JK: Several things. First, it's the age of the characters. Ellie, Al, and Hansen are all in their sixties. I wanted to show that rape and violence happen to older women, too, not just pretty young women—that all women, regardless of age, struggle with self-identity after betrayal. And that they can encounter romance, be the object of affection of interesting men.

I also wanted to explore older men's feelings about older women. We hear a lot about older men who want younger wives, but many older men are attracted to women their own age. Relationships, not the sociopath, are at the center of this thriller; in fact, the killer is, in many ways, a catalyst for the drive for love and security.

Then there's Ellie's drinking. She's an alcoholic but I didn't want her addiction to be the main point of the book. Her addiction doesn't cause the violence she experiences but it complicates the aftermath.

Last, many thrillers delve deeply into the psychology of the killer. I wanted to keep him completely unknown until the end and make the book about the victim and her relationships and how they impact the complications and final understandings of the plot.

What are you writing now? Will there be a sequel?

I have two new novels in the works. *When Your Mother Doesn't* is a relationship novel that relates the challenges of two sisters who struggle to become their whole selves after growing up with a mother who couldn't love them.

Vague and Broken Boy (thanks to singer Adele for the title phrase) is a thriller about a married middle-aged professional woman and her involvement with a mysterious man who lives on the margins of society. Her need for adventure and a new life wreaks havoc in her family and then threatens her survival when she discovers what kind of games her lover is playing. Detective Hansen has already appeared in this new novel, so maybe some of the other characters from *Fog* will too, but I don't know yet.

BOOK CLUB QUESTIONS

1. What was your reaction to Ellie's acceptance of Al's marriage proposal in the first chapter? Why do you think she accepted?

2. What did you find most believable about the main characters in the book?

3. Do the minor characters contribute well to the story?

4. Which characters did you especially like or dislike? Why?

5. How do Ellie's problems with alcohol function as an additional character in the book?

6. Road trips are a common theme in American literature. What is the purpose of Ellie's travels to France and to the Southwest?

7. The story travels through time and several locations. Did you find this added or detracted from your enjoyment of the book?

8. The ending leaves a lot open. Do you think Al survives? What do you think happens to Lenny?

9. Why do you think Ellie chooses Hansen in the end? What problems lie ahead for them?

10. A thriller keeps the tension high throughout the book. Which episodes were particularly tense for you?